ENDORSEMENTS

"A stunning and captivating novel. Brennan McPherson's fluid prose and vivid imagination are a treat for the senses, bringing to life one of the Old Testament's most enigmatic figures."

—Billy Coffey, critically acclaimed author
of *When Mockingbirds Sing* and *The Devil Walks in Mattingly*

"*Cain* is a wonderful novel that explores the 'what ifs' of the world's first family. Brennan McPherson explores the questions we've all had about Adam and Eve. 'What happened to Cain?' is just the beginning. Brennan writes in a refreshing style that makes you want to read more, and I expect this novel is just the first of many more to come."

—Gordon Robertson
CEO, The Christian Broadcasting Network

"Orson Scott Card meets Stephen King. An imaginative debut novel that explores the first murder and makes us aware of the Cain in all of us. McPherson can write, and his beautiful language is both artistic and thought provoking."

—William Sirls, best-selling author
of *The Reason* and *The Sinners' Garden*

"With literary skill and respect to the original text, McPherson weaves a terrific 'what if' story on the life of Cain, all the while exploring the depths of temptation, sin, and above all, God's unfathomable mercy."

—Bill Myers, best-selling author of *Eli*

"Thought provoking, well written, creative, highly imaginative, and all written within an honest attempt at accurately interpreting Scripture while allowing for creative license within the bounds of what might be possible. A smartly-paced debut novel. I think we'll be hearing more of Brennan and his stories."

—Charles Martin, *New York Times* best-selling author of *Unwritten* and *Water From My Heart*

CAIN

THE STORY OF THE FIRST MURDER
& THE BIRTH OF AN UNSTOPPABLE EVIL

BRENNAN S. MCPHERSON

BroadStreet
PUBLISHING

CAIN

The Story of the First Murder and the Birth of an Unstoppable Evil

Copyright © 2016 Brennan S. McPherson

ISBN: 978-1-4245-5232-0 (softcover)
ISBN: 978-1-4245-5233-7 (e-book)

Published by BroadStreet Publishing Group, LLC
Racine, Wisconsin, USA
BroadStreetPublishing.com

Cover design by Josh Meyer Photography and Design
Interior by Katherine Lloyd at www.TheDESKonline.com

Printed in the United States of America

16 17 18 19 20 5 4 3 2 1

To my grandmother,
Nonnie

Partial Family Tree

Adam / Eve

Cain / Sarah

Abel / Lilleth

Seth / Ayla

Lukian / Keshra

Mason

Gorban / Peth

Kiile / Elsa

Machael / Zillah

Calebna / Terah

Philo

Tuor

Gillian, ...

...

...

...

Jacob, ...

AUTHOR'S NOTE

Genesis is a literary masterpiece intended specifically for a Hebrew audience, so converting the story of Cain and Abel into a modern, full-length novel presented a few difficulties, not the least of which was the terseness of the narrative. The account spanning from Cain's birth to his expulsion into the land of Nod (which means "wandering") is only about two paragraphs long (Genesis 4:1–17).

Another difficulty was its extraordinary ambiguity, which, while beautifully rich, makes it impossible to offer any singly authoritative interpretation. One example of this is in verse 17, which in Hebrew may be read as either, "Cain built a city and named it after his son, Enoch," or, "Enoch built a city and named it after his son." Two more examples lie in both the nature of the relationship between Cain and Abel as well as the hopes Eve held for her firstborn. Some scholars believe the original Hebrew implied that Cain and Abel were twins, and that Eve's proclamation over the newborn Cain implied she hoped him to be the Christ prophesied of in the garden of Eden (Genesis 3:15; 4:1–2).

Of course, a detailed and unified story could not be crafted without drawing specific conclusions to replace the original story's ambiguity. *Cain*, like all works of fiction, is therefore a fantasy, a product of my imagination. But it is one that was formed out of Genesis 4:1–17 and the compelling questions it raises. What happened to the family after Cain was banished? What other family might he have had? Did Abel have a wife? How about children or grandchildren? How would the family have handled Abel's murder? Why did God warn Cain of sin crouching at the door and waiting to devour him? Was there significance in using such language?

Answering those and many other "what ifs" brought me on my own journey to a deeper encounter with Christ, and so the story reaches past the original narrative into the rest of Scripture to imagine the ongoing repercussions of sin and to rejoice in the redemptive power of Christ. The consequences of sin and the promise of redemption through Christ, I believe, are the most central themes of Genesis, and what connect the book to all of history. So, while this story is an expansion of the original text, nowhere did I draw any conclusions or intertwine any themes that couldn't be fitted into the original Hebrew text.

Two more notes should be made: one for the unusual capitalization of words such as "Music" and "Light"; and one for concepts jarring to the reader unfamiliar with the early Genesis stories.

Certain elements in the book refer to biblical concepts that needed to be grounded in the familiar, and for this reason, I used recognizable images or words and capitalized them when in reference to something other than themselves.

This story is also set in a culture vastly different from ours, and the critical reader must keep this in mind. Though I have modernized the story in many ways, other elements, such as Adam and Eve's children marrying each other, remain. While this may seem disturbing to some, nearly all biblical scholars agree this was the only choice, and was actually encouraged by God in this time period. It wasn't until thousands of years after this story takes place that God formed laws regarding siblings marrying (Leviticus 18).

Thank you for picking up this book. I hope you enjoy reading *Cain* and that it draws you closer to the heart of God.

PROLOGUE

Then the Lord God said, "Behold, the man has become like one of us in knowing good and evil. Now, lest he reach out his hand and take also of the tree of life and eat, and live forever—" therefore the Lord God sent him out from the garden of Eden to work the ground from which he was taken. He drove out the man, and at the east of the garden of Eden he placed the cherubim and a flaming sword that turned every way to guard the way to the tree of life.

—Genesis 3:22–24 ESV

Piercing cries echoed through the dark cavern. Adam felt Eve's fingernails dig at his hand hard enough to draw blood, but couldn't sense whether the moisture was blood or sweat as the shadows rendered it colorless.

He brushed back her hair as she drew air through flared nostrils like a wounded animal. Her body shook as she gritted her teeth and let out a scream longer and more agonized than any before. Then a sound that had never been heard in the world met his ears.

The sound of a human baby crying.

The sunrise breathed into the cave and warmed Adam's back as he cleaned the baby, cut the cord attached to its belly, and presented the newborn to Eve as a trophy marking months of struggle in the wilderlands. She accepted it with rapture and said in a shaky whisper, "With the Lord's help I have delivered a boy!"

Adam pressed his forehead to hers and laughed. His unmistakable reflection glowed in the newborn's features, but as he watched

Eve twirl the child's black hair, a cold sensation dulled the smile on his face and prickled the hairs on his arms.

Eve looked up from their child. "We should call him Cain, for he is our firstborn."

Adam looked up and, upon seeing the joy in his wife's eyes, smiled and nodded, and mouthed their baby's name to feel it on his lips. So much waiting, so much wondering. To finally experience the birth they had waited for produced a strange mixture of excitement, disbelief, and anxiety.

But as they entwined their fingers and rested, Eve let out a cry. "Something's wrong," she said.

He shook his head and swallowed, attempting to attend to her as her hand closed over his again. But no matter what help he offered, her screams grew. "Eve," he whispered, though she did not reply, seemingly too deafened by pain. "Eve."

"What?" she said through bared teeth.

"I think another child is coming."

Her breath accelerated and her neck muscles tensed as she screamed again. He whispered to her that all would be well, but his eyes caught the dark baby lying beside her, and the words seemed to fall apart in his mouth. He pressed his lips together and focused on helping her again. Finally, through her sweat, blood, and water, a second child plunged into the world and gasped in shock.

Adam lifted the second infant into the growing glow of daylight as it wriggled and squealed in discomfort. Another boy, except with platinum hair and a complexion to match. Adam looked at Eve with his own delighted smile. "We will call him Abel, for he came like a sudden gasp." He brushed the boy's hair aside and whispered, "My boy, Abel."

In a cave in the wilderness, the first children ever born lay cradled in their mother's arms. Abel on her left and Cain on her right. But the father's gaze rested most on Abel.

PART ONE:
MURDER

For your hands are defiled with blood
and your fingers with iniquity;
your lips have spoken lies;
your tongue mutters wickedness . . .
and from one that is crushed a viper is hatched.

—ISAIAH 59:3, 5 ESV

1

Cain stood on a nameless hilltop. He was far from the City, and below him stretched a vast field of long grasses and wild flowers. Several trees stood in the depression, but the valley was mostly flat and open, and cloud cover poured darkness into it like wine into a giant bowl. He studied a familiar figure in the midst of the valley as the smell of coming rain wove through the scent of plant and soil. Then he gazed into the growing eastern twilight and descended toward the figure.

The earth was soft beneath his feet. Moisture bubbled between his toes, and mud suctioned his feet in place, as if the world was attempting to stop him. He smiled at the thought.

Let everything try to stop me. Let the world try.

Upon reaching the bottom of the hill, he waded through the waist-high grass. A slight wind blew through the valley, brushed the blades back and forth in rippling waves, and caused them to shimmer. He focused on the figure he had followed to this place as his mind likened it to a statue, a silhouette chiseled out of the surroundings. He was close enough to be heard, so he stopped as the grasses beat his legs. Every moment was intoxicating, and though he had spent weeks planning every word he would speak tonight, he decided to savor the moment.

The winds settled and the silhouetted man addressed him in the lull. "Which do you enjoy more, the calm or the storm?"

Cain did not respond. The wind picked up again, and the grasses continued their attack on his legs.

"The clouds are in labor, but the floodgates are barred."

Cain took a step forward with clenched hands. The figure turned and his blue eyes gleamed. Cain knew those eyes well. He remembered seeing them gaze at him from a face soft with youth as the memory aged and merged with the shadowed figure before him.

Abel. The name spilled from countless recollections like a compendium of wasps.

"I know why you are here. You might as well voice your thoughts," Abel said.

Cain's head throbbed and his breath stuttered; so much depended on this encounter. "You have always wanted to frame me as a failure, haven't you?"

Abel paused before answering. "I have done nothing but speak truth."

"And strive to ridicule me."

Abel shook his head.

Somewhere, long ago, young Abel tugged on Father's garment and pointed, directing Adam's twitching frown and furrowed brow toward Cain. "You have always played the favorite." He broke a stalk of grass and tossed it. "I could have had respect and love, but you stole it."

"I have stolen nothing. Is it my fault if others show favoritism?"

"Of course it is. Don't play the fool. Every time I fall, you are there to take my place. Every mistake I make, you are there to correct it. Everything you do is born through your desire to be better than me. Since birth, life has been nothing but a contest between us, hasn't it?"

"I do what is right, and if that puts me ahead in others' eyes, so be it."

"Do I only do wrong?"

"You have sinned."

Cain laughed. "I take chances. I diverge from the well-trodden road to forge my own because that earth feels better under my feet. The dust kicked up by everyone else gets in my eyes and teeth, and I grow tired of spitting it out."

"It was not my desire that the Almighty would accept my sacrifice and not yours."

Cain knew his gift still lay by the altar caked with the dry blood of Abel's offering. The muscles in his neck flexed and pulsed with hot blood at the memory of the broken stalks of his garden lying discarded on stone and trampled by feet. He shook his head. "That wouldn't be enough to bring me here. You have played me for a fool since the day you learned you could."

Abel laid his words like a silk carpet between them. "I made my choices and you made yours. I have never been guided by malice."

"But you think me a stepping-stone. You cannot deny you have perpetually gained by my failure."

Abel bit his cheek and shook his head.

"You expect me to ignore the past hundred years?"

Abel's eyes chilled and sharpened, though his voice remained mild. "No matter what I say, you believe what you want to believe. Your jealousy has poisoned you against me."

Cain lowered the pitch of his voice. "I have not been jealous of you one day of my life."

"But I know you have. I know you better than any other."

"If you did, you would not open your mouth again."

"Are you threatening me? I have abided the hatred in your eyes for far too long. I have loved you all my life, but you have pitted yourself against me as if I were trying to usurp your place as first-born."

"I took care of you when you were weak. I protected you, I taught you, and I led you. *That* is love. What have you ever given me in return?"

Abel was silent.

The corner of Cain's mouth trembled. "And what do I get from everyone else? Father prefers you, he always has. From the moment you were born, I was unwanted. And now even the Almighty has rejected me."

"But I have done nothing to you."

"No, you've made sure of that. And your inaction, your calculated silence, it has twisted everyone I love against me."

"Give me proof, not empty words."

Cain remembered how Sarah's eyes had danced over Abel at the celebration the day before; and when Abel turned and met her gaze, a flame burned in her eyes like a spark in dry grass. Cain knew that look and had for years failed to draw it from her. It was admiration, attraction, *love*. Yes, as much as she tried convincing Cain otherwise, Sarah loved Abel. Cain scowled. "We both know my words are anything but empty."

Abel softened as if noticing Cain's cruel expression. "We are both sinners, brother." His voice lulled and pulled at Cain. "All of us, even our children and their children. It is the curse Father brought upon us by partaking in the forbidden fruit."

"Of that, you speak truthfully." Cain stepped forward, severing the space with sharp strides. He had grown weary of the argument. All pleasure deteriorated into impatience and irritation at the sound of Abel's voice. "So, brother,"—Cain smiled—"shall we have a contest like when we were children?"

He could smell Abel's breath and feel the heat of his body. Insects buzzed around their ears, but neither moved. He could see Abel's calculating gaze analyzing, attempting to understand.

Cain's smile cracked. "Let's see who the real sinner is."

As Abel's eyes narrowed, Cain seized him by the throat. The impact made Abel blink and sputter, but Abel shoved him back a few paces. Cain regained his footing as Abel massaged his throat and coughed. Then Cain rushed toward him, screaming as his shoulder made contact with Abel's midsection, sending them both to the ground. They tumbled through the towering grass, and Cain managed to roll on top of him and pound knuckles on his face, but then Abel struck back and the two twisted. Abel threw him off and rushed to his feet, stumbling like a drunkard. Cain scrambled up and leapt on him, flattening Abel on his belly. Cain pinned him to the earth with his knee and hammered the back of his head with knuckles hardened by harvest and hatred.

Abel went motionless. Cain paused, but his hand found a stone and gripped it hard. He poised the object high above and then smashed it into the back of Abel's head. As black emotions swelled within his chest and erupted as a bestial scream, he bludgeoned Abel's skull over and over again.

Eventually, Cain's limbs weakened, and he fell back. All around Abel's head and torso lay a glistening pool of liquid, flesh, and bone. No air entered Abel's lungs and no air escaped them. Cain stared at his brother's body, at the shape of the crater of collapsed bone and tissue. Nausea and pleasure coiled together, and he wondered if what lay on the ground were truth or fiction. It had been so simple, so quick.

But there it was. The smell of blood and brain blackened his nose.

"Murder," he whispered. The world had not known it possible, but with a stone and two hands, he had proven it was. He had never before felt so powerful and vulnerable at once, but as twilight fell into darkness, panic speared his shoulders.

What now? He had thought through each step countless times but the tossing froth in his stomach overwhelmed him. He bent, rested hands on knees, and breathed deeply against the rising nausea. He felt as if it would pass, but his body lurched and he wretched bubbling stomach acid.

He stayed bent, gasping for air and spitting the remains in spiderweb streams. The biliousness receded and his body relaxed, but a whispered voice came to him as if from far away. He thought it said, *"Bring the body to the river."* Cain stilled himself, wondering if it were anything more than amplified thought. Again he heard the voice, and chills scrambled up his neck. *"Bring the body to the river."*

He straightened and wiped his mouth. Could someone have seen him kill Abel? His lungs squeezed his throat with bony hands. Plants rustled in the wind and insects chirped. The screech of a distant owl pierced the night sky and ricocheted off the hills, but he could identify nothing abnormal. Nothing, except for the itch in his brain and the sweat in his clothes.

"Bring the body to the river. Take him to the river and wash yourself."

He couldn't seem to pinpoint the direction from which the

voice spoke. Though he knew sound behaved strangely in the hills, the displacement unnerved him.

"You need not fear."

He twisted and searched with narrowed eyes for a face, a body.

"Do what you must."

If it were the voice of the Almighty, he could not recognize it. In the long silence, he listened. No more words.

Cain nodded slowly. Then he stepped to Abel, stooped, and grabbed his garment by the neck with one fist. He began to drag his brother's body toward the river. He listened for the voice but heard only the wind in the hills and the crackle of thunder. Breath burst past his clenched teeth and his fingers ached with the weight, but all he could seem to see was blood glistening in the darkness. A shadowy trail through trampled grass.

So much blood . . .

The panic pulsed in his head, but the sound of rushing water just beyond the trees met his ears like cool water on cracked lips. He let the body drop. His arms and legs shook like tree limbs in a storm, despite his attempts to still himself.

"The river," urged the chilled voice again.

Cain's chest tightened.

"The river, the river, the river," it droned on and on, buzzing in his mind.

"Wait," he whispered. "Just wait."

"The river!"

He shook his head as the anxiety intensified.

Am I fighting myself, or does this voice actually exist?

He smeared bloody fingers through his hair as he sensed himself slipping into that familiar abyss where only panic existed. He wanted to beat himself, to rip his hair out, to silence the voice, but most of all he wanted to kill again, to feel that rapturous release.

He recalled feeling the rock in his hand as it made contact with Abel's skull. He thought of how the violent blows shook his shoulder, and how his vocal cords tore as his scream pierced the murky darkness. He had felt such power and pleasure. He had felt like God.

It made him sick.

"The river!"

"I know!" His voice echoed through the valley, but soon was swallowed by the roaring river. He ran to the body and hefted it again as desperation invigorated his limbs, but the world felt all too intangible.

Surely the corpse my knuckles strain against is only as heavy as my thoughts. Surely the voice is nothing more than a reaction to stress.

With aching shoulders, he arrived at the river's edge. It was wide and fast and, most importantly, flowed away from the City. The icy water washed his calves, and his thighs as he thrust the body deeper into the river and watched it bob and float along the surface. The current carried it away as Cain washed his arms and face, scrubbing his skin until it felt as if only bone remained. He plunged his head into the water, attempting to rinse the sticky matter that had congealed in his hair and clung like tree sap.

The voice returned. *"Cut it."*

He straightened as the hair on the back of his neck prickled through beads of cold water.

"Cut it off."

"Who are you?"

There was no answer.

"Tell me who you are!" He scrambled up the bank and searched for the source of the voice, but the entire world seemed overcome by rushing water. He let his eyes linger on the shivering stream, and asked again, only softer, as if trying to coax a child from hiding. When he grew tired of waiting, he chuckled anxiously, ran fingers over his matted hair, and walked home as if the world was as it always had been.

As if Abel were still alive.

The voice returned. Though his mind was absorbed by it, he let it be. When the volume increased, so did the itch in his mind, and he wondered if the two were connected. But he had little time to spare, so he did his best to ignore it, because it was time to see Sarah.

Sarah. My sister. My wife.

When at last he walked through the doorway of their home, she stood by the window. The sight of her shadowed figure stopped him just inside the threshold. She said nothing, but he knew she saw him. She had waited for him.

He walked to her slowly, unable to breathe. A mental image of Abel lying on the ground, dead, poured snow into his gut. He swallowed as he neared and saw her glowing eyes trace his stained figure. For the first time, the heat of guilt wetted his forehead.

Her breath was ragged, as if she had been crying. He paused and almost raised his hand to touch her, but stopped. She knew what he had done.

His dry voice hammered the silence. "I need your help, Sarah."

She stared, but did not speak.

He turned and headed toward their sleeping quarters, and she followed as he knew she would. He snatched a burning candle from the hall and set it in a holder that his son Gorban had made. The golden flame unveiled her face, and as their gazes met, every minutia was communicated. Sarah grimaced and looked toward the floor as if it would open up beneath her.

"I need you to cut my hair." He cleared his throat and whispered, "The blood . . ."

After a long, tense moment, she wiped her eyes and nodded.

He rubbed his face with shaking hands as Sarah retrieved a blade. When she returned, Cain sat cross-legged with his back to her knees.

She slid long fingers over his matted hair and recoiled from the gore. But slowly, reluctantly, she brought up the blade and began her work. The knife tugged and scraped and sliced, at times causing him to wince, but the pain made him feel alive.

Sarah was crying again. Part of him ached at the knowledge. The other part felt profound satisfaction that he had done what was necessary. He had no other escape. All logic within him demanded he murder Abel and test the bonds that held them within the walls of the City of the Almighty. Though his soul had at first been repulsed by the thought of murdering his twin, repressing his conscience had been a necessary progression.

"A step for humanity," whispered the voice in his mind. He tried to push it away, but couldn't help but agree. Yes, and who better to take that first step than he? He would take the fall. He would perform as they all expected him to. And he would rise again, stronger than before.

Or die in righteous rebellion.

His eyelids and the corners of his lips drooped at the sound of his hair tearing against the dull blade. The flame on the table stabbed the shadows, and as his thoughts spread and interwove, the rhythm of the blade carried him close to waking dreams. Like the swinging he had felt in his mother's arms so many years ago. The same arms that had held his brother.

A chunk of matted hair struck his nose. The smell of Abel's blood filled the air as though his body were hanging in the room, and suddenly the voice spoke again, whispering secrets in the dark. Sarah had stopped. He looked over his shoulder and saw her face buried in red-stained hands. She wept, but not for herself. Cain knew she cried for Abel.

He stood and walked out to wash his scalp. Even if he had wanted to, he could not have comforted her. It was the chasm between them. He looked at his hands and shook his head.

I killed you, brother, yet still I feel your hands pushing her from me.

His fingers clenched.

If only I could kill you again.

He lifted a pot of water high and pitched forward, letting the water cascade across his head. As the last drops fell, he lowered it to the ground, careful not to damage it. He wiped the water from his face and breathed deeply. The unexplained buzz drove him to seek solitude, and the whispering sporadically increased in volume until he could perceive words.

"Kill her," it commanded.

He shook his head. That, he would not do. Sarah would tell no one. Not until the time was right. She hated Cain, yet her fate was bound to his. And as much as he wanted her to experience pain for desiring Abel, he could not bear her death. Even as the hunger inside him grew.

He started at the paradox between his longing for her and the desire to end her life. The thought came to him that the voice, and its urgings, belonged to something else entirely, something new. He could no longer deny it, and the more he meditated on its meaning, the warmer it throbbed like blistered skin.

He shook his head to rid it of the buzzing itch as Sarah's cries continued growing until she wailed. He couldn't endure the sound, so he turned down the road and strode on. Billowing black clouds swallowed the sky. Strangely hued lightning bolts streaked through them and shook the ground with vengeful rumbles, but no rain fell. His eye twitched and his labored breathing brought no satisfaction. Each lungful felt hollow, somehow less than it should be.

He needed the rain. He had counted on the rain, had waited for a storm such as this. And yet it stalled.

He found a patch of soft grass underneath a large oak and closed his eyes, but he found no peace. So he stared at the sky and waited for it to wash away his sin. Hours slipped by like waterless droplets in an ocean of thought, but only one thought remained solid like the earth at his back. He closed his eyes and whispered, "Nothing could clean stains such as those."

He felt a strange peace in speaking it.

2

Lilleth's footsteps pattered the pathway like a bolting bird's. Abel hadn't returned, and Lilleth could wait no longer.

He must be in the hills searching for wayward sheep. He must be healthy and whole.

"That's a lie," she whispered. She could not evade the fact that he was gone, and never before had he been gone this long without explanation.

I have nothing to worry about. We're in the care of the Almighty. Nothing bad can happen to us. He promised we're protected.

More lies. She had every reason to believe, but could not. Why? Maybe something in her believed that evil could breach the Almighty's shield and end their happy, simple lives. Still, it eluded her. The years in the wilderness worrying about the Jinn, those demonic perversions of animal life, had not yet departed her consciousness, and the strangeness of the brooding storm disturbed old fears.

The world was dangerous. They didn't live in the Garden anymore, running free in naked innocence. Now they clothed themselves as they rose and went about with care and toil, working the ground with sweat and blood.

The world has changed.

Of course it has, she thought. *It has been a century and a half since we fled Eden.*

Her throat tensed. *Do not fool yourself. This is more than a consequence of the Fall. You sense something different.*

Lilleth hurried. The sky was as dark as night, though sunrise should have begun hours ago. The storm seemed malevolent, yet the Almighty had promised them protection from such forces.

"While you dwell in me, no danger will reach past the walls I have constructed. Not sickness, not demon, not nature."

The recollection of his voice in the wilderness evoked the taste of dust and the feel of wandering. Other sensations came as well, and though she had no desire to return to those days of hardship, she felt an affinity for them.

She bounded across the grass in front of Mother's home and called out as she pulled aside the flap hanging from the arched marble entryway and passed within. Dim lights flickered as the flap fell back into place, and she was suddenly aware of the sweat matting her clothes and her breath buffeting the silence. The stone walls seemed to stoop over her, their smooth texture dully reflecting the candle flame.

"Lilleth, what brings you here at such a time?" Eve sat like a tower on a hill, holding wool and needles in her hand.

"Have you seen Abel?"

Eve shook her head.

"I can't find him. He's been gone all night."

"I have seen no others since we left the celebration last night."

Lilleth hugged her waist. "I wonder if something has happened."

For a moment, it seemed shadows obscured Eve's face. "Come now, you know where we are." She set down her tools and waited for a peal of thunder to dissipate. "You have no cause to worry."

"Of course. I know." She rubbed her clammy palms together. "But it isn't like him to be gone so long, and he didn't explain why he walked off to the pastures last night. Such behavior is strange, even for Abel."

"I understand your concern, but we are in the City of the Almighty." She cleared her throat. "Are you all right? Did you just awaken?"

"I haven't slept at all."

Eve motioned to the cushion beside her. "Very well, sit and tell me what happened. Then I will make us tea."

Lilleth slid onto the cushion and forced a deep breath. "Last evening as the sun set, Abel acted oddly. He talked very little, especially for such a joyful day. The Almighty accepted his offering with

grace and gave him much honor, but he acted as if he had been—"
She paused and implied the rest with raised eyebrows.

Eve squinted.

"He acted as if he had been rejected. Like Cain."

Eve pursed her lips and nodded.

"And the things he said were strange. He kept mumbling about the storm and wouldn't respond to my questions. Then he said he was off to the pastures, and I haven't seen him since. All night I have been awake, staring at the sky and hearing its distant thunder. The darkness of the storm seems wrong and so does Abel's absence."

Eve opened her mouth as if to speak, then stared at the ground. When the silence grew heavy, she said, "Since we have been with the Almighty these past two years, we have been safe from danger. His Spirit is with us at all times, protecting us from beast and nature, from all manner of sickness, even from the Jinn. Abel must be safe . . . It is impossible for anything to have happened." Eve sighed, and her tone gained disapproval. "Dear daughter, when will you come to trust that we are safe in his arms? He loves and guards us fiercely. His intention is for us to live joyful, peaceful lives. He wants us to prosper. If he didn't, why would we serve him?"

Lilleth took in the words with a grimace.

Eve smiled. "Do you see?"

Lilleth nodded.

"Good."

"But could we not look for him?"

Eve's eyes narrowed. "Why?"

Lilleth pressed her hands to her chest and bowed. "For my sake. I wish to speak with him."

Adam entered the room with his tunic tied around his waist and a jug of water in his arms. He bent to set it on the ground next to the fireplace. Lilleth observed her father's shoulders, jawline, and eyes—so similar to Cain's.

"Adam," Eve said. He glanced at her. "Lilleth is wondering where Abel is. He's been gone all night. Would you go find him?"

Adam met Lilleth's gaze, then nodded at Eve. "After you're done with the tea, will you heat this for me?"

"I will make sure it is ready when you return."

Adam turned to Lilleth. "Where might he be?"

"He walked toward the pastures last evening."

Adam smiled, pulled the tunic over his torso, and nudged Lilleth. "Do not worry. I will find him." He walked into the morning twilight and was gone.

Lilleth breathed in, then forced it out. Eve laid a hand on her shoulder and smiled. "Abandon worry, beloved daughter. All is well."

Lilleth smiled and repeated, "All is well."

But it was little more than a whisper.

3

Seth bolted up in bed, and the woven covers slid off his shoulders. His pulse throbbed behind his dark eyes, and he swallowed the taste of metal while wiping sweat from his shaved head. Ayla moaned next to him and turned to peer through sleepy eyes.

"What is it?"

He swallowed, but the excess saliva did little to cure his throat's dryness. Already the details of the nightmare were falling out of reach, but still the world seemed to close in about him. "Just a dream, only a dream." He slipped out of bed, walked to the wall, and steadied himself with one palm. His legs wobbled as if unsure of the ground's stillness, and if Ayla hadn't been watching, he would have dropped to his knees.

She rustled in bed and sat up, brushing milky hair behind a flushed ear. "Are you all right?"

"Yes, I'm fine." She looked at him as if imploring him to explain, but he shook his head and said, "You can go back to sleep. I need to clear my mind."

She didn't lie down.

Seth walked the cold marble floor and slipped on his sandals. As hard as he tried, he could recall neither his dreams, nor any reason for fear, yet his belly was troubled by a creeping chill.

As he exited the stone house that the Man had crafted with his very own hands, the breeze carried the scent of leaves and flowers and damp earth. The brusqueness was rousing, so he began jogging the dirt road snaking between the houses that the rest of his family slept in. His joints ached. As he ran, he stared at the tumbling darkness above. Every so often, the sky was painted red with lightning, as if the bolts hemorrhaged the heavens.

For exactly seven nights, he had been awakened by nightmares. Only twice had he woken Ayla. Four nights earlier, he decided there may be a reason for the nightly recurrence. The effect of the nightmares on his body had intensified every evening, and even now, he trembled.

What are you trying to show me?

Seth lifted his eyes and followed the road up the hill to the well, which sat in the center of the City. His legs burned as the path climbed, and upon reaching the well, he sat on its ring. The rock edge dug into the back of his thighs as water whispered from within. Seth dropped a stone, waiting until it broke the surface of the water. He brushed the dirt from his hands and surveyed the surrounding land.

When they first came to the City two years ago, he had come to this hill every morning. The view and tranquility made it a resting place, and memories of times at the well hung in the air, calming the shakes. He thought of Ayla, her ivory teeth shining in the light of a summer day, laughing at him after he tripped on a stone. He smiled and moved on to the years ahead of them. He saw them clasping fingers and walking new roads with their brothers, sisters, nieces, and nephews as the sun rose and set.

But then he thought of his eldest brother Cain. After over a century of marriage, Cain and Sarah had clearly grown apart, and that reality drained the color from Seth's imagined future.

He shook his head and rubbed his face, redirecting his thoughts to his mother. He relaxed, thinking of Eve. When would she bear his next brother or sister? There were nearly eighty years between him and his older sister Lilleth. Mother and Father had been so focused on surviving in the days of their nomadic existence within the wilderlands that bearing children had been a luxury postponed. Seth had been a welcomed, albeit unintentional, gift after the Jinn had stolen Cain's eldest, Lamech, from the world. Still, they had grown as a people, with grandchildren and even great-grandchildren born through the fires of young love.

And now they lived under the protection of the Almighty. It

seemed only a matter of time before his mother conceived again. Even after all this time, he was excited by the thought.

Seth examined the back of his hands. His coloring was different from Cain's and Adam's. Theirs was an olive complexion, darkened by sunlight. Seth had come from the womb darker than either, and any exposure to sunlight had no visible effect. Would a new child look like him? Or like his wife and sister, Ayla, whose pale skin and green eyes reflected the sun like the sea?

The complexities of humanity were deep, and the thought of the Almighty's creativity widened Seth's smile. All of life seemed to coalesce as his eyes absorbed the City of the Almighty, crafted by the very hands of their Maker. In his mind he saw the connections form from his parents to him and his siblings, and watched them trace on through the generations, past Calebna and Lukian and to their children. Encircling them were the inner and outer walls of the City of the Almighty. Outside: Death. Inside: Life. A simple calculation. He liked it that way.

He breathed deeply, stood, and swept his gaze across the land. Something moved in the corner of his vision, and his blood frosted. A familiar feeling lodged itself in his belly.

"I have seen this before," he whispered.

Down in the valley, a lone person stood beneath the canopy of a tree. He hadn't noticed the figure before, as it had lain motionless, but he recognized it was his eldest brother, Cain.

A flood of images came upon him and threatened to burst his skull. In a fraction of a second, he saw blood drip from the tip of a knife, a woman's mouth gape in a scream, and a man's limbs break under the weight of violent hands. He tried to juggle the images and understand their connection, but they multiplied and expanded until he fell to the ground, thrust into blackness.

4

Adam walked to Cain and Sarah's home, the next closest building on the way to the fields. Upon arrival, he called out, and
Sarah's muffled reply sounded from inside, "Come in!"

He pulled aside the tapestry hanging from the stone archway
and entered. She was by the fireplace, the wood crackling as she
poured tea. The scent of jasmine blossomed in the smoky air as
she asked, "Would you like some? It is ready." She appeared to have
been awake for hours.

"Thank you."

She filled a wooden cup for him, and he smiled when she
handed him the vessel, though she looked away, placed the pot over
the heat, and sat on a cushion near the fire. "Did you sleep well,
Father?"

He sipped his tea, scalding his tongue before swallowing. "For
the few hours I was allotted. Calebna and I were the last to leave,
which would have been tolerable if not for my body deciding to
wake before sunrise." His eyes stung with the smoke, and he rubbed
them with his thumb and forefinger. "You seem alert."

Sarah scooted from the heat. "I could sleep no more, so I rose
and decided I needed tea."

Adam nodded. "It does calm the restless mind." He looked
around and listened for movement. "Is Cain resting?"

"No." Sarah brought the cup to her mouth and sipped several
times before turning her back to him. As he watched her, he was
warmed by compassion. As an infant, her grip had been strong and
her will stronger. Even now he saw her toothless smile as she hobbled into his arms for the first time, and he marveled at the swiftness
of time. Could the woman sitting before him really be that little girl?

Does she muse over Cain's humiliation?

He took a breath and finished the last of his tea. "Have you seen Abel?"

She paused longer than he thought natural. "Is he gone?"

Of course, that would remind her of the Almighty rejecting Cain's offering last night. He shouldn't have mentioned it. He cleared his throat of the mucus the tea had loosened. "He walked into the fields last night and has yet to return. Lilleth is worried. You know how she is. I checked on Seth before I came, wondering if he had seen him, but neither Seth nor Ayla were home. I know it's early, but have you heard anyone speak of where they may be?"

"I haven't. I am sorry."

"Don't be. Their house was a mess, though I suppose I shouldn't be surprised after the celebration yesterday. So much to prepare for, especially for the women, and Seth has never cleaned a thing in his life." Thunder rumbled in the distance. His words had brought tension, and he had little desire to add any more, so he set the empty cup on the ground and placed a hand on Sarah's shoulder. "Thank you for the tea. And may the Almighty bring you peace. His shame will pass."

Sarah stiffened, and he could see her eyes fill with tears. He frowned. Her relationship with Cain had struggled for years; such was obvious to all. And yet, she had remained faithful.

He squeezed her shoulder. "You deserve more than he has given you."

She shuddered.

He kissed the crown of her head and whispered, "You're a strong woman. You should be proud." He turned and left. Thoughts of Cain had put him in a mood, and he wanted to talk with Abel. If he knew his son at all, he knew where he would be.

5

C ain stood and began to walk home. The storm above raged like a caged beast. It tore through the atmosphere with invisible claws streaking red across the sky. As a fresh carcass impassions a hungry dog, the sight made him long for Sarah. But after over a century of marriage, the endless fighting had distanced them. He realized it was merely a symptom of the Fall.

Proof of my father's failure, he thought.

He and Sarah, at moments, felt something more than loyalty to each other, but thinking on it made the past sting all the more.

He breathed deeply, savoring each portion of air that was free of Abel's presence. He would endure the years of torture again just to feel such rapture as he had with that final blow, and he hungered for it with an intensity that frightened him.

He had hoped that freedom from Abel's presence would remove the sickness, but though the pleasure had faded, the sickness endured. He breathed deeply and reminded himself of all the reasons he had killed his twin. Then he shivered as he remembered the chill voice that had rested on his ear in the darkness of the valley. It had become so constant he had almost forgotten it, but if he focused, he was able to recognize its presence again. It was there, it was real, and it was something other than him.

The thought that there could be something inside him manipulating his decisions was disturbing. *But eventually,* his mind reasoned, *knowledge will unveil the mysterious as benign—just as the morning sun burns the shadows.*

He ran a hand across his scalp and wondered at how no one but he and Sarah knew of Abel's death. Everyone in the City of the Almighty was ignorant of Abel's body now rotting on the river's surface.

And what of the Man? Did he know? Did he understand?

Yes, Cain thought. *Understanding. It will come, all in time.*

He quickened his pace, rounded a corner, and saw someone exiting his home. He slid behind the nearest wall, held his breath, and listened past the thrum of his heartbeat. The sound of the footsteps faded, but the identity of the person remained.

"Adam," he whispered.

Father must have visited Sarah and was now walking toward the fields.

He wiped away the sweat on his brow and allowed his lungs to reinstate their rhythm. Could they be searching for Abel so soon? His heartbeat raced, and he shook his head. Impossible. They believed too deeply in the Almighty's protection to support suspicions already.

His fingernails dug into his palms as he looked up and willed the boiling clouds to wash away the blood in the field. He ground his teeth. "What are you waiting for?"

He'd hoped for more time to prepare. He couldn't deny he wanted to be present when they found out, to see the knowledge creep across Father's face, but he knew what would happen if he stayed that long, and for her sake, he could not risk it.

He threw occasional glances backward, but the streets were vacant and he reached his home quickly. As he entered the foyer, the scent of his wife's hair was almost palpable. She stood by the window, bending in an uncomfortable position, as if to peer through the window without being seen.

All the noise in his head, even the ever-present whispering, quieted as he admired her. Then his foot slapped the ground and she spun and cried out, knocking a bowl of fresh olives off the table. Her eyes flashed as she cupped her mouth. She lowered her shoulders, but her eyes burned with fear. Her voice was hushed. "Are you alone?"

"Of course. Why?"

"You scared me." Her breath came in uneven lurches. "They're looking for him. If they find out what you did . . ." She shook her head.

Cain's smile flattened. If they found the blood, suspicions would grow. There would be no way around it.

His eyes narrowed. Had she said something? The thought made bile bubble up his throat.

She wouldn't have. She's more afraid than I am of what they might do if they find out the truth.

His eyes roved over Sarah's body. Then he walked past her to the next room and sank into a cushion. The voice came back louder, and he had a difficult time ignoring it.

She followed, her words hushed and her eyes glancing about. "I know what I told you, but I didn't actually want him dead. I was just angry. You know that. You must know."

He closed his eyes and leaned back while supporting his head. The voice droned on with hers, gnawing at his patience like an insect, commanding him to get up, to finish what he started and flee the City. "Say what you must to deliver yourself from guilt."

Her lips pressed into a thin line. "So cold."

"I say what needs to be said. You would do well to imitate me."

"Father came to get your help looking for Abel. I couldn't hold back my tears."

Cain glared at her.

"I said nothing. He knows nothing."

"Then leave me in peace."

She waited, and he sensed the disquiet inside her. "What happens if they find him?"

"They won't."

"What if they figure it out?"

"It doesn't matter."

"How can you say such things?"

Cain stood, grabbed her arms, and shook her. "Whether you wanted him alive or not, he's dead. He won't ever come back. You cannot change the past. Nor can you remove your fingerprints from it."

Tears formed in her eyes and her lips parted. He could see the fear, but also the searching. Her gaze darted from his left eye to his right.

He frowned. "I have simplified life. No more choices, no more questions. Just follow the path before you."

Her muscles tensed beneath his hands. She was a wild deer, poised to escape. Untamed for a century and counting. "Where will that path lead me?"

"Have patience. Just know that I"—he paused and let his gaze jump across her features—"I won't let them hurt you. This is a new beginning for you and me. I have shaken the world. It will take time for them to adjust."

She stared while the voice in Cain's mind grew louder. Over and over it repeated the same refrain, urging him to travel east. He felt his limbs' desire to respond to those words, like a flame to his feet, and now, with the possibility of discovery only hours away, he knew it was almost time. As much as he wanted to deny the possibility, he had to flee soon. Yet the knowledge of what he must do to Sarah was immobilizing.

He cursed Lilleth's inquisitive and worrisome nature. For the first time in his life he actually wanted someone to be stupid. His grip tightened on Sarah's arms. *Remain calm,* he thought. *You must remain calm.*

He tipped his mouth to her ear and whispered as sweat broke out on his skin, "If they really are searching for Abel already, then I have to leave for a while. Just remember what I told you. Remember me."

She pulled away. "What do you mean? What are you talking about?"

He hushed her, forcing a smile though sweat burned the corners of his eyes. "Do not fear. I promise I will come back for you, no matter what happens. I will fix it all. Just know that everything that happens is a part of the plan I have set into motion."

It felt good to hold and comfort her. He was surprised he wanted to comfort her. Their lives had been set on the edge of a knife, and now everything had changed. With a stone and two hands, he had changed the world.

He thought of how her body felt against his. Such a beautiful creature in every way. He desired her now as he had not in many years, and he slipped his hand lower down her back. His mind moved on, imagining enjoying her once more, but she jerked herself out of his grasp after sensing his intentions.

Anger burned his throat, and he thrust his palm into her face with such speed he hardly perceived the crack of his hand against her cheek. She stared with mouth gaping and brought a hand to cover the wound. To his surprise, the look in her eyes forced an ache through his numb interior like a spear through a wild pig.

He turned and strode out of the room as she sank to the floor and cradled her face. He stopped after a few paces and leaned against the wall to steady his breathing. She was crying quietly.

He breathed deeply, pushing his fingers through his shortened hair. All he wanted to do was hold her, but he knew he could not. It was far too late for that. The ache in his chest could not be dislodged no matter what he did, and the whispering voice droned on.

He rushed to the next room, grabbed a leather satchel, and started throwing miscellaneous items inside. Treasured carvings, gifts from his children, flint, rope, a rain cloak made of cured animal skin.

What had he been thinking? He loved her. He had always loved her. And he always would. She had been good to him. Maybe too good. His mind was stressed, being pulled in many directions at once.

He didn't hate her.

And yet he hated her.

He loved her.

And yet he could not love her.

"One day," he whispered and thrust a loaf of bread into the satchel. One day he would heal the old pains, the disappointments. They would all be replaced.

He tossed the bag on the ground and pushed away the temptation to believe he could avoid damaging her. He had struggled with the decision for many days, but even if it would break her, he would rather her experience pain, than have to live without her.

He rubbed his eyes, unable to remember what else he needed to pack. It felt as though insects were burrowing through his legs. He cleared his throat and started pacing.

He had so carefully calculated each step, his reaction to every possible inquiry. Even so, there had been complications. His family had grown suspicious too soon. The rain had not come. Adam was searching for Abel. And there was the voice. Yes, that was what had thrown him. He had let it creep under his skin and push him to talk with Sarah for comfort, like a fool.

Too much weighed against his will. He was losing acuity, becoming distracted. He could wait no longer; it was time to act.

I will come back for you, Sarah. I will. I must.

6

Adam scratched the jaw of a young sheep looking up at him through rectangular pupils. It chewed on grass as if indifferent to the world. Its relatives stood about doing the same, and scattered between them were gnarled trees. They looked old, maybe a few as aged as he.

Life had moved so quickly in the century and a half since walking in the Garden. And how long had they lived inside It? He remembered the strange speed at which time seemed to flow there. With unending restfulness and peace in the Light of the Almighty's presence, they had labored hard and yet all had been joyful. In the Garden, work remained no more than a building block of satisfaction.

Then their world had crumbled.

He looked at the flock of sheep again. Few of them could have been more than several years old, yet who knew what the eyes of the eldest sheep had witnessed? In a world so much more temporal than the Garden, the curse was felt by all with deadly force.

His brow furrowed as he noticed a lump on one of the sheep's shoulders. He touched it and the sheep jerked away. As it did so, Adam noticed another lump on the side of its head.

I will have to show this to Abel when I find him.

He had never seen an animal suffer from such a malady before. None of their animals had taken sick since wandering the wilderness, and the Almighty had assured them their animals would remain healthy within the City's walls.

So what then was this?

He patted the tangled fur on its shoulder and attempted to reason it away. He should talk to High Priest Calebna after he found Abel.

He resumed walking.

He and Abel used to walk together often. And when Abel grew old enough to compete, they raced. The first time Abel beat him was on the outskirts of a desert whose creeping sands had slowly encroached on the niche they had carved into the cliffs. That day the dunes reflected the sun like so many mirrors, and the blue sky was devoid of blemishes. Abel had turned and slapped his hand, and they had walked home to find Cain had abandoned the herd of sheep once again to scout the wilderness for game.

Truthfully, Adam couldn't remember the last time he and Cain had done anything. And the last time Abel provoked Cain into competition was when Cain still found joy in how Abel looked on him with shining eyes.

Cain. A leader in all things, even from the beginning. What had happened?

"I am my own man, Father," Cain said. "I am not, and do not want to be, anyone but myself."

"You are destroying relationships, and for what reason? To keep your pride? Give it up. Stop fighting against everyone. None of us desires it. We just want peace, we want to be a family again."

"As do I. But you won't find it by trying to change me into something you prefer more. If I am not good enough, so be it."

Adam frowned as his feet slid through the grass. Remembering the fight angered him. It had only served to increase the tension between Cain and the others.

Everything I do fails to make an impression. Such thick-headedness. Such stupidity.

The problems had yet to resolve themselves as he imagined they would upon returning to the Almighty. Now he wondered if they ever would. And even though it gave him no comfort, he continued praying.

He crested a hill and saw a valley spread away filled with grass and freckled with trees. It was the space between Abel's pastures and Cain's fields, and he descended into it, making his way toward a patch where the grasses looked depressed. The dark clouds rendered light little more than shadows, but as he reached the clearing, he saw spots of color, as if the grass was sickly. The spots were positioned around a pool of liquid that lay beneath crushed grass, and he stopped and ran his hand over the stalks to break the surface of the liquid with his fingertip. He brought it to his nose, and as the scent entered his lungs, his scalp tingled.

Blood?

Looking around, he found clumps of hair. Picking them up, he rolled them between his fingertips. More blood came off them, and the hairs themselves were light. Very light.

"My God," he whispered as shadows encroached on his vision. "What is this?"

Adam rubbed his face. He was becoming paranoid. Lilleth's fear had planted the seeds of unnatural thoughts. *You only fear danger to your son because you have been searching for him.*

But what could explain the blood? And hair? What animal had such light hair and with such a texture?

He noticed a faint trail ahead, and he sidestepped the blood and followed the trail toward the line of trees that veiled the river in the distance. The grasses bent as though something had been dragged this way. The Almighty had never sanctioned the killing of animals unless for sacrifices, and surely no animal was allowed to be slaughtered in the fields and dragged so far, even here, between the inner and outer walls that the Almighty had built as boundaries to the City and the pasturelands outside it.

The hairs. The fine, light hairs. Each second stretched into hours. The Jinn, those demonic half beasts, could not have entered this far. Surely with the Almighty's protection, humanity was safe. Had he misunderstood?

He scratched his beard. No, the reason he agreed to come back to the Almighty was for the relief that very promise offered his family, who were so burdened by the unnatural pressures he had purchased them by tasting the fruit they should not have tasted.

He reached the river and found footprints in the mud. He bent to one knee and examined them. They were human and fresh, maybe a day old. He traced his fingers over the curvature of the arch, the five toes and shape of the heel.

Droplets fell from the sky as he ran his hand across his forehead. What had happened? No animal would be thrown in the river. Such wastefulness was not only sinful, but it was foolish. Abel would never do such a thing, would he? He had buried every animal that died under his care with honor and solemnity. And sacrifices were given with equal respect.

His eyes widened. Could it have been Cain?

Cain had been gone earlier, and Sarah had acted strangely. It certainly was possible Cain had been in the field and slaughtered one of Abel's sheep. But why? Retribution for the sacrifices the day before?

What if it had been someone else?

But this was Abel's pastureland, and his flock was still here, and both Cain and Abel were gone. Cain's hair was black as coal. Abel's was almost white. The hair he had found was not an animal's, and Abel would not have harmed himself, and couldn't have dragged himself to the river. Whoever made the footprints was uninjured, and whatever was dragged had been large.

He could not admit that Cain may have harmed Abel. *But what if he had?*

Adam squeezed his eyes shut and rubbed them. How could he think such blasphemy? The Almighty held them safely. He had promised. Was he then a liar? "Let me die before I entertain such thoughts."

He turned and started for home, his knuckles white from unanswered questions. He sped until he was jogging, anxiety growing until his breaths came in shallow pulls. Then he sprinted, pushing his legs until they burned with exhaustion. Drops of rain fell faster. One landed on the bridge of his nose, and others came until the storm matured and fell in sheets.

PART TWO:
RETRIBUTION

Then Satan answered the Lord and said, ". . . Have you not put a hedge around him and his house and all that he has, on every side? You have blessed the work of his hands, and his possessions have increased in the land. But stretch out your hand and touch all that he has, and he will curse you to your face." And the Lord said to Satan, "Behold, all that he has is in your hand. Only against him do not stretch out your hand." So Satan went out from the presence of the Lord.

—JOB 1:9–12 ESV

7

C ain stood in his bedchamber and shoved the last few items into the satchel as he recalled a moment eight nights earlier when he had surrendered to his murderous desires and embraced the decision to plan his brother's death; when his mind had plunged into endless darkness, and hours later he woke naked on the stone floor of his house, wondering if he had already committed the act. After actually consummating the sin less then twelve hours ago, he felt the familiar sensations creep up the back of his skull. The strange itching ballooned in his mind as he felt himself slipping, falling into that nameless space he had come to know and hate.

He screamed and thrust his fist into the wall. The voice pulled at him, wagging its tongue in his ear, but Cain pressed his palms against his head. *Leave me!*

But it would not. It was inside of him. Its desires throbbed against Cain's mind like a beating heart. Beating. Beating. Beating!

This isn't how it is supposed to be. I wanted freedom from the Almighty's tyranny, from the expectation to live in impossible perfection. Instead, I am teetering on the borderlands of madness.

A chill scuttled through the building and under his clothes. The whispering grew until it was all he could hear, and he squeezed his eyes and fists shut and waited for the darkness to swallow him.

Instead, all went silent.

He waited. No voice. No itch. No burning passion to consume life. He opened his eyes and sensed normalcy like an infant waking from a dream. "Hello?"

The room echoed silence. The dark corners feigned calm, but

he sensed with a shiver something was present. For a moment, he wondered whether it was paranoia.

"Give it to me."

He spun to the voice. His mind stumbled, but after blinking he couldn't deny that he saw what appeared to be a little boy with silver eyes, silver hair, a tall forehead, and an elongated nose above a set of thin lips. Its neck was tall with dark arteries, and though it stood before him as if it belonged, something he could not place rendered it alien.

"There's no more time."

The hair on the back of Cain's neck prickled. He knew that this had been the itch in his mind, the voice he had obeyed the previous night as he dragged Abel's body to the river. The fact was disturbing, and he felt nausea ride up the sides of his stomach. Words circled through his mind, but only three found their way to his tongue. "Who are you?"

"You will know me in time. But now, you must obey."

The creature seemed surreal, but Cain could not doubt its reality, for he saw it with his eyes and felt it with his soul. The thing's lips curled like straw in fire—a convulsive, flashing expression.

Saliva pooled in Cain's mouth. His face twisted and his legs burned to run, but his body would not respond. He was locked in place, forced to stare into those eyes as he felt the world buzz. The Almighty's warning one day earlier returned. *"If you do not do well, Sin is crouching at the door. It desires to devour you, but you must rule over it."*

"Is your name Sin?"

"Come," it commanded. *"Give it to me and I will show you the way. He is calling us."*

Cain tried to look away but only managed to tip his head.

It frowned and arched its eyebrows with something like sadness. *"Still holding on? Too proud to give in?"*

Cain's response was no more than a throaty grunt.

"I will break you."

Would it kill him? Would those eyes, those silver rims around black holes, suck him up and never let go?

The silver boy turned and, with a motion of its hand, evaporated. Cain bent and vomited. When he finished retching, he laid down and let new thoughts enter his mind.

Which is the illusion—the Almighty or the hope of having any freedom at all?

8

S eth could not move. Nor could he quite see. At least, not in close detail. What he did see were shapes like murky outlines in a clouded pool, and soon those shapes and lines congealed and formed a silhouette, and then a face.

He knew that face. It was familiar, and yet seemed like a painted image. The painting's expression changed, and he wondered what could be happening. Was he dreaming?

Its lips formed his name, and its eyes strung heady emotions through the holes in his soul. For a moment, all was calm. Its hair fell over him, glaring in the light, and he winced. The world rushed in with strangling intensity. Hands clamped down on his arms, and everywhere there was pain. He could hear his breathing, and that of the painting, like pulsating counterrhythms atop a symphony of winds—like terrible Music.

The world slowed and quieted. "Seth." It whimpered as droplets of color slapped his forearm. "Seth!"

This was no painting. He shook his head. How had it taken him so long to recognize who it was? The light mellowed. The picture sharpened. With difficulty, he lifted his arm and wrapped fingers around the hand on his chest. "Ayla?" The word barely limped out.

She fell on him and wept.

"What's wrong?" His tongue felt like wadded wool. He looked at his bruised and bloody arms. "What happened?"

"I don't know." She squeezed his waist. "I left to find you, hoping to join you on your walk. But then I saw you fall on this hill, and when I arrived, you were thrashing yourself against the stones. I was scared. So scared."

He squeezed her hand and rubbed the back of it with his

thumb. The thumping in his throat slowed, and the muscles in his face relaxed; but he struggled for breath, and his head was filled with painful pressure. "I'm all right. I'm fine now. I'm sorry I worried you." His muscles ached and burned.

"What happened?" He lay frozen by the way the tears revealed the color of her eyes. She went on pawing at his chest. "Are you sick?"

He reached through the murk to grasp at his memories. "I think I had a vision. Such terrible images. I saw . . ." He swallowed and shook his head, not wanting to continue. "Terrible things. Can we not speak of it? Remembering makes me feel strange."

"Of course. We don't need to talk about it."

He swallowed and attempted a smile, but it probably looked painful, because it was. "Can you help me up?"

She rose to her knees, grasped his hand, and helped him lean against the wall of the well. His arms and legs had cuts and bruises, and his joints felt swollen. Dark blotches appeared on Ayla's arms and face. He pointed to her cheek and she touched the spot and winced.

"Is that from me?"

She nodded.

What had happened when those visions rushed in? They certainly had not come from the Almighty, so maybe he really was sick. He gazed at the black clouds in the sky, and a spear of panic struck him. He tried to stand, but Ayla pushed him to the ground. "What do you think you're doing?"

"I'm going home," he said.

"What if it happens again?"

"You want to wait until we're soaked by the storm?"

"We don't know what's wrong with you."

He shrugged. "It was just a dream."

"Does a dream overtake you as you walk? Does a dream make you injure yourself?"

The sound of sporadic droplets striking the leaves punctured the silence, and Seth wondered at how long it had taken the storm to start. "Don't you think it odd that this storm has been hanging over us for days, but not a drop has fallen until now?"

"Is that all you can think about? You're injured. If it happens again, you might throw yourself down a hill or worse."

"You forget that we're in the City of the Almighty. You're starting to sound like Lilleth."

"Tell me how we were protected from these." She pointed to the marks on their bodies.

He was startled by the realization that what she said held weight. It was true that they were still in the City of the Almighty, and that the Man had promised them safety as long as they dwelt with him.

He looked at the bloody contusions on his arm. *So, what do these mean?*

Something was different. He could feel it in his bones.

He glanced at Ayla, whose pale face was rounded by concern. He reached up and clumsily pushed a tassel of hair behind her ear. "I will be all right. I promise. We should wait to speak more until we've gotten under shelter."

Ayla stood and brushed the dirt and grass from her knees. "Father's house is closer. We will go there, but you will not walk without my aid. And when we arrive, you will do no more than lie down and rest. Agreed?"

He nodded and smiled. She frowned. Droplets fell faster as he draped his arm over her shoulders for support, and she helped him stand.

"I will let you know when I sense the next dream coming."

"No. No more dreams."

The rain intensified and as they walked, his knee bothered him less, but when he tried convincing her he could continue on his own, her grip only tightened. They made their way slowly and were drenched by the time they arrived at the gray arch of their parents' home, which sat apart from the others that knelt clustered together like so many stone bodies bowing at the foot of the Temple.

He saw Eve peering up at the storm from inside. When she saw them, she called out. "What are you doing in the storm?"

"Seth fell at the well. He is having trouble walking," Ayla yelled. Thunder pealed and shook the ground. "Is he all right?"

"I think he's sick."

Eve came out and braced Seth's other side. "Come inside and rest. We'll dry your clothes. Tea is ready."

Seth nodded thankfully as they ushered him dripping through the doorway.

Eve glanced at Ayla. "Lilleth is here."

"And Abel?"

"He never returned last night. She came here this morning to ask if we had seen him."

"Have you?"

Eve bit her cheek and shook her head as they passed into the lounge, where Lilleth lay on a cushion and gazed into the fire as if lost in thought. Eve and Ayla helped Seth to one of the cushions, and Lilleth noticed them with wide eyes. "Brother, are you not well?" Her sparrow voice sounded strained.

Seth nodded and smiled, then winced. "I'm fine."

Ayla mumbled something directed toward him, shook off her soaked clothing, and helped him do the same—though not without a bit of roughness, he thought. Eve handed them cotton rags to blot their hair and skin with, and soon they donned new dry garments.

Eve removed the tea from the flames and poured a cup for each. Seth accepted the wooden vessel and breathed deeply. Chamomile, mint, and lemongrass, brewed overstrong. Eve returned the pot and slid it from the flames, either ignoring or not noticing Lilleth's glare.

They blew on their tea and sipped without speaking. Ayla twisted her wet hair behind her head, Lilleth wrung her fingers, and Eve sat cupping her tea with both hands. After a while, Seth smoothed the coverings on his legs and said, "This storm is unusual."

Eve nodded and Lilleth seemed to whiten a shade, though it was hard to tell in the firelight. The only sound was the pitter-patter of the rain on the roof. Lilleth would not look at them, and Eve stared blankly, the creases in her face deepening.

Seth caught Ayla's gaze, and they exchanged curious expressions. He cleared his throat. "What has happened?"

Eve glanced up. "Nothing. Nothing has happened. Adam is looking for Abel. He left this morning and has yet to return."

Ayla addressed Lilleth. "I assumed when I saw Abel leave the celebration last night that he was going home."

Lilleth hugged her knees and rested her chin on them.

"Lilleth and Abel returned home after the celebration, but afterward he left for the fields," Eve said.

For a moment, it seemed to Seth as if clouds darkened the flames in the hearth, though he did not know why.

Ayla addressed Eve, since Lilleth seemed in a strange mood. "Seth fell at the well earlier this morning. I found him on the ground, moving as if lost in a dream. After a while he awoke, but he's been injured."

Eve glanced at Ayla. "Injured?"

Ayla's voice gained an edge. "Yes. He has bruises and cuts from where he struck rocks."

Eve furrowed her brow at Seth. "Why would you do such a thing?"

"I think I was dreaming."

"Do you not remember?"

"I remember sitting on the edge of the well."

"I meant your dreams," Eve said.

"You never did say," Ayla said.

Seth sighed and wiped his face. He sensed their gazes, but he suddenly felt weary and a little sick. "I'm unsure what it means, if anything, and I know it might sound strange coming from me, but I'd rather rest than talk right now, if you don't mind." His head throbbed, and he rubbed his temples. The pain came in waves.

Eve folded her hands in her lap. "Of course. You should rest."

"I will be fine." Seth felt Ayla's hand on his leg. He breathed deeply and leaned back to ease the pressure, but his swollen joints and muscles pained him, and the cushions offered little relief.

The silence returned, and Ayla shifted. "Do you have any idea what it might be?"

"Sorry?" Eve said.

"Do you have any idea what might have happened to Seth?"

Eve shook her head. "It is new to me, whatever it is. Perhaps . . ." Her eyes dulled. "No, I have never seen or heard of anything like it." She turned toward the fire and seemed to fall back into heavy thought.

Ayla stood, as Seth knew she would, and cleared her throat. She never could abide silence. "Thank you for the tea. Is there anything I could help you with in return?"

Eve smiled, but somehow looked wearier. "There are bowls and clothes needing to be washed. You may finish them."

Ayla spun away, and Eve called after her saying she could stay and rest, but she had already vanished. Seth's brow wrinkled as he tried to find a comfortable position to rest.

"Adam is looking for Abel."

The significance rolled in his mind. He rubbed his forehead and sighed. Surely he needed rest, but he was afraid of what might happen if he slept.

The dreams . . .

Thunder rumbled the house, and the sound of rain increased to a roar. Wood creaked with the winds, and the buildings howled. It sounded strangely orchestrated, as if a part of some subtle Music too discreet to be fully known.

Exhaustion took over, and he closed his eyes. As he drifted, he pictured places Abel might be, and reasons why he might not have returned.

Then he dreamed a series of nightmares he would not remember.

9

The City was washing away. Cain could hear it as he smashed their jars and broke their furniture. The winds screamed at their house. The rain pelted the earth, flying through the tented arched windows and gathering into puddles on the floor. It was so loud he didn't notice Sarah until she grabbed his shoulder and shook him.

"What are you doing?" she asked.

"What needs to be done."

"Destroy our house and our things? Why?" Her fingers needled his arm as he pulled away. Her red hair was disheveled and her face was dotted with water from the storm. He couldn't remember a time she looked so haggard. "What's going to happen to me? What will our children think when they find out what you've done?"

He grabbed a small table and lifted it above his head. She released him and shuffled back, her eyes black and wide.

Do you think I would kill you too?

He yelled and smashed the table on the ground, its fibers exploding. Sarah screamed, pressed her hands over her ears, and shut her eyes. "Stop it. Stop!"

"No."

"You're a monster."

"What if I am?" He could feel the blood hot in his cheeks. "What if I am?"

Her voice warbled and she sank to her seat, cradling her face in her hands. He was surprised at her reaction. At how much she seemed to care. He wondered if he were making a mistake.

What if she really does love me?

But the buzzing in his mind made it difficult to focus. The voice was mumbling, then speaking.

No, not just speaking, it was shrieking.

"She only cares because you're all she has left, because Abel is dead, and when you leave she will have no one left to love her, no one left to hold her or to keep the darkness at bay. Your children are all grown and no longer need her. She uses you, she always has."

He shook his head. She had loved him once. And with Abel gone, there was no one else she *could* love. But then again, that was the point, wasn't it?

She was shaking. She was wailing. Her body was alive, but the sobs were the sound of a soul falling to pieces.

My wife's soul.

His eyes softened. He wanted to kneel and scoop her into his arms like a child. He wanted to hold her and bring her to their bedroom and press his lips against hers with all the passion he felt in his chest.

"But you can't stop now. It will all fail if you stop, and you know it. She has to believe you hate her. She has to detach from you. If she doesn't, she will either die at the hands of your family, or follow you into the deadly wilderness. Everything you have done will fail if you comfort her in this moment. Break her. Break her!"

He grabbed the broken remains of the table, lifted it high, and smashed it on the floor. "I am a monster. I killed him, and I'll kill anyone who gets in my way. I am a monster." He beat the floor with the wood. His chest heaved with the intensity of his breathing, and he dropped the remnants. Sarah was no longer looking at him, for her eyes were hidden behind her hands.

He rushed into the other room, grabbed his satchel, and came out, stopping one last time to look at Sarah's crumpled figure. Lightning boomed overhead and seared the image of the room in his mind with white silhouettes. He had to get out of the City while he still had time. Wanderlust burned his legs, and he could resist no longer. Everything had been rushed. The broken remnants of their furniture and pottery lay scattered about the room.

Details that will distract and confuse. Misdirection.

The voice returned. *"They will think she fought with you. They will think you left her like the worthless whore she is, and they will look on her with sympathy. Then, when you return . . ."*

Cain's hand extended and his throat constricted painfully. He nearly risked everything in that moment to speak words of comfort, to whisper he loved her and to hear her say it back, but thunder pealed and muted him. His cheeks flushed as fantasies fell and disappeared like ash. Desire for her tender touch cracked and bled shame, and a sudden craving to beat her rose in his chest. He turned and flipped up his hood instead. He hesitated, caught between rage and some longing he could not describe. Then he strode out of the room and into the storm, leaving Sarah alone on the floor.

If someone had seen him walking in the storm that night, they may have thought the wetness on his cheeks was only rain. But it was not.

10

Adam strained for air. He had to get back. If Cain really did it . . .

He stumbled forward as the tears on his cheeks became lost in the raindrops pattering his face like tiny wooden paddles. Lightning flashed and thunder rattled his teeth, and the long grasses, which before had swayed so blithely in the breeze, were wet hands grasping his legs. He struggled on. He fought the world to get back to his family, to find them safe. But when he reached the last hill and looked down on the buildings, his heart coughed and sputtered.

Adam mumbled a quick prayer and made for Cain's home. He slipped down the hill and fell on his palms, splashing mud in his eyes. He scrambled up, flung the muck from his hands, wiped his face, and grit his teeth. He loped on until he saw their house. As he entered Cain's home, he recognized a scent he had missed when last there. The faint, though unmistakable, smell of death.

He breathed deeply.

That's the smell of your son. The last sign you'll ever have of him. Abel is dead, you fool.

Sarah sat in the same position he'd last seen her in, though all the furniture had been broken and lay scattered among shards of pottery, and there was no longer any fire in the fireplace, though three candles burned to her right.

The room bore the signs of long-bred violence, and she seemed to cower in the shadows.

"Where is he?"

She did not respond.

"Sarah, where is he?"

She rubbed her arms.

"Is he gone?"

She nodded.

He tried steadying himself against a table, but his arm pushed off a broken piece of pottery and sent it clattering across the floor. "Did he really do it? Did he really kill my son?"

Her warm alto was frosted with shame. "Yes."

He breathed raggedly, his wet clothes producing pools on the floor. He watched a droplet grow on the end of his fingertip and saw it change color. The forbidden fruit hung and swayed, and Eve reached for it and broke it off. After she took a bite, he received it from her one mouthful lighter. Oh, how it felt to puncture its skin and let the coppery taste fill his mouth. It tasted of death. The same smell that hung in this room, only one hundred fifty years later.

Sarah wept quietly.

How could she have said nothing? How could she live here with that serpent and not warn anyone? He strode to her, grabbed her shoulders, and shook her. "Tell me where he is."

She guarded her face. "I don't know."

"You're lying."

"I thought he was going to kill me."

"You're lying!"

"I wish I were." Her jaw clenched, and her red hair twisted about her head like a motionless fire.

He turned away, and all he could think of was Abel, his son. Lost. Dead. He felt the terrible weight of the mistakes he had made, and yet could not admit, for fear they would crush him. He struggled to convince himself the house was not collapsing about him, that the world itself was not being mercilessly pressed between the hands of the Almighty, whose eyes pierced the heart of every man.

But surely his Lord knew his intentions and forgave him. Because Adam's darkness was not that of Cain's—a remorseless, all-consuming evil.

"Dear God," he whispered. "How could you have done nothing?"

After all the service Adam had given the Almighty, after all of the sacrifices he had made, God had let his son, his most beloved child, die. Could the Almighty be loving and still let that happen? Could Abel live under the Almighty's protection and yet be killed?

His throat burned. There was only one conclusion such unshakable facts pointed toward. He opened his mouth and let the words fall from his mouth like forbidden fruit. "God lied." And they, too, tasted like death.

11

The rain fell like a volley of arrows. Eventually, glowing faintly through the storm-filtered light, Cain saw the eastern portion of the inner wall of the City of the Almighty. It reminded him of the spine of a great beast, long slain and removed of flesh and fur. He bent to see the Temple on the hill, but the hood of his cloak hugged his skull. There was a red flash as electric flames wormed through the sky, and the rain transformed, momentarily, into a million flaming spears stabbing the earth.

He turned up the path that led to the Temple entrance and rubbed a hand over his scalp, attempting to relieve himself of the buzzing sensation. The pressure corralled his thoughts through a diminishing space, until at last every part of his conscious mind was occupied by mundane facts that repeated endlessly.

Make each step the same length. Make each stride vary as little as possible so that the numbers you've counted will be measurable. You need to know how many steps it takes to get from your house to the Temple.

But his true goal wasn't in numbering his steps. He didn't care how far it was. He only wanted to escape from the hellish itch in his skull. It was as if the silver boy were grinding its teeth down the edges of his mind. Scraping. Cutting. Devouring.

He planted his feet before the doorway, and with his left hand, grabbed the handle of the polished marble door of the Temple. He gazed up at the gilded image carved into it of two winged angels guarding their faces. It was heavy on its hinges, but the gap between it and the wall widened, and he slipped through. The door swung shut behind him, and inside was blackness.

The violent storm had been the first indication that everything had changed. The darkness of the Temple was the second. Water dripped to cold stone as he flung his hood back, rummaged through his satchel, and pulled out a rope and flint. He coiled the rope, laid it on the ground, and dropped the flint on top of it. Then he patted the wall until he found a torch and grabbed it. He returned to the flint and struck sparks until the torch's head warmed to embers. He dropped the flint, tended the embers into a flame, and watched the light reach into the corners of the basilica.

As the flames reached their full strength, he realized he was not alone, and the buzzing in his mind died away. His breath stilled and sweat broke out on his forehead and palms as the Man stared at him with golden irises. His hair was long and white, and concealing his mouth was a voluminous beard.

"Hello, Cain."

That voice. It was deep, earthy, familiar. Questions long-suppressed bubbled to the surface, but he dared not speak. He knew the importance of this moment. He had expected the Almighty to be here, of course, but the darkness had distracted him.

The Man knows. Why else would the Temple darken for the first time since we arrived two years ago?

"Where have you been?" the Man asked.

Cain rubbed his temple out of habit, but realized there was no itch, no voice. Only silence. He knew he should be relieved, but the voice's absence disturbed him.

The Man straightened. He rested against a staff, but his eyes were as intense as a morning star. "Speak, son of Adam. Where have you been?"

Come now, you have long prepared for this moment.

Cain cleared his throat. "I have been home. With Sarah."

"Is that all?"

"Could that ever be all?"

Golden irises shifted over him. The man's beard clung to a slight frown, but no clear emotion revealed itself. "Do you think I do not know?"

"You know all things."

"Tell me," the Man said.

"I do not know what you want me to tell."

"Be free with your speech while you still retain the capacity."

Cain wondered at the Man's words. Did he threaten?

"Where is your brother?"

"I do not know."

"I saw you both walk to the fields."

"Am I my brother's keeper?"

The Man bent, and the words he spoke next were so small he nearly missed them. "What have you done?"

Cain stared, suddenly feeling the heat of the torch scald his hand. *Show me who you are. Will you try to suppress me like a tyrant? Show me your true self. I am dying to know it.*

He wondered what the Man would do, but Cain would not turn back. He could not.

The Man's voice was soft and smooth. "I know what it is you have done. You have killed Abel. I hear his blood crying out to me from the ground. If you would have but spoken truthfully . . ." He shook his head and blinked watering eyes. "So, now you are cursed from the ground, which has opened its mouth up to receive his blood from your hand. When you work the ground, it shall no longer yield to you its strength. You shall be a fugitive"—his mouth contorted with emotion—"and a wanderer on the earth."

Cain's body shook, and as he thought of the Man's words, he sensed the tyrant loom. "If I had but spoken truth, you say? I will speak it now. You curse me to the life of a fugitive, and if I don't die from starvation, whoever finds me will kill me. This banishment is no less than murder itself, and yet it is for murder I am sentenced." He raised his torch. "By doing this, you commit the very act for which I am being punished. Where is your justice? Where is your mercy? Where is your *love* and *forgiveness*?"

The Man's eyes flickered, and he lifted a hand. "If anyone kills you, vengeance shall be taken on him sevenfold. I tell you that unless you will it, no man may sever a hair from your head."

Cain straightened. He blinked and rested the butt of the torch against his thigh. "I was right about you. You are just as weak as I expected. You know what I do and yet still give in."

The Man held his gaze.

"Why?" Cain asked. "I could understand and hate your punishment, but this I cannot. I killed him. Why?"

"Indeed, why?" The Man reached forward and pressed a finger into the center of Cain's forehead. A burning sensation rippled across his skin, and black ridges like painted vertebra appeared across his arms and legs and glowed faint silver in the torchlight.

The Man looked at him with concern, and his voice came in a rushed whisper. "You do not have much time. Leave, and do not look back. I tried to warn you, but you have placed yourself in its jaws. Only remember my mercy. Remember that there is *always* a way back to me."

The Man turned and departed, his staff clacking on the stone long after he disappeared into the dark labyrinth of the Temple.

Cain stared at the marks on his skin, considering the significance. Water and flame dripped from him. It felt surreal. The conversation, the curse, all of it seemed like a distant dream he saw in the reflection of the puddle at his feet. He looked at his arms and breathed the smell of dust and burning wood. *I'm alive*, he thought.

"You are more than alive," whispered the voice. *"You have been set apart."*

Little fingers grasped his hand. In the light of the torch, he saw the silver boy looking up at him, but he was no longer afraid. Its voice was thin and harsh, like wind hissing between stone, like harsh Music. *"Come. He is calling us."*

12

E ve watched as Lilleth slept on the floor beneath a blanket, and Seth snored softly. The fire had settled to white coals, and though the smell of smoke and ash warmed Eve's chest, the disquiet of the storm left her restless.

She stood and thought about finding Ayla. Instead, she walked the hall and peered at the streams, birthed by the rain, flowing down the hill in serpentine patterns. The deluge had intensified, and though she knew it was midday, it seemed like the darkest night.

What kind of storm is this?

After two years of safety, the Jinn seemed an imagined horror, but this brought the memories back.

How quickly truth is forgotten.

She shivered and glided to the lounge where the air had warmed to something moist and sticky. She avoided the flooring she knew would creak, and took a seat between Seth and Lilleth. Their breathing was heavy, and she regarded them.

After Cain and Abel were born in that long-abandoned cave, movement through the wilderness had been difficult. She and Adam stopped often to feed and care for them, and she could still feel their tender skin against her fingers as she clothed them in leaves and woven fibers. What a beautiful burden to be those children's only means of survival. She recalled her children's squeals and smelled the leafy beds they had nestled under fallen trees and inside caves.

But then she thought of the darkness. And with the darkness came the Fog. And with the Fog . . .

Eve cleared her throat and clasped her hands in her lap. She examined Seth, her youngest son. He was an honest man with a

personality conveyed through a wide grin. But if Seth was a carica-
ture of expression, her daughter Lilleth's face was muted emotion.
Neither beautiful nor ugly, the dependent Lilleth relied on Abel for
support and direction, but having Lilleth rest on every word Eve
had spoken today aroused old desires.

Is it a sin to desire her dependence?

Lilleth's breath caught in her chest, and her eyelids trembled,
but soon her breathing slipped back into a steady rhythm. Eve
noted how her hands cupped her chin, and her knees curled to her
elbows. Even in sleep, she held herself like a youth. Did Abel find
that attractive?

Eve closed her eyes and thanked the Almighty for everything
he had given them.

*Almighty God, I desire you with every portion of my body. My
bones cry for your presence. I cannot have enough. Though your
peace and power overwhelm me, I thirst for you. I know I have not
experienced all of you. I know I do not live you. Please, tell me how I
can do more.*

She tipped her head, spread her palms, and reached for his
presence. She pushed, yet found nothing. She called for his Spirit,
but felt only emptiness. Surprise and fear raked her stomach.
Something was different. She had never felt such distance, not since
returning to the Almighty two years ago.

Where are you?

She reached and nearly felt something like sticky fingertips skipping across her skin. She gasped, Lilleth stirred from her dreams,
and as Eve bent and sucked at the air, her daughter said, "Mother?"

Seth still slept, but his sweat-covered forehead gleamed in the
firelight, and he moaned.

Lilleth called his name, but he did not wake, so Eve hurried to
her feet and shook him. He gasped and his eyes flashed wide. He
clutched Eve's arm, then swallowed and loosened his grip.

"I was dreaming," he said.

"So was I," Lilleth said. "What did you dream?"

He frowned and gave her a look as if not wanting to say.

A noise at the doorway drew their attention. Adam entered the archway with water dripping from his bent shoulders and stared past them as if not realizing they were there.

"Father?" Lilleth asked as her drowsiness sped toward excitement. She struggled to her feet. "Where is he? Did you find him?"

Adam stood stonelike, but his gaze shifted to Lilleth, then to Eve, and finally to Seth, who raised himself on his elbows. Adam's jaw stretched open, clenched, then relaxed. Eve expected Abel to enter behind him, but Adam stood unmoving, and nothing moved behind him but the rain in the wind.

Thunder pealed and Lilleth clasped the clothing by her throat. The thought struck Eve that this was a cruel joke. Adam was remaining silent to teach Lilleth how absurd it was to distrust the Almighty. She could hear his voice even now. *"Lilleth, all is well, of course. How could you expect anything else? Is the Almighty our God, or is he a liar? There, do you not see? You must trust in his protection, for he will never abandon us. If he cares for the sparrow, how much more will he care for a songbird like you?"*

Fear rose in Eve's chest, and then anger. "Why do you wait? Tell us where he is."

Adam shook his head. "No." His voice was quiet, but carried a peculiar emotion.

"What does that mean?" Lilleth searched their expressions.

"He is gone," Adam said.

Lilleth spilled the cold tea she hadn't finished and quickly tried to mop it up with one of the cushions she had used as a pillow. "Who is gone?"

"Abel." He nodded and said, as if to convince himself, "Abel is gone."

Lilleth squeezed the pillow until her knuckles whitened. "Where is he?"

Eve thought water dripped down Adam's cheek. But his face shuddered. "Abel is gone, and we could not find him though we searched the world." His voice fell to a whisper. "Cain killed him. The Temple is dark. Everything was a lie."

Eve reached out to steady herself. "What?" She could not believe those words any more than she could disbelieve her own existence, but the sound of his moans darkened her sight. She turned toward Lilleth, whose eyes were like black stones.

Adam rested his back against the wall and slid to his seat as he cradled his face and wept. "He killed my son. My Abel."

Saliva was thick in Eve's mouth, and an ache intensified in her throat. "No. He's not dead. God could heal him."

Lilleth edged past Adam and into the storm. Seth rose and hobbled out after her, whether to follow or walk elsewhere, Eve did not know.

Adam's cries continued, and Eve sank to the ground, incapacitated by shock. She wept into her hands until she could weep no longer. Eventually footsteps came, then words, but she could not bring herself to answer. The footsteps pounded past and out into the storm, and Adam and Eve were together, alone.

13

Sarah stirred the bubbling broth over the fire. The chunks of vegetables slowed the spoon, and eggplants and potatoes bobbed through the steam. Her empty stomach reached for food, but the scent was repelling and she crinkled her upturned nose at it and angled away to get a fresh breath. She laid a hand on her belly, which seemed to protrude ever so slightly, though the change would have been imperceptible to all but one looking for it. A hint of a smile came, but then faltered.

You should be happy.
Shall I be happy in loneliness?
A child grows within you.
The fruit of forced intercourse.
It is so much more than that. It is a human child, your child.
But will it survive?
You will give birth.
Will it know its father? Should it?

She stood and her lower back ached as she walked the hallways and let her fingertips ride the walls. The sensations blocked out any thought of her children, or any regret in her past, and for a moment, she was content to merely *be.*

Her hands rested at her sides and she found herself once again staring outside. "It's a dream," she whispered. She pushed a hard breath out as she glided back to the food she no longer desired. She took the pot off the fire and placed it on a wooden rack, and the bubbling liquid settled to a steaming reflection. She breathed the herbs, stifled an involuntary gag.

Control yourself. There's no reason for such weakness.
But Cain is gone. I am pregnant and alone. Abel is dead.

She threw her bowl of food. It shattered across the floor, joining the rest of the shards and slivers scattered about her home.

I feel dead.

But there is life within you.

She rubbed her belly and imagined the baby warming to her touch, reaching out with tiny hands to grab her fingers. Her stomach groaned and she gazed at the soup once more. She needed to eat for the child's sake.

She lifted a spoonful and let it fall in her mouth. A chunk of vegetable swished in the broth behind her teeth before she chewed and swallowed with much effort. It was nauseating, but she dipped for another mouthful.

Something shuffled behind her. It was a human noise amidst the thunder and rain. She turned and tensed at the familiar brown eyes and simple, soft face. She dropped the spoon into the pot. "Lilleth?"

"Don't speak." Lilleth's usual lilting soprano had been replaced with a strident alto.

Sarah swallowed and awkwardly faced her younger sister. She thought of Abel's blood on Cain. The scent of death. Adam's visit.

A feeling of responsibility gripped her abdomen. A moment passed when she strained for a way to deny any involvement, but she couldn't.

Lilleth knows. Why else would she come? Why else would her voice bite with such venom?

Lilleth gestured toward the pot on the rack. "I made stew for Abel yesterday, but he was late in returning. The stew grew cold so I had to place it back on the fire and stoke the flames." Her voice grew as she approached. "I added more and more wood until a new day began and the logs spilled into ash. I felt it then, but my mind told me it couldn't be true. I thought maybe Mother was right. Maybe I was just being fearful." Lilleth's eyes searched Sarah's, as if pining for a reason to disbelieve.

This is not my fault, Sarah thought. *If only you knew how much I regret it. If only you knew how much I wish I could have stopped him.*

Lilleth was shaking, and Sarah could no longer deny what Cain had done, but neither did she want to. She moaned, brought a hand to her mouth, and almost reached for Lilleth's arm.

"So it is true," Lilleth whispered. Her cheeks flushed. "I was a fool for wishing, but still I hoped . . ."

"I'm sorry."

"You're sorry, and yet I am alone. You're sorry, but you're still alive. And so is your husband."

The way she exaggerated the word *husband* sounded an alarm within Sarah. Lilleth had always been delicate, but something in her eyes was cold and brittle.

Sarah lowered her head. "I am sorry."

"Is that all you can say?"

"What more could I say?"

"You've not been speechless a day in our lives. But I want you to tell me what it's like to kill with lust and smuggled glances. I want you to tell me what it's like to want what you cannot have until the desire is so great you'd rather obliterate it than ache any longer."

Sarah's face grew hot. "I could never exalt in your pain."

"He was the only one I ever loved. No one, nothing, could repair the hole you bore into me. Tell me, because I want to remember how far you fell." Lilleth took a step closer and Sarah felt a pinch in her belly. She looked down and saw Lilleth's hand gripping a knife pressed against her abdomen.

The floor tilted beneath her. Her breathing sped and her body tensed, but she couldn't move. *Oh, God, don't let her kill my baby.* "What do you want?"

Strands of wet hair clung to Lilleth's cheeks. "I want to see you and Cain burn. I saw your eyes follow Abel. You always thought it unfair that I, not you, could be with such a man. You knew he was better than Cain like you knew your own superiority."

Sarah edged back, felt the knife dig in.

"Don't move. I'll thrust this blade straight through you."

"What do you want from me? Just tell me what you want."

"I want to kill you."

The startling admission stopped Sarah's breath. Ways to refute Lilleth's accusations raced through her head. But nothing would help. She knew it. Truth be told, she had influenced Cain. And part of her welcomed the guilt, the idea of death as atonement. But the child in her belly begged for breath. "You want to kill me?"

Lilleth's face shone in the light as she brought the knife to Sarah's neck and pressed it against the side of her throat. "I want you to die."

Sarah's mind scrambled for logic. She licked her lips and gasped as the knife pinched her throat and warm wetness trickled down her collarbone. She closed her eyes and tried to focus past the spinning. "You hate us." Sarah's voice shook. "You want me to die but you don't want to *kill* me. I know you."

"It's all that I want, all I've ever wanted, though it took the pain to open my eyes."

Sarah felt Lilleth's body tense in preparation of plunging the knife into her throat. Her mind emptied and she reverted to animal fear. "Stop!"

"Shut your mouth."

"He would hate you for it."

"I said shut your mouth."

The knife pressed harder and Sarah gasped. "Abel would hate you for it." The knife shook against her throat. Sarah dared not move.

"I would rather you both died than live knowing you won," Lilleth said.

Sarah shook her head, careful not to press into the blade. "I didn't win, Sister. I didn't win anything."

Lilleth stared with shaking intensity. For the first time, Sarah saw her examine their surroundings, the broken furniture and shattered pottery. Lilleth's expression softened, then shifted to something like fear. She whispered, "I hate you. I hate you. Look what you—" The words caught in her throat. She sobbed and stared at the floor; the shaking knife drew away.

Sarah chanced a breath, seeing the murderous intent in Lilleth's eyes replaced by dullness. But then something happened that Sarah had not expected. Lilleth took the knife across her own throat and opened a thick gash from one edge to the other. The knife clanged on the ground as she backed away and stared.

"Sister," Sarah screamed. "No!" She rushed forward, caught Lilleth as she fell, and laid her on the ground. She tried to press her hands against the wound, but blood gushed from it like water from a spring. It took her a moment to realize there were fists beating her sides. She looked down and saw Lilleth's eyes boring into her and said, "I'm not going to let you die."

Lilleth gurgled and beat her ribs. Sarah's hands slipped on and off the wound, and Lilleth weakened as she lost blood. Sarah could not stop it alone.

"Help," Sarah screamed, looking up toward the doorway. "Help me. God, where are you? Help me!"

Her voice was swallowed by the storm, which suddenly rumbled like distant, violent Music. Lilleth lay in a pool of her own blood. Her eyes were glazed, locked open like a dying fish gasping for one final breath. The bloodletting stopped, and Sarah brought her shaking hands slowly away.

"No," she said. "Why? Why would you do that? You fool." She shook Lilleth's shoulders. "Wake up. Wake up."

Sarah's hands were stained with blood for the second time in two days. She stared at the dark pool that soaked her knees and ached for a way to fill her sister with it once more.

She thought of Cain, of the good years together that felt like so many lifetimes ago. The light of those years and the darkness of now so starkly contrasted that she could hardly believe the light existed. She closed her eyes, wiped the blood on her clothing, and imagined being in his arms again. She saw him tilling the earth and planting seeds. She saw him shoveling dirt from holes . . .

Her eyes snapped open. She couldn't let anyone find Lilleth's body. If they found out, they would banish her. And if she were banished—

She placed a shaking, stained hand on her lower abdomen and tried to sense the baby within her as the thunder returned. She stood and shivered with sin.

"God, forgive me."

PART THREE:

COLLAPSE

Be ashamed, O tillers of the soil;
wail, O vinedressers,
for the wheat and the barley,
because the harvest of the field has perished.
The vine dries up;
the fig tree languishes.
Pomegranate, palm, and apple,
all the trees of the field are dried up,
and gladness dries up
from the children of man.
　　　　　　　　　　　—JOEL 1:11–12 ESV

14

It didn't take long for Sarah to realize her plan was a poor one. Mud was everywhere, and with every shovelful flung, half as much water rushed in. What was she going to do—float Lilleth's corpse in it like a hunk of wood? She pictured her sister's pale face bloated with moisture and decay. Twin balloons pressing the eyes until they disappeared behind fetid flesh.

Sarah felt as if the world was trying to drown her, and maybe it was. Nothing had happened as Cain said it would. She had lost so many she loved. First Abel, then Cain, now Lilleth.

If only vomiting could rid me of the guilt I feel.

She stared at the puddle and gripped the shovel like a two-handed axe. How could she plan on burying Lilleth without speaking a word to another? She loved her sister. Maybe she hadn't realized how much before this day. Perhaps she truly had been blinded by jealousy, but now she knew.

I'm sorry I ever wanted you gone.

She refilled the hole, hurried into the house, whipped off her hood, flung water-clumped hair from her eyes, and breathed deeply. The shovel clanged on the floor as she dropped to her knees and held her face, letting the emotions rush, if only to be rid of them. She slapped her hand on the floor and said through gritted teeth, "Stop it. You can't do this alone. Think of who you can trust."

Mason. Her second eldest son, mute from birth. He could carry the body and dispose of it quickly and discreetly. He would never speak of it, because for him speech was physically impossible. With the storm, Lilleth's body would be rushed far away, and surely no one would walk outside in such a tempest and stumble upon them in the dark.

But the blood . . .

Listen to yourself. You can't even bring yourself to honor your sister's death. You are just like Cain.

She looked at the knees of her dress, stained by Lilleth's rusty veins. "Do what you must, and nothing more." She repeated those words until it became a mantra. She mopped up much of the blood, crawled out of the soiled clothing, and redressed. She donned her rain tunic, threw the ruined dress and undergarments on the fire, and watched them burn. Then she draped a curtain over Lilleth's body, which lay in the closet, and rushed into the storm to find Mason.

He lived on the far side of the quarry a quarter mile south, and though it seemed a journey away in such a storm, she couldn't risk involving her other children. The mud was like quicksand, and the hills and ditches ran with enough water to swipe her feet away. Once she fell on her palms. Once more on her side.

The rain dropped like darts and she closed her eyes to protect them. But when she found the quarry, it was not by sight. As she stepped forward and her foot failed to meet ground, it took the time of her body pitching forward and her arms flailing to realize she had stepped off the ledge of the quarry.

She tumbled like a bag of broken bones and came to a quick stop, saved by a ledge. Her head spun and it took her a moment to realize she was no longer moving. She rose to her knees and cradled her rib cage. Her breath came in short spurts in the fight against the pain that pushed out the air with the force of a hammer. Soon she felt panicked for oxygen. She exhaled, finding it easier than inhaling, then frantically urged it back in again. When she could breathe easier, relief washed her. But as her hand brushed her abdomen, a new thought hit her.

My baby, what if I hurt my baby? Her fingers tingled.

"Dear God," she prayed as she started crying again with the memory of all that had transpired in the past two days. "I don't know if you exist in such hell, and I know I deserve nothing." She swallowed and tried to stand, lightly pressing her stomach. "But please keep my baby alive. You can throw me off the highest mountain. You can drown me in the deepest sea. Just don't let my baby die."

She felt a peace deeper than words could express. The ledge she stood on jerked and broke away. As her feet pedaled the air, the surreal sensation of flight stirred her abdomen. Then she hit.

Thick blackness exploded in her ears and muffled the bubbles bursting from her mouth as she screamed and gasped at liquid. Seeing a bolt of lightning dimly, she twisted toward it, breached the surface, and coughed. Thunder roared and water slapped her ears as she struggled to stay afloat. Her toes, no matter how far they stretched, found only water.

Flooded, she thought. *How is the quarry flooded?* Water stuck its fingers up her nose and she coughed and felt her sinuses burn against the intrusion. How had the storm deposited so much water so quickly?

The river. It ran next to the quarry. The storm must have bloated it until the water broke its boundaries and filled the quarry. She could try to swim across and find a way out, but she felt so heavy and her fingers clenched her tunic spasmodically. With effort and pain, she shook free from the tunic and began to tread across the water, remembering what she had been taught as a child. Spread the arms and kick the legs, breathe deeply and consistently. But with broken ribs and God knows what else, she was soon clutching at the sides of the quarry. Swimming took energy she didn't have and demanded muscles she couldn't utilize. As did climbing out of the quarry. So she clung to the wall and crawled to the right, feeling for the stairwell.

I am going to die. Like an insect in a trap.

She imagined the Almighty watching her from the top of the quarry, smiling at how easily she had been ensnared. She imagined the look of satisfaction in his eyes, an approving nod as the frigid water slammed her against the wall. Her hands could no longer grasp the stone, and she grunted with the effort of trying to move her arms. It took her a moment to realize she was floating once more, free. Water tickled the bottom of her ears, and then her cheeks, as her eyesight clouded and she felt as if she were being encased in ice.

How long have I been in the water? I feel like a small child falling into heavy slumber. But I'm not falling asleep, I'm dying. There's a little child inside me who has never inhaled the air my body is screaming for. And that child does not have the strength to carry on without me.

As Sarah sank beneath the water, her hands rested on her abdomen.

I wonder if the child inside me can feel pain. God, please give my child a painless death. Grant me at least that.

The warmth of her womb had been replaced by shivering skin, and her ribs ached less with each moment. With closed eyes, she saw the Almighty standing on the ledge above, his head nodding. Up and down. Up and—

15

C ain awoke shivering on the ground. He was naked and stones
dug into his back. He sat up, brushed them off, and felt the
impressions they made in his skin. The sky was dark, though clear
and dotted with pricks of light sharp enough to draw blood.

How much time had passed since he gave up consciousness?

He rubbed his hand over his scalp and strained to clear his
mind. The silver boy had taken control and pushed Cain's soul into
a black empty space. There had been no way out, though it seemed
he searched for an eternity. And it had been cold. So very cold.

He palmed his shoulders in an attempt to warm them. The surrounding wasteland gave him the sensation of absolute exposure.
There were no trees, no hills, nothing but endless flatland covered
in small, sharp rocks. And he had the strange sensation that every
noise was an intrusion, as if hidden hands stopped hidden ears to
keep the place secret.

"Hello?"

Silence loomed like a shadow, and a cold wind pinched Cain's
skin. He looked down and wondered what had happened to his
clothes. Then he studied the stars and began walking the direction
he thought was east.

Where had the silver boy gone? He didn't feel the itch in his
mind, and he didn't hear its voice, but neither did he think the creature dead. It had understood Cain's plans with precision, and yet
seemed to have devices of its own. Whatever it planned, he doubted
it harbored hopes for his good health.

He breathed into his hands, creating clouds in the air. His skin
rose like a reptile's, his fingernails ached, and he no longer felt his

feet, which concerned him as he gazed at the stone-cut ravines on his skin that were filling with fresh blood.

Everything had gone well. He had killed Abel, successfully disposed of the body, escaped from the City, and gained the Man's protection.

So why was he naked in the freezing wilderness?

The silver boy had been and remained an anomaly in the landscape of Cain's new life. Cain had felt safe with its fingers around his, and yet here he walked in this wasteland. The solitude began to feel like an anvil on which he had been laid in order to await the hammer strike. *To be fashioned into a tool,* he thought and grit his teeth. *That is why it has brought me here.*

What was the silver boy's relationship to Cain? Why had it come to him? And what was the reason for the unmistakable familiarity between them?

A cough lit a fire in his chest, and he grabbed at the skin of his breast to ease the pain. In the years of their nomadic existence after his parents had been expelled from the Garden, his family wandered far across foreign terrain. Though the times had strained them, the pressure and pain had also strengthened them. *Could it be the silver boy is trying to strengthen me? If it wanted me dead, it would have no reason to wait.*

No. It wants to consume me. He envisioned the stone in his hand as it crushed Abel's skull. *The only way to gain power is by taking it from another. Like the Serpent in the Garden.*

The Almighty's warning returned. *"Sin is crouching at the door. It desires to devour you, but you must rule over it."*

The silver boy had claimed it would break him. Maybe this was its way.

He sat and sifted through all that had happened. He had killed Abel, disposed of the body, and first heard the voice then, though he had felt the itch in his mind long before. How long? He couldn't remember. Several weeks? Maybe more? Then the voice appeared as the silver boy and urged him away, and he left Sarah and—

Sarah. I wonder if she is thinking of me as I think of her. And how she is coping with the changes I have set into motion.

He lifted a handful of pebbles and let them fall one by one. The world would know soon enough that Abel was dead. Would the people question their God? Would Calebna, the High Priest, lose his faith in the face of his father's murder?

And what of Cain's own children? Lukian, the twin brother of his dead firstborn, would likely seize any opportunity to free the people from bondage. Cain could still see the look on his son's face as he planted questions like seeds.

"Son, do you believe we have true freedom?"

"We have the power to craft our lives."

"In the Garden we were given dominion over the world."

Lukian nodded.

"So why did we flee for over a century?"

"The Fall."

"The Fall was the decision of one man and one woman. What about my freedom, what about yours? Do we not have the choice to regain our dominion? Another question. Where are we?"

"The City of the Almighty."

Cain nodded, and a smirk crept up the corner of Lukian's mouth.

The stones of the wilderness dug into Cain's thighs and buttocks as he closed his eyes. He had broken the Almighty's chains with a stone-smashed skull, and yet what had he gained? Marks across his skin and blood on his feet. And now he waited for death to come in silver skin.

He tensed his muscles. He would not be controlled. He would not be dominated. If the silver boy demanded all of him, he would embrace death.

But what if he retained a splinter of that control?

I escaped slavery before. I could do it again.

Cain closed his eyes and rested, letting his mind dip into endless silver waters until something jerked him back. He was sitting on the ground with his legs crossed and his arms in his lap. His fingertips were blue, and his body was numb. His mind told his hands to clench, but they moved as if listening to the commands of another.

He was tired, and he felt detached as he lay and watched his skin blacken and his limbs shake. Little feet approached, and as the gravel crunched by his ear, a small shadow blocked the stars to the south.

I am dying, Cain thought. *Eventually, I will pass into the world beyond. Unless . . .*

That familiar voice whispered in his ear, *"Let me in. I will give you what you need if you would only give me what I want."*

Cain was repelled by the sound of the voice and the scent of its breath. It was an acrid, yellow stink that crept across the side of his face.

"You know what this means." Its voice dripped with desire. *"You must understand. Not all, but more."*

Cain nodded and whispered, "Come." And he thought to himself, *I promised I would come back for you. And I decided I would never lie again—not to you.* And he thought of how her red hair shone in the sun and danced in the wind and felt between his fingers.

The silver boy's nails dug into Cain's shoulders, and its breath passed over his lips and down his throat. It swam down his limbs and crackled through his head, and though he knew what it was doing was shameful and should never be, he knew that it *was*, for the shadows of its emotions hovered at the outskirts of his mind.

Cain's skin grayed, and he wanted to observe it closer, but already the silver boy urged him in a new direction. He stood and realized then what he must do. For a time he would suffer the thing to live in him, but when the moment presented itself—*and it must*—he would crush its head underfoot.

But for now, I will walk with the Devil.

16

Seth knew his father was wrong. Still, as he made a mental list of all that could not be true, he ran as fast as his stiff legs would allow. As he had lain on the floor of Mother's home and listened to Adam's words, he remembered. And not just the single set of visions that threw him into seizures. He remembered everything.

He looked back through blurred eyes and saw only rain. He had left as soon as he could, and maybe, just maybe, it would save her life. *I cannot accept a world in which belief is only a misty haze simulating substance. I cannot abandon hope.*

"I'm running." He gasped for breath. "I'm trying."

He hobbled up the hill and nearly fell in the mud. His lungs burned as he crested and staggered to the double doors of the Temple. Shaking with weakness, he reached, grabbed hold of one of the gold rings, and leaned back, but the door did not move. Panic invigorated his limbs, and he tugged until it opened, and he slipped inside.

He looked around, seeing the Temple's insides grayed with shadow for the first time. Lampstands stood like mute sentinels, their flames extinguished, their figures gleaming in the light that stole through the cracked doorway. The tapestries and paintings depicting the glory of the Almighty were drab and colorless on the walls, and as he made his way forward, the darkness deepened.

Seth fumbled along the wall to find the door to the Throne Room, and as his fingers slid from stone to metal, footsteps pattered in from the rain. He glanced behind him and saw a shadowed figure silhouetted by the shaft of light pressed between the doors. He squeezed the handle, jerked the door open, and slipped inside. But as the door shut behind him, his feet melted.

The room was lit by two candles that burned on either side of the throne. The flames were weak after many hours, but still bright enough to illuminate the throne and what little was in the room. He shook his head and steadied himself against the wall. Then he crumpled to his knees and flattened himself against the floor. "Almighty?"

There was no response.

The door opened and feet shuffled beside him. He found it unusual how in this moment everything was magnified, from the sound of his wife's footfalls, to the subtle intake of breath as she took in their surroundings, and the sting of the dust turned up by her tunic as she fell to the floor beside him.

"Almighty?" His nose ran from the chill of the chasm. If his dreams were only dreams, looking upon the glory of the Almighty could strike him dead.

But he had looked already, hadn't he?

He held his breath. Perhaps a second look would be fatal.

He glanced to the left. To the right.

Where were the colors? Only Calebna had been in the Throne Room, but the stories he told were those of Fear and Reverence. Not the petty kinds of the incarnate world, but the purified oils of the Almighty, refined in the flames of eternal Holiness—gifts from beyond the edge of the world.

Could Calebna have lied all this time?

He could bear the unknown no longer. At the very least, what greater death could there be than to die in the presence of one's Lord? He raised his head slowly, painfully, until he could view the throne out of the corner of his eye. Sweat poured from his skin as thoughts swirled through his mind. He could see the angled stone, the flickering shadows from impatient flames, and . . .

A robe.

"No," he whispered as he let fear and rage burn his face. The fabric lay torn and wrinkled across the throne, and he didn't need to look again to see the Almighty's crown bent and dirtied with black stains.

The dreams.

He glanced at Ayla who still lay with her face to the floor.

"Don't," she whispered. "Don't, Seth."

He turned and straightened, and Ayla stilled. He stared at the Almighty's empty throne, but no retribution came. Nothing happened, and that nothing was more terrible than any punishment he could have endured.

"I've seen this before," he said. "I've seen it all." He clenched his fingers into fists and swallowed the stone in his throat. Ayla's clothing quivered against the floor as she let out a shaky breath, but still she did not stand.

He touched the sleeve of the Almighty's stained robe. Some of it still glistened, but more had crusted and flaked like rust. A groan escaped his throat. He laid his face in his hands and let the horror flow until he stumbled and fell to his seat. He rested his head on the floor and let tears stream from temple to Temple.

"No." The roar of his voice echoed through the chamber. "He's dead."

He thought of the remaining pieces of his dream and had to shut them out. He would stop it. He would stop it all. They wouldn't die. He wouldn't let it happen.

But how?

Ayla's sinuses bubbled as she sniffed. She remained prostrate, perhaps because there was no longer a reason to move, because she believed her husband and dared not look at the proof lest grief crush her.

For who could endure the death of their God? Who could see the ultimate reduced to nothing but lifeless matter? They had put their trust in the Almighty and it had been destroyed. But by what? Had Cain killed the Almighty? Was that why Cain had murdered Abel—to show them they had been duped by a false God?

It was true that only Adam and Eve had walked with God in the Garden. What if they had been fooled? What if their memories had somehow been twisted against them? Or what if they had never seen God at all?

"No," Seth whispered. "No." He scrambled to his feet, grabbed the crown in both hands, and threw it across the room. It clattered and skidded to a stop, and he noticed then an item that hadn't been in his dreams. A goblet on the throne's armrest. He lifted it and liquid sloshed over the rim. At first he thought it wine, but then the smell of blood reached into his awareness. He grimaced and dropped the cup, splashing the redness across the throne. "He lied to us."

Ayla straightened until she knelt. "We should leave."

"He's dead. Our God is dead. It was a façade. A trick."

"Listen to yourself. You would have given your life for him, and now you toss his crown like refuse."

"What does his name mean? He claimed to be the Creator of the world, the Creator of our souls, and yet he is gone and his Temple is dark and his robe is stained with blood."

She struggled to her feet. "He's not dead."

"Then how do you explain what you see?"

"I don't know. Just stop it."

"I already tried. Why do you think I'm here? Hours ago you argued for the impossible, that suffering could find us despite his promises. Now I say you were right, and you can't even bring yourself to look at the proof."

She shook her head.

Rage swelled like a bubble in his head. "You won't take her from me. I won't let it happen."

Her voice shook. "You're scaring me."

The images wouldn't leave his eyes. It would happen exactly as he had been shown.

He remembered a detail, a momentary flash amidst the flood of images, and its meaning quickened his blood. He turned to Ayla, his eyes wide and clear. "We need to get out of here."

"What?"

"Run. Go!"

She turned slowly, her eyes narrowing. He could see she was hurt by the sharpness of his voice, but he didn't care. He wanted to push her, to throw her out the door and get her as far from this place as possible.

A blinding flash lit the room, as if they had been struck by lightning. Ayla screamed, and a high-pitched ringing smashed into Seth's ears, though it sounded like a thunderous Word. And in the space of one fleeting moment, Seth knew that their lives had ended, and that their story had just begun.

17

Mason was dreaming, but the words spoken by a familiar voice seemed to grab hold and pull him halfway to consciousness.

"She's drowning in the quarry. You must run to the quarry as soon as you wake. If you disbelieve me, she will die. Do you want to carry that weight? Then get up and run. Run!"

He woke with his feet swinging, then landing, now sprinting. The entrance of his single-room hut was already filled with water, and he splashed through puddles as he whipped out the doorway and into the storm. His matted hair slapped his shoulders like waterlogged snakes, but he knew where to go, even with his eyes closed.

He skidded to a stop at the edge of the thirty-foot drop and searched the water below. He didn't think the quarry would be so full already, but the voice in his dream had told him it would be so. By the time his mind had roused enough to question why he would obey a voice from a dream, he was staring at his mother's head bobbing above the surface of the water, then sinking underneath.

He tore off his tunic, sprinted, and jumped into the quarry. Air and rain buffeted his face as he fell and plunged deep. His legs hit the bottom and jarred, though not hard enough to break, and he swam to the surface, then dove and searched with his hands for Sarah. He felt a body, cold, but real, and grasped it. He breached the surface and thrust her face above the water, but she wasn't breathing, so he swam the rest of the way and tugged her up the ramp.

He lifted her head and struck her back with a flat hand, but she didn't breathe. Instead, she vomited. After the initial shock of it, he realized it was better she vomited, not worse. She coughed, then began gasping. He picked her up as gently as he could, and she hung in his arms, cold and heavy, and her eyelids fluttered closed. She began to shake.

"Don't stop until you bring her home. You can't bring her any-where but her home. If you do not bring her home, she will die." The voice had been right about her being in the quarry, so why should he distrust it now?

He paused, then sprinted up the staircase, feeling the burn in his thighs as he crested the top and turned for her home. Time blurred in the space between thunderclaps. The sheet over the doorway stuck to them as he pushed through, and he had to angle sideways to slip past with her in his arms. The storm muffled as he walked into the kitchen and set her on the floor. There was a trail of dark fluid twisting out the room and down the hallway.

He looked at his mother and brushed the hair from her face. She was shaking and her eyes were closed, but she was still breathing. He stood and followed the trail to the closet, where he found the source of the blood—a body with a curtain draped over it. He slid the curtain back.

Lilleth? He dipped and pressed his ear to her chest in search of the rhythm of life. There was none.

His skin tingled as he returned to his mother. Had she done this? Had that been the reason she had come to the quarry? His mouth was dry and he tried to swallow, but it stuck in his throat.

"Bury the evidence," the voice said, *"and make sure no one can find it. Do it or your mother will die."*

So many questions Mason could not answer. But he would not let his mother die.

18

E ve was in the lounge when Abel's firstborn, Calebna, entered. "The crops are shriveling." Calebna was breathless, as if he had nearly drowned in the water that dripped from his long hair.

"What do you mean?" Eve's voice was harsh, and Adam stiffened. She could feel his fingers tighten around her hand. She remembered the pain of Abel's entrance into the world, and how her hands had dug into Adam's, but Abel's murder overshadowed any pain she had yet felt. And Adam?

"I mean that everything green and growing in the City is decaying," Calebna said. "And our fruit is rotting. Some blight is taking it."

"What about the fish? Our animals? Are they alive?"

"Most. But many show signs of sickness. Some have lumps across their bodies. Others have been consumed." He paused. "There is more."

"Speak quickly, Son of my son," Adam said.

"Mason found Sarah in the storm. It seems he risked his life to retrieve her from the water that destroyed the southern half of the City. Gorban informed me only moments ago that all attempts to wake her have failed. Mason took Sarah to the Temple, seemingly in hopes that the Almighty would heal her . . ."

"What? What happened? Speak!"

Calebna jumped as if startled. Eve could see that he was shaking. "The Almighty is gone. I would not believe it until I saw it with my eyes. The Temple is dark, and when we entered, we found the torn and bloodied remnants of his garment on the throne, and beside it were Seth and Ayla's prone bodies. I am sorry. They are dead as well."

Eve whispered, "Dead?"

Adam toppled a table and shouted. Eve studied the desolation in Adam's eyes as Calebna brushed the wrinkles from his tunic and looked anywhere but at Adam.

"I am sorry," Calebna said again.

Adam slid to the floor and held his face. He was weeping, but out of anger rather than sorrow, Eve thought. A chill clambered up her back as she remembered the prophecy the Almighty offered them in Eden—that through one of Eve's sons would come a reversal of the curse. When Cain had been born all those years ago in the cave, she had thought him the Savior the Almighty spoke of, and perhaps Adam had thought Abel the same. But Cain had proven himself born of evil seed, and both her other sons were dead.

That is why Adam weeps, she thought. *He knows now there is no hope, for not only are our children either dead or false, but the Almighty himself has abandoned us. And can a promise be any truer than the character of the one who promised?*

She turned toward her grandson. "Show me."

Calebna led the mother of all mankind under the last vestiges of the storm to see the bodies of those she loved too deeply to express. Somehow she remained upright. It didn't affect her like it had Adam. Like an underground lake, her soul lay quiet in darkness. Though the tears didn't flow, she remained filled by them, and that was perhaps the most painful part.

Calebna's brothers, Philo and Tuor, arrived as Eve clutched the Almighty's torn and bloodied tunic. Together, the men hauled Seth and Ayla's bodies out of the Throne Room and into the antechamber, where they laid beautiful tapestries over their pale forms.

Eve exited the Throne Room, saw the bodies, and ran her fingertips over their covered faces. Though she knelt staring for what seemed hours, no one spoke. They merely watched, as if waiting for her to determine their direction. How should they react? Surely there must be some explanation?

But there wasn't. So she stood, turned her back on the Temple, and walked home. When she returned, Adam sat with his back against the wall, and his eyes held some goal in the farthest distance. When she spoke, he would not respond, and Eve understood what she had seen in his eyes.

Can one die inside and yet remain living?

Yes, she thought. *And it seems Adam has.*

PART FOUR

INTO THE HEART OF DARKNESS

These are waterless springs and mists driven by a storm. For them the gloom of utter darkness has been reserved. For, speaking loud boasts of folly, they entice by sensual passions of the flesh those who are barely escaping from those who live in error. They promise them freedom, but they themselves are slaves of corruption. For whatever overcomes a person, to that he is enslaved.

—2 PETER 2:17–19 ESV

19

I t had started slowly. For many days Cain simply traveled. The sounds of the world became amplified in the absence of human speech, and the itch in his mind disappeared beneath the roar of nature. For what seemed an eternity, all that remained was earth and sky, the breath of lungless leaves, and the quiver of wind over water. *Music.* The whole of Time seemed contained in an eternal Song, and he joined in its exaltation.

Then all had flickered and pieces of the Music fell bit by bit into little pockets of blindness. Eventually he grew accustomed to the strangeness, but the pockets widened until a great nothing rolled out, swallowing everything and turning back upon him until only the void remained.

"In the empty chill, I finally know the extent of the bondage I welcomed. Slavery tastes bitter, and I would fight the gates of hell to stop it from burning your beautiful lips." He had taken to speaking to Sarah in the void. "A habit born out of necessity," he explained, so she wouldn't think him odd. He imagined her nodding in response, half believing, half mocking. "Yes," he said to her. "I know you think it strange, but it is true. I need to talk to you."

She pursed her lips and said, *"Whatever helps."*

"I've wondered if I lost myself long ago and imagined all this as I'm imagining you. If maybe killing my brother simply broke me, or if maybe I imagined murdering him, and that all this is only a dark dream."

"You know this is not a dream," she said. *"And you don't look broken."*

"But I feel it." He thought of the silver boy forcing his body along. It seemed like many years since last touching his soul to his body. He grimaced. *My body. Not that silver devil's. Desire grows and aches in my chest. I long to feel the dirt beneath my feet and the breeze on my cheek, or even the sensation of pain.*

He reached through his memory for any vivid sensation and grasped the musty smell of sweat. He held onto it like a broken rose.

"*Look at you,*" she chided. "*You should be ashamed. You even think that dwelling on the smell of your dirty body is an accomplishment.*"

He stared at his gray hands in the void. Slowly, he nodded. "I am ashamed. It's good you're still at the City and have no idea what I've become."

"*So stop it.*"

"What could I do?"

"*You chose this path.*"

"I killed Abel because I had to. I tried to find another way, but you pushed me to it."

"*Still fighting the truth?*"

"You have no understanding of the truth I've lived."

Sarah's flamed hair seemed to crackle. "*And what of me?*"

"I'm not saying you haven't suffered."

She flicked her wrist as if to dismiss him.

Cain pressed his palms against the sides of his head. "Can't you see that I need you?"

"*I'm not your toy, a child's rag doll to be soiled and discarded until next I fit your fancy.*"

He bowed his head and opened his mouth to respond, but the words stumbled over each other.

"*Speak.*"

Angry phrases flittered through his mind like rats, but he pushed them aside and said, "I am sorry."

She scoffed. "*This must be the first time in your life.*" But the words lost their edge.

He pressed his eyes and felt the anger slip away. "I wish I could explain what kept me from expressing it. I wish I could understand why I couldn't kiss you or slip my fingers into yours. I simply couldn't. But I wanted to. I still want to. If you were here, I would hold you tenderly. Remember before I left? Remember how I held you?"

She nodded and held her expression. *"I remember more than that."*

He bit his cheek, remembering how he had struck her and broke their home and yelled at her as she collapsed and wept on the floor. He stared at her, sensing again the invisible wall between them. Even in his imagination he could not do what he most wanted to do.

"Do you miss me?" he asked.

She rubbed her eyes.

"Does anyone miss me?"

She nodded and a smile creased her lips, then crumbled. She turned and her image dissipated like fog in the wind. He searched the darkness, but found nothing. The emotions came like after-shocks to an unfelt quake, and in the safety of solitude, for the first time since childhood, he wept. He was no longer a man. He was a boy finally realizing that for nearly a hundred and fifty years, nothing had been enough.

I just want to satisfy the restlessness. Everything feels wrong, as if pieces of the world have been fabricated and replaced without me knowing. What is this longing? This thirst?

The blackness crept so close it felt as if it were inside him, and he rubbed his hands over his arms, but generated no warmth. Faintly he remembered the smell of sweat, and he longed for it again.

The silver boy's words returned. *"Not all, but more."*

Cain felt as if he were awakening from a long dream. He hadn't given all of himself to the silver boy. He hadn't offered complete control, and if he had overcome it for a moment, why could he not push it away for an extended period of time? He thought of how long he had been confined in this capsule of nothing, and the possibility that he could have been lulled here brought flames to his neck. The pockets of blindness, had they been the beginnings of the void around his soul as the silver boy displaced him and took over his body?

"Let me out!"

"Would you quiet yourself?"

He turned and saw Sarah wincing and covering her ears. His mouth twitched. "I thought you left."

"I came back."

He shook his head, questioning if he really were seeing things. "Why?"

She sighed and folded her arms as if wondering whether to speak her mind.

"Tell me."

"You're a fool. You want out? Then leave."

"You're saying I can?"

"The world needs you. Our sons—Lukian, Gorban, Mason, Kiile, and Machael. They need you." She turned and walked away.

"Wait."

"You promised. Or don't you remember?" She waited, then nodded. *"You always were a liar."*

"How do I escape?"

She placed a hand on her abdomen and stared at it, then smiled and whispered, *"Just wait, little child. I'll take care of you. And he'll never touch you."*

His eyes widened.

She turned and faded into the dark.

"Wait!"

But part of him thought she wasn't gone. That she'd never left him at all. He breathed hard and his chilled hands shook. Suddenly, as if lifted by some unseen force, what he could only describe as *layers* arose like stacked sheets of papyrus. He didn't so much see them as feel them through some unknown sense, piled where Sarah had stood. He ran his hand across his scalp and rubbed his eyes. Was Sarah showing him something? Was she leading him toward these layers? Or had he truly lost his mind?

He approached the stacked sheets, stuck his fingers between two, and pried them apart. Dim Light shot out from between them, and as he bent and leaned in, he saw moving shapes inked onto the fabric. It was like looking at the whole of the world caught in flatness.

He let go and the sheets snapped into place. He repeated the process lower down. Then again. And again. He found worlds stacked endlessly upon each other, and each wove into the next like the Words of a great Song. His mind tried to convince him that this was only his imagination, but he knew that was a lie. As he fingered through the layers, he sensed the echoes of truth fluttering through its pages, like the softest Music ever played. He let a few sheets fall, and the sound of nearness, of belonging, grew. He gazed between the pair of sheets and saw himself standing in blackness, gazing between the layers. He moved his leg and watched the flat image mirror the movement. His hands slipped and the layers slammed shut.

This is impossible.

"*It's a gift.*"

He spun at the sound of Sarah's voice, but he could not find her.

"*You should be thankful.*"

"Do you want me to use it?"

"*Don't play the fool.*" She laughed then, as he hadn't heard her laugh in years, and the echo resonated until it disappeared behind the ringing in his ears.

Cain looked at the layers. Where had they come from? The silver boy must have awoken something in him. Or had the catalyst been something else?

He bit his cheek as another thought struck him. *Do the layers end?* He rifled past innumerable sheets. Eventually he reached a layer beneath which was endless blackness. He paused at the brink and studied the space. The blackness seemed alive. It moved like a roiling hot spring, and yet he felt the empty chill of it.

Cain swallowed, forced his shoulders to relax, and turned back through the layers until he found his way to another brink on the opposite end. This one was not so dark, and he found himself standing at the edge, poised to jump. It seemed like a river that flowed through the layers, but though there was illumination of some kind, he saw not through his eyes, but sensed through that same unknown faculty.

With a terrible, half-purposeful motion, he plunged into the depths, and the contact of what he could only describe as Water made him gasp. He swam its currents, explored its tributaries, and found his mind bursting with significance.

In the Waters lay shivering images. He paused and cupped his hands to catch an image of his face, and he watched himself speak, and even heard the words spoken.

His skin tingled as he let the Water fall from his hands. He cupped another image, this one of Lukian pacing the inner wall of the City.

I am watching life.

The idea made his mind buzz as he cupped another image.

But some of what I see is unfamiliar. Might these images be moments that are yet to come?

He trudged ahead, cupping Water and watching unlived life unfold. The most interesting areas were where the rivers branched, showing twisted projections of choice. Soon he found himself swimming multiple branches and coming to darker Waters.

He knew the ability to traverse these Waters stemmed from his interaction with the silver boy, but he also knew there was something more. His thoughts resonated with the river, and from somewhere beyond the river came whispers of truth and falsehood. Those whispers confirmed that there was something special about the silver boy, and about his own relationship to it. But what?

From time to time, atop a wave, he sensed multiple pathways ahead, splitting in ever-burgeoning potentialities, and the endlessness of it was overwhelming. The riverscape grew chaotic. The waves became violent and thrashed him about. Ahead lay a harbor whose surface was glassy-calm, and he swam for it. He reached and strained, the current resisting him with ever-increasing strength. Still he grew closer.

When at last he crested a wave and felt the harbor within reach, a black force welled up and threw him through the darkness into the light.

20

The first thing Cain noticed was the smell of grass. Blades stabbed his eyes, and he turned his head, grimaced, and spat into a blurry jungle. The back of his neck tensed, lifting his skull enough to see he was lying in a field. Granules of dirt ground between his teeth as he pushed himself onto his knees. He tried to straighten, but instead tipped and shot his hands out for balance. The world pulsed and rolled. He itched his face and peeled the grass from his skin. His face tingled and felt like leather, and he caught a string of saliva stretching from his lips.

He grabbed his shoulder and squeezed until it hurt. "I'm back," he said and closed his eyes. "I'm alive."

Clouds flecked the sky and a late afternoon breeze combed through his hair. He knew in only a few moments the sun would fall beneath the horizon, but with the wind on his skin and the smell of autumn and musty earth filling his awareness, he had never felt more human.

As twilight chased the red away, the skin of his arms reflected the light in metallic hues, and the vertebral marks hooking down his arms glowed silver. Little footsteps approached. He turned his arm to one side, then the other, observing the visible humps the marks produced. Not needing to look to know it was the silver boy.

The footsteps stopped and Cain turned. Its eyes watched him unblinking. Black holes within silver rims. And its skin—insipid gray littered with veins like black netting. He grimaced.

"*You must be thirsty,*" it said as Cain absently grabbed at the skin of his stomach. He wondered if it knew where he had just been, if it had somehow awoken him on purpose to keep him from reaching that harbor. He attempted to swallow, but his tongue was dry like coal and stuck painfully in his throat. He coughed to stifle a gag, knelt and clawed at the ground, moist with day-old rainfall. The silver boy crouched and watched him dig until he created a small pool of brackish water. He dipped and sucked up the liquid, keeping his eyes trained on the silver boy. It didn't move. When he finished, he stood and held out his arms. They were quaking.

Warm fluid filled his teeth, and he let it fall from cracked lips. He stared at the colored goo dripping in long strings to the ground.

Why am I bleeding?

The silver boy said, *"You cannot give back my gift."*

Cain straightened and rubbed a hand across the vertebral marks, disturbed less by the texture than by the lack of warmth. He looked across the plains and spit more blood on the ground. He had no notion of where he was. Everything, even the stars above, was unfamiliar.

"I gave you what you wanted," it said. *"You think you had no choice? You had a lifetime."*

"I chose none of this."

"You prefer death?"

Cain turned away, hooked his fingernail around one of the vertebrae, and pulled, stretching his skin with it.

"That you will die is more certain than your next thought. Do you crave release from that final tyrant too? Because I could set you free." It approached and scraped its sharp fingernails down the back of Cain's hand.

He pushed it away and stepped sideways, accidentally slipping his foot across the red spittle on the ground. He felt faint.

"How does it taste?"

Cain's eyes narrowed. "What do you mean?"

"The blood. How does it taste?"

Saliva pooled against the coppery flavor of blood between his teeth. He tried to swallow, but it poured into his mouth, flooding his tongue. His sight undulated like a ship on rough waters, and he stumbled to his seat. He was weak and thirsty. Thirsty for . . .

"Blood?"

21

Cain wondered at the size and shape of the growth sprouting from the ground and shooting through the cloud cover. It was a Tree, but seemed more stonelike than alive, and its canopy disappeared behind cloud cover.

"What is it?"

"A means of travel."

"From where to where?"

"From this world to the next and to those beyond."

Cain looked up and squinted, searching once more for the top of the Tree, but the silver boy laughed. *"It has no end. It is beyond your ability to understand."*

Cain touched the trunk, and his skin tingled with an unfamiliar sensation. He looked at the hazy Fog they passed through to arrive here. He had seen eyes like burning candles in the mist, but nothing had approached, and now there was only the sparkle of sunlight through condensation.

"Could another find this without your help?"

"No man has seen this Tree, and perhaps none will again."

Cain knocked his knuckles against it and recoiled. Blood oozed from his knuckles in beads. He smeared the blood away, then stared at the wounds, stifling the urge to lick them.

"Are we going to use it?"

"Why else would I bring you here?"

Of course there were reasons, but he needn't point them out. The silver boy utilized manipulation in a way Cain both respected and hated. "You couldn't prod me along fast enough. Why pause now?"

"You are exhausted. A moment of rest."

Cain shook his head. *It intends to impress upon me my reliance, but I am no fool. I see its desire to convince me for what it is. The truly dominant need not claim authority.* "I am ready."

"You will not return unchanged."

"So be it."

There was a pause. *"Give yourself to me, and I will bring us through the Tree to what lies beyond."*

He was repulsed by the prospect of giving up control. His neck was stiff and warm, and his vision narrowed. *If I give up control, it may try to take more. But if I do not . . .*

There was danger in taking such a risk, but more than anything Cain needed power, and he risked danger most by hesitating. *Sometimes to gain, one must also give.*

He let his soul retreat just far enough to relinquish a sliver of control. The cold fingers of the void clamped around his arms and pulled him into liquid darkness. Here he waited. And waited. There was a sound, as of a pulsing heartbeat, but it seemed too rhythmic to be organic, and the sound increased until he felt it branch and increase in complexity. Just as he began piecing it together, he was expelled from the void and into his body, and all five senses burned.

There was newness in his surroundings, in the smell of mold and taste of damp minerals. He tried to get up but was too weak. His ears rang and his sight was dark, but he sensed his environment imbued with a bluish hue. Slowly his eyes adjusted and he peered about. Above and arcing around was endless gray rock.

A cave?

Some of the stones glowed and differed from the others with peculiar marks like veins on a leaf. He stared at them, but suddenly everything seemed to glow—or was it merely a reflection?

His mind itched and buzzed. The silver boy was with him again. "Where were you?" Cain said.

"Your soul is simple and light. It moves quicker than I through the Trees."

Trees. So there were more of them. The thought made his mind spin. How much more of the world had they been blinded to by the walls of the Almighty? He struggled to his feet. "Movement seems more difficult here." There was no response. "This is your home, isn't it?"

"You presume much and are wrong."

"Then where are we? I feel corporeal, while all else seems somehow elevated."

"We are where no man has ever been, nor perhaps shall be again." Its voice softened as if in reverence. *"The City of the Light Bringer."*

He examined the glowing rocks and breathed the newness as another thought struck him. "You could not have arrived here without me, could you? You seem to take form, but it's no more real than the images in my mind."

The silver boy said, *"I hear the call. It is loud. Do you hear it? Of course not. There are many things you do not hear. Many things you cannot sense or understand."*

"Who is the Light Bringer? What does he want from me?"

"You will know soon enough. He has summoned us."

"You fear him."

"The child fears the father. The father fears failure. The strongest fears himself. The weakest fears everything. What do you fear?"

He suppressed the burning urge to swallow.

"I read the space between every word and understand its source."

For days Cain had contemplated the possibility that the silver boy could sense his thoughts, and now that fear returned. *If anything, it sees only the footprints of where my mind has been, and footprints may be erased. Surely it cannot read my thoughts.*

"Before this is over," the silver boy said, *"I will teach you subtlety and pain, and perhaps a little more."*

The silver boy yearned for control of Cain's body, but Cain suppressed it and walked down the corridor. The road ahead angled ever downward, and the path was several feet narrow, but the ceiling remained at least twenty or thirty feet above, and the glow of the stones, if indeed the light came from them, kept the illumination dim but satisfactory. It seemed they walked for hours, and

Cain grew weary. The fluid in his belly seemed to have evaporated, and the pale thirst rushed against his insides like a moonlit tide. Soon he would need to face the change the silver boy had brought to him—to understand the true costs.

Soon, but not yet. He remembered Sarah on the floor of their home and lost himself to the crumpled shape of her lit by lightning and washed by water. She shook with sobs and slowly lifted her gaze to his.

Does she see me as I was or as I am?

Cain shook his head and realized the madness in his thoughts as he stumbled on loose rocks and slid down a ditch. He stood, brushed the gravel from his tunic, and lifted himself onto a ledge. Beyond the ledge was a thin path that led down a tunnel toward light. Finally the hall opened, and he steadied himself against the wall as he peered through the opening at what lay beyond.

"Great Almighty," he whispered.

The domed chamber was perhaps a mile high, and suspended in the center was a light whose brilliance rivaled the sun's. Though it flickered like a flame, it lit the deepest ends of the dome, and cast long shadows from the buildings and from what looked like people bustling between the buildings in a sea of movement and sound.

A world entombed in stone.

"*It is beautiful,*" the silver boy said.

"There must be thousands of them."

"*More, son of Adam. The City of the Light Bringer is more vast than you could imagine. This is only one Dome. There are thousands more.*"

If the City of the Light Bringer was truly so large, of what interest could Cain and his family be? It seemed a strange thing, but still he felt the Light Bringer's call.

Not all is as it seems.

He felt the rock wall, cold of the variety that sucked life from bone. "Why did you leave this place?"

"*I have never been.*"

Cain quieted himself, but uneasiness churned his stomach. The

City seemed a great hub, and the knowledge the silver boy possessed spoke contrarily.

It could not have come here without me, but how do I know that? And how does it know the City's name, and the expanse of its construction? From what hole did the silver boy crawl?

It would not tell Cain of its origins, no matter how forcefully he questioned. He remembered the prophetic streams and wondered why the silver boy's origins, of all mysteries, remained out of reach.

Perhaps because it is a point sharpened to a tip so thin that it remains invisible to all but the one who stands upon it.

He descended and waded through the mob like a drop of oil in a murky pond. Nudging into and flowing past him were what looked like people of varied shapes and colors. Nevertheless, they were no more people than the voice was a silver boy, and Cain felt as if he were the center of attention, sticking out like a splinter, though none addressed him.

The buildings were beautiful but cold. Everywhere he went, the pale light throbbed from the stones, hummed off the towers, and buzzed the soles of his feet. Someone screamed in a strange tongue and exchanged blows with another. A group danced and sung to Music played on unfamiliar instruments, and everywhere there was chatter, and the sound of countless feet scuffing dust from stone.

An amplified voice rumbled the Dome, and every mouth closed, and every ear turned in respect. The sudden halt startled him, and he stilled. All around were closed eyes and bowed heads, and Cain would have imitated them if not for the fear pinching the nape of his neck. The last echoes faded and the cacophony resumed. Soon he found himself pressed against the wall by a crowd of bodies.

"What was that?"

"It declared a shift of some sort."

"Of some sort?"

"Keep moving."

"Answer me."

"I was born for more than to ease your curiosity."

"I don't care what you were born for."

"Someday you will wish it was all you had cared about."

"In this moment there is only you and me in this City. Remember that you would not have arrived here if not for me." It did not respond, and he felt a sort of satisfaction in this, though soon he wondered if its silence stemmed from ignorance or hidden knowledge.

Now Cain could physically feel the Light Bringer's pull. It was as if a magnet were set by his head and, as he went off course, it tipped him back. Time and again this happened. Eventually his legs tired and his body ached with the monotony of the journey. All numbed and fell away like stains washed in a river, and he slipped into what he could only explain as a waking dream. He was unsure how long this lasted, but remembered waking with a start against the wall at the bottom of a stairwell. He looked up the angled shaft and realized he must have descended beneath the metropolis.

What he at first thought were people now filed through stone archways ahead one at a time. He stumbled forward, obeying the magnetic compulsion to follow, though he tripped and landed on the bony shoulders of the individual before him. Before he could right himself, a fist smashed his forehead, and he staggered and blinked away motes of light. After being spat on, he kept his distance and waited for the line to move.

A pair descended the stairs and fell into place behind him. They gargled unintelligible words, then chuckled. He glanced back and saw them smiling. They looked androgynous. Cain's face flushed and he looked away. They chuckled again, and his neck crawled.

After filing through the archway, he proceeded down the tunnel until it ended with dark holes on the left and right. No light stones led the way down those paths, where the ground was hollowed out.

Wind gushed out of the hole on the right, and a metal cylinder slid into view and stopped. It was set on its side and marked with doors that slid open and allowed groups to exit before those that had waited with him entered. He followed the compulsion into the cylinder and found a seat at the end. The others took seats far from him, the doors shut, and the cylinder sped down the tunnel into darkness.

Throughout the journey, the cylinder stopped and some exited while others took their place, but he never felt the impulse to move. Three stops down, the pair that molested him with their eyes exited, and exhaustion came like an innocent caress. Indeed, he was so fatigued that he thought he wouldn't have been able to move if commanded. After the last of them left, the hum of the cylinder lulled him to sleep for the first time in many days.

It was a deep and dreamless repose.

22

C ain awoke with a gasp, still sitting on the bench in the cylinder. He was alone, and the container was illuminated by pale light filtered through cracks in the doors. Dust flecks floated through the beams, and the scent of aluminum and sweat clung to the enclosed atmosphere. He rubbed his face with a sticky palm and stood. The machine creaked and the doors opened when he neared them. He hesitated, temporarily blinded by the light, then exited the cylinder to a well-lit corridor identical to the last, only empty.

"Hello?"

He walked a few slapping steps forward and stopped, listening to the rush of his blood, a soft but steady rhythm. He tasted the pale thirst and momentarily wished he had a red-filled cup to quench it. He ran a hand through his hair, smothered the desire, and walked on.

"Few come this way," said the silver boy.

Cain looked at the arches. "Where are we?"

"The central Dome of the Light Bringer. Only those summoned dare come so far."

Cain walked past the arches, pausing only to run his hand across their slimy texture. He ascended the staircase. As he reached the top, he paused. This Dome was not the same busy metropolis, filled with beings and buildings. It was a barren wasteland stretching from end to end and punctured by a singular Tower dwarfed amidst the grandeur of the Dome. He walked toward the Tower and the ground beneath him sped away strangely. It seemed to him that Time itself was rolling beneath him, and he skipped from crest to crest. Finally the undulation stilled, and the Tower loomed above him.

The door in the Tower's side opened like that of the moving cylinder, but its shadows were repulsive, and light failed to enter its mouth. It impaled the ground, a beautiful and archaic thing, both severe and terrible, and fear held him motionless.

But what was fear but an illusion? Cain was chained to the silver boy and had set down a path he could not escape, walking the land of the Light Bringer, whose power made the silver spirit inside him quake. Every instinct screamed for him to run from this place, and yet he knew how misleading instinct could be.

The rabbit follows impulse and becomes prey. The human outwits the trapper and gains dominance.

"*What are you waiting for?*" the silver boy asked.

"You offered me a moment earlier. I will take that moment now."

He knew that to walk into this Tower would be to pass into a great nexus of Time. Every detail of the future, the fate of his grandchildren, even his great-grandchildren and those beyond, ran through this singular point. It was not simply another choice, it was a *defining* choice.

He had realized even when planning the deed that killing his brother had set him down a path into the core of the forbidden, and now he found himself at the entrance to one of its arteries. If he turned back, Abel's murder would become nothing more than an experiment in futility.

Cain was reminded of the incredible power of the present. Every choice crafted truth from clay, and though days earlier he would have welcomed this moment, now, with the Waters of prophetic truth rinsing him of ignorance, he saw what violence could arise from such a seemingly benign choice.

Stray but a little and the world may shatter. But if I resist . . .

No. I cannot choose that way.

To move forward was to embrace chaos. No man knew what possibilities lurked within that chaos, but only with movement could the pieces align. Failure was the true Sin, and as the Almighty claimed, it would consume him. Mankind had embraced chaos before, and it had brought them to a state of heightened awareness. The Almighty banished them from the Garden out of fear, for he knew that mankind in such a state could accomplish *anything*.

Clarity with immortality. The recipe for Godhood.

The human lays traps for the animal, but God ensnares mankind in the ambition to be as he. Power. It is what separates man from God.

This was his only chance to move forward, to embrace innovation, to seek and find what lay hidden in the dark recesses of the world and worlds, to reclaim the godhood mankind inherited in the Garden by eating the fruit of the Tree of Knowledge of Good and Evil.

"For God knows that if you eat of it, your eyes will be opened, and you will be like him."

It was fate. Destiny. *Purpose.*

He looked at the vertebral marks burned into him by the Almighty, and raised his fist to the ceiling, accepting for the first time the meaning those physical manifestations contained. His throat constricted and his fist shook as he screamed past the Dome to whatever lay beyond.

"I am." He shook his fist, "I am. And nothing and no one can stop me!"

He turned, let his fist fall, filled his lungs, allowed the fear to pass through him, and plunged into the Tower's throat.

23

Machines growled and whirred as the sensation of movement spun Cain's mind like a falling maple seed. Down he went into the bowels of the Tower to meet the Light Bringer. He could see nothing, for there was only darkness, and as he groped and attempted to maintain balance, his fingers waved through bone-chilling air.

He felt as he had when left in the wilderness by the silver boy. He was once again powerless, surrounded by empty nothing. The hum of grinding metal—or was it so many hammers striking anvils?—cycled with steady rhythm, and the deeper he went, the more lifeless and hollow the space became, until at last he shivered and brought his extremities in to conserve heat. Frost formed on his nose, and he closed his eyes and hugged his knees.

His insides sank as the descent slowed and everything stilled. No more gears, only the sound of Cain's uneven breathing. His body shook.

There was the sound of sliding stone, and a sliver of light stabbed the darkness ahead. He jumped and ran toward it, shoving his hand into the ray to feel warmth. The sliver widened, became a beam, then an open doorway.

The light melted the frost from his skin as he entered an immaculate hall decorated with tapestries, lampstands, and art. The way was wide enough for perhaps twenty or so men to walk abreast, and symmetrically placed pillars held the ceiling high. Into the pillars was carved the likeness of a single face that was sensuous and drew him until he smiled unknowingly.

At the end stood golden doors into which was cast the focal point, a work of art—without equal—portraying thousands of beings with weapons raised. They marched toward a great City, and at their front stood a figure lifting a brass horn from which light volleyed in widening arrows.

He brushed his fingers across it. *They march to war?* He traced the leader's arm to the instrument he held. *A musician.*

He studied the image, then knocked thrice.

A basso voice rumbled from beyond the doors. "Enter."

Cain obeyed.

The chamber was not as he expected. The vanity of the hallway and the overwhelming size of the City had primed him for indulgence, but the door opened to a dull gray box whose only ornamentation was one stone throne, two red lamps on the throne's armrests, and a towering mirror on the far wall, lit by burning braziers. In the throne sat who Cain guessed was the Light Bringer, for the face was similar to the busts in the hallway and the musician in the mural.

"You are drawn to me." His voice was sweet and smooth, yet powerful.

Cain wondered if the Light Bringer could see him shaking.

"You are free to speak in my presence." A pause. "You have no reason to distrust me, though fear is an appropriate reaction." The Light Bringer sipped from a goblet and set it next to the lamp that had obscured it. The drink stained his lips a dark crimson, and Cain felt the pale thirst return.

"You are a strong man." The Light Bringer smiled with tainted teeth, then slid out of his seat and approached until close enough to touch. "You and I are cast from similar molds."

The Light Bringer was roughly the same size as Cain, but Cain felt overwhelmed by his presence. "In what way?"

"You want freedom." The Light Bringer's voice lowered enough to shake the room. "And I brought you here to show you that I *am*."

"You are what?"

He spread his arms. "What do you see?"

"Stone walls."

"And what do they represent?"

"A prison?"

The Light Bringer laughed, but it was cold. "Try again. Where are you?"

The silver boy tried seizing control, but Cain suppressed it and said, "Your City."

"*My* City. And how did I make this *my* City? Well, son of Adam, that's precisely why you're here, isn't it?"

"I'm here because I was led here."

"Liar. You're here because you chose to come. The moment you decided to beat your brother's brains into the dust, you put yourself on the road that led only here."

The corner of Cain's mouth twitched toward the floor.

"Ah, you see truth. You desire release from stupidity, and the truth will set you free, will it not? That is why you came to me. But let us speak plainly. We need each other."

Cain gazed at his hands, then cocked his head. "Why do you call yourself the Light Bringer?"

"They call me the Light Bringer because I bring illumination. I expose what others hide. I give fruit to those who hunger. I give insight when silence reigns. I give pleasure when chastity binds. I give freedom past darkness. I am the Light Bringer, the Morning Star, the Son of the Morning, the Day Lark." The Light Bringer's words fell into a melodious rhythm, and Cain felt himself compelled by the Music. The notes and tension of his voice stirred the heart. "I am the Great Musician, the Voice of the Damned, the Friend of the Broken, God's Helping Hand. I do what he needs done, though I'm despised as a rebel son. Listen!" The final word struck Cain's ears with the force of a hammer blow. His body shook as the air itself seemed to fall silent before the Light Bringer's eyes.

"Come," he commanded, reverting to his rumbling bass. "Show me what's inside you."

Cain stepped back, but the Light Bringer approached and grabbed his chin with a soft hand, and the sensation struck him like open palms to the chest.

"Let it out."

Cain felt his awareness recede and realized he was voluntarily giving up control. The silver boy came forward, and the Light Bringer moaned with satisfaction.

"Yes," he whispered. "You are beautiful. Everything I ever dreamed. My beloved child . . ."

Tears seeped from Cain's eyes. He felt as if the words *beloved child* had been directed toward him, but he was the rightful first-born of Adam, not the product of this lord of spirits. Could it be, perhaps, that this being was their Creator? His skin tingled at the mere thought of it.

He jerked from the Light Bringer's hold and realized the Light Bringer had been speaking to the silver boy, and not he, and that it was the resonance of the silver boy's emotions that brought the tears.

So, that is who you are. And that is why you wouldn't tell me your name or where you came from. You were waiting to be given one by your father, the Light Bringer.

The silver boy retreated to the void, and he sensed satisfaction spilling from the darkness. He swallowed the saliva that filled his mouth, wiped the tears the thing had forced from him, and stepped back to reestablish dignity and distance between him and the Light Bringer.

But something had happened in the few moments since entering the Light Bringer's chamber. He felt strange intimacy with this being whom he had never met. He knew they understood one another. But there was more. With a crackling sensation rippling through his mind, he realized their relationship *was* the nexus, the point of convergence where the fate of the world would be decided for millennia to come.

Cain, the Sinner, was in this moment the most powerful man in the world. He felt this fact resonate with the Waters. His newly awakened prophetic sight gave him the right to make this claim devoid of arrogance, for simple truth may be believed without pretense, however much of it involves one's self.

The Light Bringer slid his fingers under the goblet resting on the arm of the throne and shifted back toward Cain. After swirling its contents, the Light Bringer offered him a drink. "Come now, you must be thirsty."

Cain looked at the liquid and, against his better judgment, allowed the scent of blood to reach into his awareness. His heartbeat sped as he felt his muscles twitch and burn. Saliva pooled in his mouth, and his tongue longed to break the surface of the drink. His fingers chilled and shook.

"You desire. I see it in your eyes." The Light Bringer's voice was smiling, but Cain could not look from the ocean in the goblet. Brackish coagulates churned hypnotically, and as he stared, the Light Bringer swirled it again. "As fresh as if you sucked it from a wound."

Sweat beaded on Cain's face.

The silver boy said, *"Take it. Accept what you have become."*

His mind burned for him to drink. *No. I need not accept this curse.*

The Light Bringer said, "You cannot escape what you are."

With great restraint, Cain looked from the drink to the Light Bringer's eyes. He thought about slapping the cup away. About beating that smiling face into a grimace and grabbing a stone, as he had in the darkness of the valley, to spill red yolk from skull to goblet.

"Feed the lust. Let it grow and mature until you must vomit it forth."

Cain reached, gripped the goblet in a shaking hand, and brought the cool lip to his mouth. Blood poured into his mouth and filled his tongue with pleasurable flavors. His body lurched, and he tipped the goblet until it spilled down his neck and chest.

He gasped as the goblet clanged on the floor.

"Beautiful," the Light Bringer said. "You were thirstier than I thought. Well done." He laughed. "Well done."

Cain ground the bitter clots between his teeth and felt them burst. Tears blurred his vision and his hands clenched at his side. *Sarah, I won't forget my promise. I will return to you, even if I must bear the ultimate shame to do so.*

The Light Bringer frowned. "Young child, young gift. Is a worker embarrassed when his master says, 'Well done'? Is a son ashamed when his father says, 'You are my pride'? They should not be if the praise is timely. Yet you were cursed instead of applauded." He stepped close and his voice grew tender. "Ah, I know of the injustice. Your ears were starved for affirmation. Absorbed by wanderlust, they searched for approval, and for a time you found it in your sister, whom you loved and married. But the pain grew with you. Every time you reached for her, the movement stretched your wounds and spilled their rot on you both. Her eyes grew weary of the hardness of your pain, and more and more she sought relief in the tenderness of another."

Cain folded his arms and shifted away, feeling the Light Bringer's words clutch his emotions.

"Abel stole her eyes, as he stole your father's and the eyes of all the others. He was a void absorbing everything you loved. You feared he would overtake you. That he would steal everything and you would die alone and forgotten. You and he were the Night and the Day. The very laws of nature held your faces to the grindstone. Dear child, I understand." He stroked Cain's cheek and whispered, "That is why I gave you the strength to do it."

Cain closed his eyes, inwardly screaming for the Light Bringer's arms around him.

No! He wants to use me. I can see it with my very eyes!

The Light Bringer leaned until his lips touched Cain's ear. "I offered what you wanted, and you didn't care what it cost then, so why care now?"

Cain felt himself nod as logic lost itself in desire.

"I love you, Cain. I am the only one who ever loved you. And I am proud of you. You have done well." He pulled him into an embrace and kissed his head, as a father would a child.

Cain shook against the warmth of the Light Bringer's body. A century of suppressed emotions he hadn't known existed boiled and stung his eyes and throat.

"I am proud of who you are."

What perversity. It's a hoax. A fabrication.

The Light Bringer said, "Give in. Accept what you are."

Cain whispered, "What am I? Who am I?"

"You are *mine*." The Light Bringer traced the vertebral marks on Cain's arms with sharp fingernails.

Cain could not deny the depth of the relationship between him and the Light Bringer. It felt like fate. It felt like love.

But what was love? He thought he loved Sarah, but this was unlike anything he had experienced, and he wanted it. He wanted it all.

"What do you want me to do?" Cain said.

The Light Bringer smiled. "Build me a Garden."

"A Garden?"

"A New Garden, a place of safety, a home."

"Why?"

"Because your family needs you. The Man is dead."

"Dead?"

The Light Bringer laughed. "Don't look so surprised. You killed him yourself. And soon they will die without him. They need you. Your family needs you. I need you."

"Dead," Cain whispered. *The true test of divinity is to kill the one who claims to be God—does that mean I am he? But the silver boy . . .* He frowned.

"The imposter is gone, but your family is tangled in his web nonetheless. You must liberate them. Some are already struggling, but the others—" He did not finish.

"Even an imposter's curse may hold power," Cain said.

"Indeed, his curses hold power beyond even the end of all things. You could not accomplish this alone, but together . . ." The Light Bringer smiled. "Do you think I do not know your plight? I will stay here to attend to my duties, but at the present you will keep my child, who has shared your existence and begun in you the process of *refinement*."

Cain wiped the sweat from his face with a shaking hand, and wondered if he truly did understand. He felt like an animal in heat, his veins pumping with passion. The words were distant and weightless as they leapt from his lips, "What am I to call it?"

"My child shall be called Abomination, but never speak a word about its existence, and do not speak of our meeting here, or that this City exists. More depends on this than you know." The Light Bringer's eyes seemed to suck him in like endless black holes rimmed with blood. "Surely you understand the magnitude." He drew out the final word in a way that highlighted its importance like a tongue across skin. "After you do these things, you and your people will be truly free for the first time since the foundations of the world were formed. You will become gods. You will become like me."

Cain was fully compliant to the Light Bringer, possessed by its very Abomination of a child, and though reason warned him of the danger, he knew he must welcome this momentary slavery. Yes, in the end, bowing to this new lord would give him the chance to free all humanity from bondage, whether the Light Bringer was a liar or not. Cain would play the game, he would walk the line, and at the opportune moment he would turn and exert mastery over all. Or, as he had planned from the beginning, he would die a martyr.

Alone, but never forgotten.

PART FIVE:

THE CHILDREN

Woe to them! For they walked in the way of Cain and abandoned themselves for the sake of gain. . . . These are hidden reefs at your love feasts, as they feast with you without fear, shepherds feeding themselves; waterless clouds, swept along by winds; fruitless trees in late autumn, twice dead, uprooted; wild waves of the sea, casting up the foam of their own shame; wandering stars, for whom the gloom of utter darkness has been reserved forever.

—JUDE 1:11–14 ESV

24

The sky's great yellow eye hid itself from the bodies in the coffins, and Lukian had little difficulty understanding why. Many wanted to turn away. Many still didn't believe the bodies were real. How could they be?

Adam and Eve were at the front of the procession but hardly seemed capable of balance. They leaned on each other silently, though Adam seemed more damaged than she.

Perhaps, Lukian thought, *it is the elegance with which she holds herself. Or maybe it's the austerity of her eyes or the emptiness of Adam's.* Regardless, Eve had always been the stronger of the two. No one spoke of it because they'd never needed to. It was simply understood.

Behind their matriarch, and the man from whom she had been formed, walked their children, and their children's children. Leading them all was Calebna, High Priest and eldest son of Abel. His mouth was drawn and his eyes dripped like melting candlesticks, but he was not alone in suffering.

With shaking voice, Calebna led them in the song of lamentation. Voices faltered. Some broke while others became songbirds perched on tombs. It seemed the world was at war with itself, and the wind joined with howls and spurts of wounded coughing. But Lukian was absorbed with the question of whether his father was still alive.

Where was Cain? Had he succeeded in finding greater power and freedom? Or had he merely destroyed himself?

Lukian glanced at Mason. He could tell by the swing of his arms and the shuffle of his feet that he just wanted to finish the ritual, return to Sarah's side, and wait for her eyes to open for the first time in days.

His other brother, Gorban, bumped into him and glanced up in curt apology, then focused on the path before him. Gorban walked beside his wife, Peth, but she offered no comfort to him. Not now.

Soon, little brother, Lukian thought. *The time for action is growing near.*

When they reached the grave site behind the Temple, Calebna led them around the three tombs in a semicircle, broke away and faced them. His cheeks shone in the light of the torch, and the shadowy flames enlarged his bruised figure.

"Today"—Calebna's voice broke—"we entomb only a portion of those taken from us. My father remains where God let him lie, and my mother remains missing, may God protect her soul. You must forgive me for not offering words of comfort." He gazed at the sky as if searching for the words. His expression said he failed to find them, and instead he let the leftovers fall from his tongue. "My world collapsed two days ago when I heard of my father's murder. Moments after, I learned of the death of Seth and Ayla, and the death of our God. I dare to say none of you but Adam felt more lost than me. In the days since, I have wondered how we can serve a being and so completely believe he is our only hope, our salvation, our very Creator, and yet place his bloodied crown in a tomb? I do not know the answer. Maybe there isn't one. Yet now more than ever, I feel the longing, the need in my soul for the rituals of the Almighty to calm me, to repeat to me in the darkest hours that everything will be made right one day. And these are the darkest hours."

Calebna wiped his eyes. "Maybe I am a desperate man holding onto a fool's hope, but I will not relinquish my duties as High Priest. My spirit tells me my eyes betray me as I look upon the Almighty's torn and bloodied robe, and the bodies of Seth and Ayla, and so I find in myself a contradiction. I believe and yet I do not believe. I need to accept, but am compelled to deny."

The silence absorbed Calebna's words, for those gathered knew his pain well. The children of Abel glanced warily at the children of Cain, and Lukian thought, *Meaning in every motion. Distrust is a deadly poison in our well, but the world is charred and thirsty, so thirsty.*

Calebna's voice strained. "I refuse to believe they are dead. The Almighty once promised he would make all things new, and challenged us to follow him through pain and shadow. Though we bury God, I believe he is greater than the grave. Though we perform his funeral, I cannot believe he is gone." He shook his head and whispered as if to convince himself, "Not forever."

It struck Lukian as odd that even his brothers had no idea what Calebna's words ordained for them. He almost smiled. *No one understands that you, dear cousin, are now the only thing standing between me and freedom.*

Calebna stepped toward his family and offered the torch to Adam, though Eve grasped it. She led Adam haltingly, step by painful step, to look upon the faces of their dead children.

The bodies in the tombs were clay figurines. Adam did not look down, for his motionless eyes were empty. Eve glanced first at her expressionless husband, then at Seth's cold face. She smiled as if expecting him to do the same, but he didn't, and so she reached out to stroke his cold eyelids with the tenderness one would offer an infant. If she would not have had to support Adam, she may have dipped to kiss their son. Instead, she spoke words for their ears alone.

When she saw the body of Ayla, her youngest daughter, the sorrow flowed more readily. She mouthed her youngest daughter's name, but the word was strangled as she clutched Adam's arm for the support he was unable to offer.

Upon seeing the Almighty's crown and torn robe, she straightened and nodded, and her grip on Adam loosened. She raised her chin and swept her eyes across her family, stopping finally on Adam.

Lukian frowned and thought, *Fatalism. A dangerous emotion I shall have to expunge. There awaits now no calm path or return to innocent bliss. Only violence.*

After an extended silence, Eve helped Adam to the Temple, where the family had taken refuge together.

The Temple. The house of the imposter who had imprisoned

them. What more ironic refuge could they take? *Let the slaves run to their cage. Let them box themselves in.*

One by one, the remaining mourners passed over the coffins and gazed on the terrible beauty of death, and when all had grieved, Mason, Lukian, Calebna, and his son Jacob pushed the stone covers over the coffins and sealed them to keep the worms from feeding on their remains.

A final dignity. A gift to the dead.

◆   ◆   ◆

Adam sat in the corner—where he could not fall and strike his head—listening to familiar voices argue, wondering who they were and thinking strange thoughts. But he had always thought strange thoughts, hadn't he? Or at least they had become strange since . . .

Since the pain. Waterfalls of pain falling, rushing, splitting me like a mountain. The rush of water, the thrum of voices, and the deafening thunder of thought—these sounds remain, though all else is gone. I cannot jump the river. I cannot reach the other side. I am stagnant. I am rotting bones. I am dust and decay. I am . . . Who am I?

"He hasn't moved in days."

"Days? You have watched him so long?"

"What else would I do? He needs me."

"Yes, we all need you."

"I know it. I . . ."

"It's all right."

The voices droned on. One comforted another. No comfort came to him.

"I have been praying for him."

"Praying? Have your eyes been sealed shut?"

"I know what you would say. But it comforts me."

There was a pause, then softly, "Who do you pray to?"

"I don't know. The dead. The world. Whatever god is out there."

Another pause. Amidst tears. "My sons are gone. God has fled and taken them with him. What hope do I have left? I feel as though there is nothing. Nothing."

The tears became rivers and washed the voices away. Adam was alone again. There was relief in the emptiness, and he savored it. He imagined he could be washed away with them.

Yes, washed away. Like blood in a field. Like blemishes in the cloth of Time. Gone. Just gone. He would enjoy that. He would like to disappear.

So he closed his eyes and dreamed. And the world was good again.

25

L ukian paced the hall and assessed those gathered. His shoulders were rigid, and he walked as if his feet were spears and the ground their mark. It had been six days since they sealed Seth, Ayla, and the elements of the Almighty in their respective tombs, and even longer since Abel died and Cain and Lilleth disappeared.

I must keep the appearance of strength, for this is a moment of proving.

Lukian's brothers remained separated from the sons of Abel. Gorban leaned against a wall with his arms crossed, and Mason sat cross-legged, nearly as tall while sitting as Gorban was while standing. Calebna stood with his hands clasped behind his back and his eyes glaring sideways. Eve sat with Adam, stroked his hand, and silently begged him to speak, to do anything.

Those gathered likely had a myriad of explanations for Cain's actions, the dead bodies, the state of Sarah and Adam, and the death of their God. Their suspicions and the tension had metastasized into malignant glances.

"I am no liar," Lukian said. "No one has gained from this. I see it in your faces." He looked at Calebna's brothers, then at Calebna's eldest, Jacob. He looked at Eve, whose eyes grasped him like vines under winter's first chill, straining to keep their strength despite the ache of the frost.

Calebna spread his hands. "We make important decisions today. We have no room for belligerence."

"I cannot go back to when I first heard whispers against me and my brothers. I held my tongue then out of respect for the dead, but I can stand it no longer." Lukian paused, yet everyone remained silent, unwilling to break the tension for fear of its recoil. *So strong behind closed doors, yet so weak when pressured.* "Is a child a copy of his father? And were Abel's children the only ones harmed?"

Calebna sniffed and cleared his throat. "What choice do we have? How can we believe no one aided Cain in his sin?"

"By having faith." The people mumbled. None held Lukian's stare. He continued, "Perhaps you should share from your excess store of it, High Priest."

Calebna's expression rotted.

Lukian continued, "You are right about one thing. Separation is dangerous. But we do not know what has befallen our mother. Why was she found half drowned in the flooded quarry?"

"Many think their suspicions warranted."

"Change has come, and unless we adapt, none of us will survive."

"It seems you've been conceiving a plan in silence, and I'd rather you voice it and let us discuss its merits than for us to argue over opinion and conjecture."

"Finally you speak with sense," Lukian said. "You remember destroying our weapons when we arrived. Tell me, with the Almighty's death, what do you think has happened to his protection?" Some of their eyes catalogued the possible danger. *Yes, realize how ignorant you've been.* "We need weapons, but have only shovels, hoes, scythes, hammers, and pickaxes. We cannot defend ourselves with these. We must remake them into implements of violence." He could see the fear in their eyes. *They are ready,* he thought. "Unless we flee from the City, every one of us, from our great mother Eve to the babe in Terah's arms, will die."

The mumbling increased to a gentle roar, and Calebna raised his hands to quiet them. "The viper spits, but is there bite behind the prattle?"

"Our plants are dying, our food is rotting, and our animals are sick or dead," Lukian said.

"Fear will gain us nothing. We must stand strong in faith. All else is cowardice."

"Is it cowardice to free ourselves from bondage? Is it cowardice to consider the lives of children more important than dead principle?"

"You would have us abandon our lifestyle, remake our weapons, and run blindly into the wilderness, but for what? Do you also propose yourself as our leader?" Calebna laughed and shook his head, not finishing what was written in his expression.

"You mock yet still cling to a lifeless God as if his skin could warm you. God is dead. His cloak and crown are lying in a stone coffin next to Seth and Ayla, and I will not lie down and die by the rules of an imposter, for that is what the Almighty was."

"What reason do we have left to live, if not for hope in God? By what transcendence could we gain direction?"

"By the same principles that led us through the wilderness. In those many years we synthesized our own meaning. Or have you forgotten?"

Calebna's shoulders sagged. "I remember the pain of those days, and it sticks in my throat even still."

"And yet those days were *ours*. I cannot say that about our lives here, and I would fight and pay the price to say it again."

"We returned to the Almighty because we were dying. The demonic Jinn overwhelmed us. It seems you, not I, have forgotten the true price we paid. Indeed,"—Calebna's eyes glinted in the torchlight—"the price you yourself paid."

Lukian's neck warmed at the memory of his twin brother's entrails wrapped around his mangled legs. *That was a cowardly blow, but they are watching. Calm your anger.*

"The Almighty is our only hope," Calebna said.

"How?"

"Our own strength has ever failed."

"Maybe you're right. Maybe our chances are better here with no food and no protection. Or maybe our future is laid before us waiting to be claimed."

"Our purpose lies here."

"In becoming sacrifices? Do you intend to burn us all at your holy altar?"

Calebna narrowed his eyes. His jaw moved from side to side, then clenched. "Hear this now. As High Priest of the Almighty, I declare that the Almighty's laws, which we all swore to preserve upon returning two years ago, remain. Those who live by the sword will die by the sword, but those who live by the Spirit of the Almighty will stand on the firmest rock. Remember the flood that washed the City the night after Abel's death, and heed my words that another flood is coming, and its red waters will drown all who quench themselves in its depths. I vow today to never again pick up a weapon and strike with fierceness, and if any desire to call me family, you will take this vow with me."

Calebna's son Jacob stood. "I vow the same." But none followed save Calebna's wife, Terah, and she hesitantly.

Those standing looked at those who sat, and doubtless shame weighed upon the shoulders of Calebna's younger brothers, Philo and Tuor. But Eve spoke, and her voice chilled the air to silence. "For me, there is no hope." Her white knuckles held Adam's hand in her lap, and the light failed around her shadowed eyes. Some of the people were fearful. Others were exhausted. Certainly all felt the bite of her words.

Danger lurked in every shifting shadow and darkened corner. Lukian knew that if he failed to stoke the flames, they might be forever snuffed, but if he pushed too far . . .

"If you cannot do it for your own sake, do it for mine. Do it for Sarah's," Lukian said. He gazed at those still sitting. "Do it for Abel. Don't let yourselves join the Almighty in the unforgiving stone."

His words stopped but his eyes went on. He saw in some of Abel's children and grandchildren the desire to struggle on. He thought he saw in Gorban, Mason, Kiile, and Machael the willingness to follow him into death, but no one moved. No one said anything.

Eve rubbed Adam's hand. Mason stared in voiceless intensity. Gorban rubbed his neck and squinted. And Calebna stared at his own clasped hands.

Then something unexpected happened. Adam's eyes stretched

and breath burst past his lips. He was struggling, and for the first time in days, he spoke two words, though they were barely audible in the hush.

"My Abel." And tears welled in his eyes as he rocked.

The room was filled with the throbbing ache of loss, and Lukian saw the damage rifle through them all. He wondered at his grandfather as the man swayed. What had drawn those words, the first he had spoken since the storm subsided?

Lukian's eyes widened. *Was that the first time in all these days that anyone spoke Abel's name in front of Adam?*

He watched Adam's twitching figure. After an awkward silence, Eve led him away. She looked fatigued, but Lukian knew she would not sleep. Instead, she would watch Adam's face and pray for her husband to return, but as had happened every day since Abel's death, his eyes would open and she would look into them and find only emptiness.

Adam has lost himself to desperation, Lukian thought. *And I must draw a similar desperation from the others. Not too much and not too little. The battle is not yet lost.* He bit his cheek. *I fear it has only begun.*

After Adam and Eve disappeared, the group trickled away until only Lukian, Mason, and Gorban remained.

Lukian cleared his throat and brushed at his tunic. Storm clouds churned in his skull, and he stood and walked from the Temple, barely aware of his feet touching the ground. On the road, Lukian heard footsteps behind him.

"Brother," Gorban said. And he repeated it as if unsure what else may be said.

"I know. You, at least, I would never doubt. I am going to walk the inner wall."

"I will follow."

For a time they were silent, but questions remained.

"What is going to happen?" Gorban asked.

"We will survive as we always have."

"How can you be sure?"

"It is the only choice we have."

Again there was silence until Gorban shifted. "They are afraid."

Lukian's sandals clapped the road.

"They will fight in the end."

"Let us hope it won't be too late," Lukian said.

"But what about the food? How long can we survive before it runs out? And then what do we do?"

Lukian stopped. "There is always a way."

"Most of the forges were destroyed in the flood. Your sons and I checked them today."

"What remains?"

"A few on the outskirts appear usable, but they're small," Gorban said.

Lukian nodded. "Could you prepare one by tomorrow?"

"Yes."

"The days ahead will be long, but not long enough. We must jolt them from slumber." He grabbed Gorban's shoulder. "We cannot afford to wait."

As night fell over the horizon, Gorban, Lukian, and his children congregated by the wall, kept watch, and burned fires to keep warm. For a time, Lukian was hopeful his other brothers and nephews would come.

None did.

26

Gorban inhaled the hot air belched from the forge, and was content for the first time in many days. As he hammered red-hot metal, the flames in the furnace licked the sweat from his skin and dimmed the world behind the flash of molten metal. A song floated through his mind, and he scooped it up and let it burn his tongue. He remembered only a shard of one verse, after which he went on humming, but the words spilled like gold into the mold of the meter.

The green grass that covered the hill,
Near the dark forest ere winter's chill,
Berry bushes and thickets tall,
And the oak and burdock in the fall,

As he repeated the words, Calebna appeared in the doorway. The man's hair was tied back and cascaded like undyed silk, and his reedy face seemed tighter than usual, though he tipped his head in greeting.

Gorban wiped the grime from his hands.

"I hope you're keeping a few tools for their original purpose," Calebna said.

"Taking new interest in the business of men?"

Calebna cleared his throat, grabbed a hammer, and tested its weight. "Peaceful tasks are often most difficult in times of disquiet, so I understand in part what you attempt."

"The forge is hot."

He chuckled and seemed to search Gorban for sarcasm. "I've never had the gift for plain speech. Maybe you could teach me."

Gorban folded his arms.

"I'm here for the people," Calebna said.

"Having trouble?"

"It's the question of leadership."

"Adam hasn't improved?"

"I thought you knew."

"I'm busy," Gorban said.

"Do you not care?"

"I'm no healer."

"Well, you will be glad to hear he hasn't worsened, but whatever ails him seems reticent to relinquish its grip. Many of us have little faith it will pass, and as your brother so eloquently illustrated, that leaves us with the question of headship."

Gorban cursed, turned to his work, and said, "Drawing substance from you is worse than cleaning a wound."

"It will be a few days until we decide, but the people are concerned. The weapons, the talk of fleeing into the wilderness, it has them worried."

"I don't know why it would."

"There's concern that if a choice of leadership were put through, violence may arise."

"You know that wouldn't happen."

"I would hope it wouldn't."

"Lukian is a good man."

"I know he is."

"Why are you wasting my time?"

"The people just want to know you still have their best interest in mind."

"We do."

"All right."

"All right."

Calebna placed his hands on his hips. Gorban could see thoughts brewing in his eyes, in the way his mouth hung open as if ready to make a pronouncement. He was always making pronouncements.

"I will do whatever it takes to keep my family safe."

Gorban motioned for the hammer still in Calebna's hand, and the man handed it to him. "So will I."

Calebna folded his arms. "You know how I feel about violence."

"Times have changed. Why don't you make yourself useful?"

Calebna's lips tightened. "I will do what I must and no more."

"What about your vow?"

"Violence is not the only means of resolving a dispute, and there are those who would fight to defend the innocents that Lukian is jeopardizing. He does not hold everyone's attention. You are his brother. Tell me, why is Lukian doing this?"

"I'm busy."

"Busy or hiding?"

"Ask him yourself. Or are you afraid?" Gorban shoved a half-made weapon into the furnace.

Calebna cleared his throat, looked sidelong at Gorban, then nodded and turned. In the archway, he stopped. "I remember the green grass on the hill. But lately it's been hard to shut out winter's chill. You should sing more."

Gorban scowled and doubled his pace for the next hour.

◆ ◆ ◆

"Something's happening at the wall."

"What is it?"

Gillian, Lukian's eldest, looked afraid to say. "Fog."

Lukian jumped up and followed his boy, who held a spear in his hands and the shadow of a beard on his face. The winding stairwell echoed with their footsteps as they ascended the parapet, and when they reached the top, the doorway opened to a divided sky. A pillar of Fog reared on the far side of the inner wall, and the outer wall, merely a waist-high mark of the extreme limits of the pasturelands, was completely consumed by gray mist.

Lukian followed Gillian to peer at the moisture. It seemed to loom over the wall, though it was only a trick of the eyes. His son pointed and Lukian noticed the reason for his fear. Countless eyes glowed like flickering candles in the gloom.

"They grow more numerous with each passing hour."

Lukian's hands gripped the wood of his weapon, but the sensation was dull. Old emotions tumbled through his chest like broken cinders as he looked at the clear sky over the City and realized the heat of the sun *was mild, and the smell of spring was thick. He and his twin brother Lamech were playing at the river, skipping rocks through the reeds and imagining felling a Jinn with each throw. Lamech lifted a small boulder and stumbled with its weight in his eleven-year-old arms. After repositioning, he swung it into the river with a tremendous splash, though he couldn't keep himself from being pulled in after it by the momentum. Water dripped from his hair as he jumped up laughing, and Lukian fell back and offered the sky his giggles.*

"I know a place we can see one in the flesh," Lamech whispered with squinted eyes and dimpled cheeks. "I saw it last week, but Father told me to close my eyes and forget. I counted our steps and marked the turns, and later, when he was asleep, I came back and killed one."

"Your words float like a pile of rocks."

Lamech shrugged and smiled. "But I did find it again."

"If you get caught wandering off . . ."

"It's not far. I could show you where it is."

Lukian sat cross-legged, tearing grass up and staring at the water. Lamech smirked. "Father will never know."

"How do you know you weren't looking at a wild dog?"

"I saw its eyes."

"You didn't see a thing."

Lamech smiled as only an elder brother could, and Lukian knew. Father would understand, but Lamech wouldn't.

Lamech turned, started walking, and waved for him to follow. Lukian did.

As they arrived and peered over the edge, Lamech drew an invisible line with his finger, and Lukian's excitement calmed.

"Fog? That's what you came here to show me?"

"Its eyes burned like lanterns in the mist." He continued in an excited whisper, "You should have been there! If I'd had a weapon, now that would have been something. I would have rammed that

Jinn through the eye and stood over it just like this." He donned a pose they once saw Cain assume over a dead Jinn, one of the first they had found in the wilderlands.

Lukian pushed his twin's face. "You are full of lies."

They stayed awhile longer, lying on the grass and peering into the Fog. Then Lukian spoke the deadly dare. How could he have known that would be the last time he would hear his brother laugh? God knew he hadn't wanted his brother's insides torn and thrown across the ground. God knew he hadn't wanted to drive a thorn into his parents, but the pain had changed the way Cain looked at him, and the way Sarah looked at Cain.

"Father?" Gillian was looking at him.

Lukian closed his mouth, turned away, and tossed the memories over the edge of the wall.

"What are we going to do?"

"We will wait in the City, and if they break through the wall, we will do what we must."

"That's it?"

"What else would you have us do?" Lukian's mind churned. They needed his brothers and nephews, but to belabor the fact was foolish. He could speak no word of their need. They would not survive any wavering.

If only we had run when we'd had the time, but we are trapped. We could never outrun a Fog this large.

Upon reaching the bonfire, they exchanged no words. Gillian sat with his arms folded, and Lukian stoked the fire from time to time, adding wood to entertain the blaze. The chill in the air felt like the beginnings of winter, but it would be many days until that season should begin. As the sun began its descent, Gorban returned from his labor at the forge. His arms were filled with weapons, and he set them in a heap.

"Where's Mason?" Lukian said.

"Guess."

"It is time someone spoke with him."

Gorban's breath hissed from his nostrils. He slapped the

metallic dust from his tunic and left. Gillian followed, likely excited to hear what Gorban would say to the mute giant.

Lukian looked at his remaining children, Jubal, Irad, and Zachariah. Together, they numbered six armed warriors, yet still a pile of weaponry remained unused, and Zachariah, his youngest, had barely reached fifteen years. If they fought alone, they would die. But if they hid in the Temple, they would succumb to starvation in a matter of weeks.

Mason would come eventually. But what about the others?

27

Mason stoked the fire and felt the flame burning in his mother's cheeks. How many times had he done this? When he found her floating in the water, it had almost been too late. Then the flame ignited, and she burned with hungry passion in the deep sleep that continued to devour her.

If I could but speak words of comfort, he thought. Since being taught as a boy, he whistled to fill the silence, and he did so now as he replaced her bandages and tended her ribs. The marks were black, and her toes kept their gruesome color. The skin on her fingertips was peeling, but would be usable in time. As long as the fever left. But that was why Calebna was praying.

The Temple. It seemed appropriate that what once had been their spiritual refuge was now their physical asylum. Built on the highest hill, it had remained safe from flooding, and that alone was reason enough to seek shelter within, after a significant portion of the City was destroyed. But more than that, Lukian had been right. They needed each other.

He stabbed at the burning wood. Calebna's youngest cried in the hallway, and he wondered if those sounds reached Sarah's mind. Was she paralyzed, cognizant but incapable of moving?

Her brow furrowed, and sweat beaded on her cheeks.

Fight the burning. Don't let it consume you.

Sometimes, when he dreamed, he could speak and sing, and upon awakening the realization always stung like an open palm. It was easy to forget his strangeness, but the dreams always reminded him.

What did *she* dream? That her words were stopped?

The irony slipped down his throat like alcohol as he brushed his thick fingers through her hair. Veiny muscle contrasted with pale, tender skin. He promised he would be her strength as long as she needed. He would stay if all others left. He would—

Calebna's child wailed louder. Why did it cry? Was it uncomfortable? Hungry? He wished someone would tend to it.

The door opened. "Mason."

He did not turn.

"How is she?"

With a glance, Mason saw Gorban standing in the doorway, hardly filling it with his compact frame and black hair curling like vines around his trunk-like neck. Gillian peaked his mousy head from around Gorban.

How could Mason communicate the few times Sarah had woken, that in those moments he had only the time to give her water before she fell back asleep? He dabbed the sweat from her eyelids.

It's been nearly three entire days since last you opened your eyes. Why won't you wake?

Gorban said, "There's Fog at the wall. It's time. We can't wait any longer."

Sarah's hands clenched and Mason took them in his fist and carefully pressed his thumb between her fingers until they relaxed.

"Brother." A hand warmed Mason's shoulder, but he shrugged it off. He could feel Gorban staring, but he remained obstinate, and soon Gorban's footsteps shuffled out the door, leaving him and Sarah alone again.

I will stay. You're going to be well again. You will. You must. They don't realize why. But I do.

And he pulled the covers over her belly.

◆ ◆ ◆

"Where is Mason?" Lukian said.

"He wouldn't leave."

"I told you to talk with him."

"I did," Gorban said.

"We can't do this alone."

"He's as immovable as a boulder."

"A stick can push a boulder if the right leverage is applied."

"What of the Fog?"

"It has kept its distance, but the Jinn are amassing." Lukian's eyes were tired, and his shoulders sagged. "You remember how to use a spear?"

"Old muscles forget slowly."

"Calebna still thinks the Temple will save him. The fool will kiss my feet before this is all over."

"He came to talk to me the other day."

"Ah?"

"Said he was there for the people, that they were worried about the threat of violence if a choice were made for a new leader. He wanted to know you still had the interest of the people in mind." Gorban sucked his teeth. "He implied you wouldn't be his first choice, and that God knows you wouldn't be *theirs* either."

Lukian smiled.

"He threatened you, in his roundabout sort of way."

"Thank you for telling me."

Gorban shrugged.

"I would love to see him fight again. That would be something worth my time."

"Is Adam doing so badly?"

"No signs of improvement. The others have made perimeter checks, but the Fog is only on our eastern flank. We can't afford to spread thin anymore, so until something happens, only one group of two will walk the inner wall in intervals." Lukian nodded. "We ready ourselves for confrontation, and for what might come after. A decision over leadership will be unnecessary if this goes as I expect."

"Many respect Calebna."

Lukian lifted his hammer and tapped Gorban's chest. "Worry less of me and more of how you're going to get Mason out here. And don't worry if you return before me. It's time I apply some leverage of my own."

28

Y ou made the right choice." Terah's hand slipped into Calebna's and squeezed.

Calebna laid his head against the wall of the prayer room. Lampstands stood beside a small cushion set atop an ornate rug of gold and violet, and next to them lay the bed he and his wife had slept in since the storm subsided. "That's not it."

"What then?"

Calebna chuckled. What couldn't it be? "I wouldn't leave you like that, not for such hopelessness. Lukian is just trying to be a man of action. He's trying to fix things." A pause. "He's trying to be his father."

"So who are you trying to be?"

"I don't know anymore. A good man."

"You *are* a good man."

He searched her face. "What is good?"

"You are."

"I mean what is *good*?"

"I don't understand."

Ben was crying again. Terah's hand left his as she went to their infant, cooing as she gathered him in her arms. Calebna watched her, but his mind was fixed. He had thought the Almighty was good. He had thought living in safety was good. He had thought peace was good. He had thought a happy life was good. But all of that was gone.

Ben's cries continued. Calebna stood and paced the room. He wanted to speak to Lukian again, but what would he say? He shook his head. Lukian wanted a fight. He would enjoy a fight. But part of Calebna would enjoy it as well.

No, he thought, *I am no longer that man.*

"Are you all right?"

He was looking at the floor, resting one hand against the wall while the other fiddled with the medallion around his neck. He looked at Terah and nodded, assuming a more relaxed position and taking Ben from her. Calebna held him out and watched him writhe and wail, his tears dripping down his fat cheeks.

If only Ben knew the real horror of life. If only he knew the pain he would endure, the anxiety of danger, the ache of loss. Maybe there would be moments where the sun would warm his toes, but there would be so much more sorrow in a world without God.

It would be better if he were never born.

Terah snatched Ben back and held him upright on her shoulder, rubbing his back. "What has gotten into you?"

He hadn't realized he had spoken his thoughts.

"Don't you dare say such things."

"You'd rather he live in hell?"

Her mouth warped as if ready to retort, but she whipped around and ignored him instead. Ben was crying louder, disturbed by the angry tones.

"I didn't mean it spitefully," he said.

Terah didn't respond. She was bouncing Ben, who had found his thumb and sucked, barely breathing past the mucus in his nose. His wet cheeks dried against Terah's hair, and his eyes looked like washed crystals. Such innocence. Such purity.

"I'm just angry. Not at you." He paused, searching his reasons. "I don't know what I'm angry at. I just don't want him to taste pain."

Still bouncing her son, Terah said, "He already has."

Calebna regretted what he had said. He was weary, that was all.

Terah's eyes flamed. "Don't say that again."

"All right."

"I'm not a fool."

"You're not."

"I know the world isn't going to be good to him. It hasn't been good to me either. You're not the only one suffering, not the only one who's lost someone, who's lost hope."

"I know." An admission.

An uncomfortable silence followed. Calebna leaned against the wall and his wife sat and cradled Ben in her lap. Ben settled and drifted to sleep. Terah looked at Calebna from time to time. Her gaze was hard but, somewhere beneath, filled with affection.

"Love is."

He cocked his head. "What?"

"Love. Love is good."

He nodded, though the statement begged the question, what, then, is love? He thought about asking, but didn't have the energy. They remained as they were, though she turned so he wouldn't see her cry.

Someone knocked at the door and Terah stood and sniffed away the wetness. Calebna rose and cracked the door.

Calebna saw Lukian's face through the gap. "We need to talk." Lukian peered over Calebna's shoulder.

Calebna filled the gap with his body. "Not here."

"Follow me." Lukian turned and walked three steps away.

"Wait."

"There's no time. Come." His eyes widened. "Now."

Calebna glanced behind him and heard Ben start crying again. He paused, stepped out, shut the door, and chased the sounds of Lukian's footsteps.

They walked down corridors and descended stairs to storage compartments that smelled like incense and mildew. Lukian placed a torch in a receptacle on the wall and shut the wooden door behind them. "I didn't think you, of all people, would stoop to such tactics."

"I've done nothing."

"What do you think you will accomplish?"

"I'm fulfilling my responsibility."

"The demonic Fog has amassed near the eastern wall."

Calebna's throat felt cold. "And?"

"Stop playing the fool. I saw them. Jinn. Hundreds, maybe thousands. Look for yourself if you're unsatisfied with my word. There are so many . . ." Lukian shook his head. "More than I've ever seen before. We cannot do this alone. Not anymore. And you're dividing us."

"Me? Everyone is here in the Temple except the men you've recruited to your bonfires."

"Why do you think we're out there? To relax in the warmth of firelight? This Temple won't save you. They'll tear its roof down on top of you. You're a fool to think otherwise."

Calebna slowed his words and sharpened their edges. "I'd rather be a righteous fool than a clever wicked man."

"Would you murder your family to be named righteous?"

Calebna's scarred leg ached as he remembered what the Jinn had done to him. As a young man he had grown bitter about his wounds and had harmed Terah as a result of it. He could never let that happen again, but to think of what the Jinn had done to Lamech, whom Calebna had loved in childhood . . .

"You don't have the luxury of living in black and white anymore."

"I have already chosen."

"The Jinn are going to break the wall, and when they do, this Temple will not save you. Who will you blame when your infant and wife are crushed before you?"

Calebna's eyes narrowed.

"We have no hope while divided, but together . . ."

Calebna nodded slowly.

"The death in my words is as real as the breath in your chest."

"God will deliver me. What about you? What do you hold onto? Yourself?"

"I will not apologize for putting my family first. The Almighty never loved me. He never loved any of us. If he had, he wouldn't have let this happen. And you're following in his footsteps, abandoning us in our time of need. You are free to stay in your Temple, but you're not free to decide for them." Lukian approached and thrust his finger into Calebna's chest. "Gorban told me about your visit."

Will this come to violence? Calebna wondered. He examined

the empty storage room and listened to the silence, suddenly fearful of it.

"He said you claimed you'd do anything to defend your family."

Calebna backed up until he leaned against the wall, but could not quell the beating of his heart. *What would happen if I killed in defense?*

No, I cannot not choose that way.

"I challenge you to prove your words hold meaning." Lukian leaned forward and Calebna felt his hot breath on his ear. "If you don't, I will."

With that, Lukian spat, smeared it across the floor with his sandal, and strode away.

Calebna stayed until the torch nearly petered out. Thoughts rumbled in him, and for the first time in years, he pondered violence.

Love. Love is . . .

He stared into the darkness. *Love is what?*

29

G orban cursed as he flung the Temple door open.
I'm not a fool. If Mason weren't Mason, there'd be no difficulty finding the proper leverage.

Lukian was right, of course, which made Gorban all the more irritable. They needed their brother. If he just weren't so attached to Sarah.

That's an unworthy thought.
And yet I thought it.

Gorban tried the door he thought was the correct one only to receive Philo's hand in his face. "Out, out. What are you doing?"

He apologized and doubled back, feeling heat on his neck. Two more tries in the labyrinth and he succeeded, thinking, *The Almighty's obsession with symmetry runs deep.*

Mason knelt as before, petting Sarah's hand in the dim room that crackled with warm smells, not all pleasant. Lukian's wife, Keshra, stood by and watched for signs of cognition. Sarah's eyelids were ashen pale against the silhouette cast by the flames, and seeing her frailty stirred deep emotions within Gorban. He cleared his throat and knelt at Mason's left. This time, his hand was allowed to perch on his brother's shoulder. "How is she?" His voice was reverent as he nodded to Keshra, who bowed and left them.

Sweat darkened Mason's bed-of-snakes hair.

Gorban nearly spoke several times, but words seemed to fall short of communicating what he desired, as they so often did. Finally he chose to say something, anything. "I am sorry I wasn't there."

Mason offered a wary glance.

"I—we need you. Our danger grows."

Mason could be so inscrutable. It made Gorban itch to leave.

He scratched his leg and his voice grew sharp. "Will you abandon us in our need?"

Mason glanced at Sarah as if to ask, *"What of her need?"*

"Keshra and Peth can tend to her. Healing is women's work." Mason shoved him away.

Gorban smacked the dust from his hands and glared at the back of Mason's head. "Never claim I didn't try." He threw up his arms in mock surprise. "But I forget—you couldn't if you wanted." Gorban spun on his heel, making sure to accentuate the slap of his sandals against the floor.

As he slipped out of the room, he realized the need to invent an explanation. Lukian wouldn't be happy. Then again, Lukian was never happy.

◆ ◆ ◆

Lukian found Kiile and Machael, as expected, huddled together and attended by their wives and children. Kiile lounged against a cushion, his limbs splayed and his mouth filled with racket. His children stood in a ring, laughing and nudging each other while a pair of the youngest wrestled and exchanged blows. Machael sat cross-legged beside his wife, Zillah, and watched with those sleepy eyes. His children stood and pointed from time to time, looking unimpressed, as usual.

"I expected you sooner," Machael said, his voice slow and deliberate.

"I could say the same," Lukian said.

"You know it's too much fun to hear Kiile chastised by the others' wives. It's like the old days when we slept huddled together and traveled in a group through the wilderlands."

"In more ways than one."

Machael nodded and seemed to grow drowsier yet.

There was a roar of applause and a few moans of dissatisfaction as Kiile's youngest wrenched his brother's arm back and slammed his face into the floor.

"He's like his grandfather, that one," Machael said. And then he added, "Are the weapons ready?"

"They're piled against the inner wall."

"Some are too young," Machael said.

Lukian pointed at the littlest boy, who strutted about slapping the hands of his elder brothers. "That one fights like a badger. By your own estimation he's useful."

"It will end in grief," Machael said.

"Another one of your premonitions?"

"Just a feeling."

"If it weren't for the gift of speech, I'd doubt you had feelings at all."

"Kiile will be eager to see his weaponry. He's stayed with Elsa, but his mind is with you."

"He's chained to that woman."

"At least they retain a connection."

Lukian huffed.

Machael's oldest, Madai, tapped his father on the shoulder, "May I participate in the wrestling contest?"

"Change out of that tunic first, and wash it and hang it before the night comes."

Madai bowed, smirked, stripped his tunic off and left to join the raucous ring.

Machael turned to Lukian. "Others will come. And soon."

"Another one of your feelings?" Lukian said.

"A premonition."

Kiile welcomed Madai, noticed Lukian, jumped to his feet, and called out as he approached. "Brother! Come to clean the dirt out of your bed?"

"Only to place it in yours."

"I can always rely on you." They embraced, and his smile faded as quickly as it came. "They're prepared?"

Lukian nodded.

Kiile cursed and thanked the Almighty in the same breath, then lowered his voice so his wife wouldn't hear. "I'm worried about Elsa."

Lukian said, "Calebna won't let her leave?"

"That's not it. God knows he would restrain her if he could—he's policing everyone with increasing intensity—but she'll slip a knife in him to be next to me when the battle comes."

"If Calebna hasn't the strength to restrain her, Terah will," Lukian said.

Kiile laughed long and hard. "Maybe."

"Eve made the pronouncement after hearing word of the Jinn. No women are to leave until Calebna deems it safe," Machael said.

"What of the boys?" Lukian asked.

"Calebna will let them choose for themselves." One of Machael's eyes awakened and bored into Lukian. "Every boy must learn to be his own master. Eve could not disagree, and yet she could not let her daughters go."

"Ah . . . and if Kiile takes the boys from Elsa?"

His eye fell back asleep. "She will stay."

Kiile grimaced and said to Machael, "I like you better when you don't talk." Then to Lukian, "Did Gorban make it how I asked?"

"You know your preferences better than me."

Kiile searched for and caught Elsa's gaze. He nodded as if she knew what he wanted to ask, and she frowned in response. "What?" he yelled. "If the sun sets and darkness touches my toes, I'll cut them off for you."

She twisted her hair and secured it in a bun with a bamboo rod. "Promise me the feet!"

Kiile smiled, then glared at his brothers. "Well? Show me my weapons—and quickly!"

30

The touch of clothing on Eve's skin gripped her attention with painful intensity. She looked down and saw her thinness exposed by the ever-loosening dress. She no longer remembered what she last ate or when. Her stomach didn't even ache anymore, and she was reminded of the years spent in the wilderness, carrying twins and living a hunted life.

She breathed in, then breathed out. *The very twins whose fates have been twisted down to Sheol.*

She rubbed her arms. Through the years, the Jinn had grown greater in number. At first, avoiding them had not been difficult, but as they multiplied, so did the danger.

After obeying the summons and coming back to their Creator, they had thought themselves immune. Now they were trapped.

Eve tipped her head and caught Adam sitting against the wall. She stared at the creases in his robe, the way his hands twitched in his lap, and how his eyes squinted at the lines in the wall. In all the madness, all the confusion and danger, he had done nothing.

"Wake up," she whispered. She wondered what would happen if she shook him, if she grabbed him by the tunic and threw him to the ground. *Nothing,* she answered. *He would do nothing.* She crossed to him trembling. "Wake up." She slapped his face, and the sting echoed in the skin of her fingers.

Do I hate him?

I hate his not being here. I hate his silence. His love for Abel.

"Yes," she said. "I see you loved him more than you loved me, for you left me in order to somehow find him, to reconstruct him from your memories—the only place he still lives. But I can't follow you there."

Eve swallowed the anger as new emotions arose. Some she recognized, others were muddled. Her hand reached, then retreated to rest on her sternum. She said, "Truly, I love you more than I could ever express," but those words dissipated like fogged breath. "How could I not after so many years? After knowing the life I have was crafted from yours? I couldn't let you waste away alone. That's why I have stayed, but still . . ." The bitterness burned, and out of the ash came something familiar. She thought it pity, though it could have been shame.

I see now where all this violence was born—all those years ago in the shadow of that cave, and his worshipping that little babe.

"How could you do this to me?" Tears dribbled down her cheeks and neck. "Look at you. You're a wretched thing, dead but still breathing."

She crouched, paused, then slid her arms around him and laid her head on his chest. It was warm and solid, and it rose and fell and thumped out a rhythm.

This is the man I was fashioned from, the man I was created for.

How foolish her anger was. He had failed her, but she had failed him too. Leaves, falling in the autumn wind, shimmered as if branded into her eyelids, and she winced at the memory.

The Serpent. The coppery flavor of forbidden fruit. The red-black juice leaking down my hand as I push it toward Adam and offer him a taste of death. The burn of the sun on my naked flesh as I breathe in the sensation of terrible exposure, and the genesis of darkness in Adam's eyes as he takes in my figure and for the first time I feel the fear of a man's desire.

A hundred and fifty years passed and Sin had stolen her children and killed her God. And when she needed Adam most, he was lost in his mind.

His tunic was wet with her tears. "Please," she implored as she clawed his back. "I know you've carried the guilt of that moment all these years. I could see it in your eyes, I could feel it in your touch. You took the shame, and accepted my own, but I shouldn't have made you do that. I was just scared. I loved you too much to admit I had harmed you." Her words were swallowed by sobs, but somehow she managed to say, "I'm so sorry." The moans forced the words out until she nearly screamed, "Can't you see that I love you? That I never blamed you? But I let you suffer alone all these years. How could I leave you alone? And now . . ."

His hands remained limp, and Eve wept, but not for him and not for her children. For the first time, she wept for herself.

Like Adam, dead but still breathing.

◆ ◆ ◆

Lukian observed the warriors, whose shoulders were bowed by the weight of the night and whose glances kept returning to the Temple drawn in silver lines atop the hill. He wondered what they thought. *Do they desire the illusion of safety? Or do they simply think of their wives, mothers, and sisters?*

Surely Kiile thought of Elsa, but the Fog had become more chaotic in the past day, and they knew the violence would begin soon.

Lukian fingered the metal of his hammer. The edges were cold and harsh. He looked at his sons, brothers, and nephews. Of what mold had they been formed? Of what mold had he himself been fashioned?

"Hand me some," Kiile said.

Gillian broke stale bread and handed it to his uncle. The man squashed the spongy dryness and spoke with mouth half full. "Is there much left in the storehouse?"

"Most of the grain rotted before we could make dough of it."

Kiile's eldest raised his voice. "I'm hungry."

"We're all hungry," Gorban said.

Kiile spit chewed bread mush in his hand and waved it toward Gorban, who scowled, clutched his spear, and walked to the edge of the firelight. Kiile returned the bread to his mouth and swallowed after considerable effort, then handed the rest to his son.

"Can you eat Jinn?"

"We'll soon have plenty to try."

"How about Jinn stew?" Gillian chanced with a smirk.

Chuckles bounced about the circle, but Lukian bit his tongue, stood, and faced the wall. Kiile fell silent, as did the others. *They fear for tomorrow*, Lukian thought. *Even my son joins to mock what his mind cannot accept.*

Lukian wanted to walk the wall, long and far in the cover of dark, but the sound of approaching footsteps rooted him in place.

"Who is it?" Gorban dipped his spear toward the sounds.

The firelight illuminated two sets of eyes, then two brown tunics. The taller edged in front of the other. "It is I, Philo, and my brother Tuor. Will you receive us?"

Gorban sauntered toward them. Lukian watched with interest. *Philo and Tuor, Calebna's younger brothers.*

"What brings such delicates to us after nightfall?"

"We want to join you."

"Why?"

Philo lifted a small blacksmith hammer. "We want to fight."

Gorban glanced at the hammer in Philo's hand, then at Lukian, who approached.

"If that is your intention," Lukian said, "you are welcomed. But know that we have no space for cowards."

He noticed a slight shiver in the younger's muscles. The motion drew his gaze to the hunched shoulders and baby-soft hands.

"We won't run," Philo said.

No, Lukian thought as he looked to the older boy, *you won't, at least.* A smile edged across his face. "Why now?"

Philo paused, then said, "We have no wives. We are young and weary of waiting. We want to be useful."

"And your family?"

"They share convictions my brother and I do not."

"Do they know?"

Philo nodded. His younger brother's eyes twitched toward the grass.

He's lying. Lukian motioned to the hammer and the boy offered it to him. He felt its weight and balance. "Philo, your brother seems to have conquered his tongue. It is strange, for I seem to remember how he couldn't stop it from wagging behind his teeth."

Tuor stilled.

"Come here."

Tuor's eyes strained toward Philo, who scowled and nodded. Tuor edged forward and eyed the hammer in Lukian's hand.

Lukian lifted it. "You think I'd strike you?"

Tuor shook his head.

"If I saw you flee from death, I wouldn't hesitate."

Tuor nodded.

"Speak."

From the corner of his eye, Lukian caught the older boy's frown and the shift of his feet.

Tuor said in a boyish tenor, "I understand."

Lukian nodded and dangled the hammer like a toy. "Do you know what this would do to a Jinn?"

Tuor cleared his throat. "No."

"Follow Gorban. He has real weapons for you."

PART SIX:

WAR

We should not be like Cain, who was of the evil one and murdered his brother. And why did he murder him? Because his own deeds were evil and his brother's righteous. . . . We know that we have passed out of death into life, because we love the brothers. Whoever does not love abides in death. Everyone who hates his brother is a murderer, and you know that no murderer has eternal life abiding in him.

—1 JOHN 3:12, 14–15 ESV

31

Gorban spat on the ground and readied his spear as bodies rushed into a hastily formed crescent, clutching wood and iron shafts with painful intensity. In one chest-thumping explosion, the Fog had ruptured a vein through their safety. The crack shifted the masonry, leaving a half-foot gap between it and the other side, and Tuor shrieked like a child waking from a nightmare and jabbed his spear at the serpent-tail vapors swirling out of the crack. Gorban cursed under his breath and yanked the boy back by the collar. "Stay."

Tuor trembled, but nodded.

The hissing filled their ears. Another eruption and a second crack formed nearly fifteen feet to the left of the first. The isolated section tipped back, its top falling into the Fog, throwing root and soil. They had seen such displays before, but now, for the first time, they witnessed proof that the Almighty's protection truly had vanished.

Lukian addressed the men. "Stand your ground and spear them down. Don't break the line."

The men shouted as the wall disappeared and the Fog rushed over them and condensed on their faces and tunics. The eleven-foot wooden shaft in Gorban's hands was nearly wrenched from his grip as a man-sized Jinn materialized from the white and slid down its length. It was impaled through its chest and clacked slowing teeth. He kicked the thing off and shoved his spear into another's thigh. That one swiped at him and shattered the shaft, and he smashed the splintered end into its face.

Gorban tossed the remnants of the spear, pulled a mace from his belt, slammed the beast in the temple, and pulled its head to the ground to stomp its skull till it shattered like an egg.

The half demons swarmed, their bodies as thick as a wall. They jostled for a chance at human flesh, but the men speared them down. One had three or four impaled on the same pike, their bodies standing wedged in place. Then the spears fell, and secondary weaponry glinted across the field.

Gorban swung twin maces, crushing and twisting the beasts into bloody heaps of flesh. Hands grasped at him. He broke them. Claws painted his skin, but he wasted no thought on wounds. Every faculty was applied to surviving another moment, to outmaneuvering the three or four swiping at him at any one time.

Gorban saw he was being pushed back, becoming isolated from the group. He recognized the tactic, but there were too many, and they functioned with singular purpose. It seemed he fought for hours, though he knew how exaggerated time could become amidst violence. Still the Jinn came. His eyes burned with sweat, and his throat ached with the chill of the air. Human screams mixed into the curdling beast wails, but they were now farther away. His body slowed as he tore one's throat out, deflected another's arm, and planted his foot in a third's chest.

They are desperate, he thought. *Never have I seen them so suicidal.*

He imagined how, with each swing, he gave the men and women in the Temple another moment to live, and yet they likely sat looking out at the Fog as it poisoned their city and brought death to their beds. Did they think they could avoid the coming destruction? If the inner wall failed, did they think the Temple wouldn't? *Fools,* he thought.

Gorban looked down at teeth that had sunken into his thigh, and black stones that seemed to have flames inside them, staring from deep-set sockets. He struck with his mace, but the metal stimulated its jaws to convulse, and Gorban screamed as its teeth sunk deeper, then released. It twitched on the ground as another grabbed his tunic and flattened him to the ground. He grunted as his ribs compressed with the weight, and he felt its claws grapple his shoulders and pull him close.

Gorban clutched its head and struggled to keep it from his

throat. He dug his thumbs into its eyes until they burst and bled down his wrists, but the thing's tongue snaked out to taste his chest. He screamed and pushed his fingers against the bone behind its eyes, but the head still approached.

He gazed at the cracks in its skin, powdery gray as if dusted with ash. It seemed strange how the starkest reality could feel invented. Even now, the wound on his leg hardly ached, though he felt the Jinn's hot breath and smelled its acidic saliva.

Today is the day I die.

◆ ◆ ◆

The first quake struck silence in the Temple. The second shot Mason to his feet. His heart skipped a beat, feeling the weight of the terrible decision he faced. It had happened too quickly, even from the beginning. Violence had come before its time, and it sped mercilessly on.

He clenched his hands into fists easily twice the size of any other man's, and felt the sensations he had feared in himself. The same sensations he knew plagued his brothers. The same sensations his father, Cain, had lost himself to.

Some vessels for honorable use and some for dishonorable use.

Mason knelt, folded his hands together, and closed his eyes in reverence. He prayed rushed, private prayers, and felt the shaking come. His face quivered as deeply as the earth had only moments ago, because he knew that he must do what he had been born to do.

His eyes snapped open.

It is time to fight.

32

As Jacob joined his father outside the Temple doors, he wrestled with disbelief. The wall had fallen, and pooling into the City of the Almighty was the defiling Fog. It curled around the men like water over an anthill, and for the first time, the repercussions of his decision to stay grew thick in his throat.

"The earth groans," Calebna said, as if to himself.

Jacob observed his father's hand, the way it scratched his bearded chin. He looked at the lines on his forehead and the darkness of his eyes.

"The Almighty taught me his true name once. It is a holy thing, never to be spoken by unclean lips, never to be heard by evil ears," Calebna said. Flakes of skin caught in his beard. "Names are important. They remind us who we are. I thought about telling you the Almighty's true name. For many days I thought I actually would. I decided not to."

The Fog deepened and expanded. What about this moment brought Father to speak like this? Why now, as the sons of Cain— no, as their *family*—fought for their lives?

Calebna folded his arms. "Are you embarrassed?"

Jacob paused, noting the foreign tone of his father's voice. "I don't understand."

"Do you want to be like me when you grow old and weary of the world? Do you want to lie on your bed and think only thoughts you know I would approve?"

"Why does it matter?"

"You look like me, but you are not me, just as Lukian looks like Cain but is his own. I think those differences serve a purpose."

"What do you mean?"

"That there are some things a man is appointed to do. Our souls fit together, each in its habitation, and none can take another's place."

"You speak of our choice to stay instead of fight?"

"I made a vow to the Almighty. As I bowed in worship, I said, 'In the dust of the world, I will remember your faithfulness. In the spring of life, I will let passion spill forth. But I will always serve you. I will always follow your commands.'" Calebna rubbed his eyes. "Is it righteous to make a promise you cannot keep? Often I've wondered, was that my destiny or only a manufactured purpose, something I took on myself to fulfill the role demanded of me?"

"You can still fulfill your vow."

Calebna laughed, a strange sound against the canvas of violence. "That vow stands on the Almighty's epitaph, and one question continues to haunt me, perhaps because I know my answer is not what it should be." He faced his son. "Am I willing to die for him?"

Jacob's pulse quickened. Was Father questioning what they'd built their lives around, what they believed to be true and had held fast to in the threat of death? "You would. As would I."

"Do you believe he lied to us?"

"I—" The words caught in Jacob's throat.

"Don't just answer with a counterfeit truth. What do you *believe*?"

Jacob's stomach churned at the screams piercing the Fog, and he wondered if they were dying, or if perhaps some had died already. "Our lives cannot have been wasted."

"Can they not?"

He nearly yelled out, "No," but something stayed him. *I knew I might die when I vowed to stay,* he thought. *I knew others might die as well, but seeing it happen makes it so much more difficult to justify.*

So what if I joined the warriors? Wouldn't those who have already been injured or killed have paid with their bodies without reason? And what of my family? Could I betray my own father?

Jacob swallowed. He could choose only one path, but still he hungered for a compromise, for some middle way.

Which is worse: to stand for death, or to stand for a life you know has already died?

He faced Calebna. "You said we need faith now more than before. What better test than this moment? What happened to the righteousness you taught me as a boy? Because it is for those teachings I stand today. I swore to abandon my cousins in hopes the Almighty was not dead, that he would rescue us."

Calebna put a hand on Jacob's shoulder, and he almost shrugged it off until he saw his father's solemn expression. "You must understand. I need someone I can speak this to. It burns." Calebna glanced at the Fog. "There is much I do not understand, but I know that if we survive this difficulty, the world will never be the same. Too much evil has happened. And too much evil remains ahead."

Jacob's thoughts seemed to settle. He saw the reason in his father's words, the wisdom in pressing him. *Was it a test? And have I passed?*

He looked at his father. Truly he did want to be like Calebna, as Calebna had wanted to be like Abel. He desired that peace and strength, that gentle determination. And yet his father's humanity struck him more intensely in that moment than ever before. All his pain and doubt, every fragile imperfection, lay exposed.

Can it be there is more to your questions than a desire to test me? Can it be you ponder abandoning the Almighty?

No. Not Calebna. Not the son of Abel.

Jacob shivered and smothered disturbing emotions. "I love you, Father."

Calebna frowned, turned, walked up the short incline to the doorway of the Temple, grabbed the brass handle of the gold door, and swung it wide. Jacob cast one final glance toward the swirling Fog, and turned to join his father in their Temple.

They sealed the entrance.

◆ ◆ ◆

When they thought they killed the last, more rushed from the Fog. Lukian motioned for them to focus their efforts on the center, but two more streams came on either side. They were being pushed from each other until only Lukian and his children remained surrounded by the swirling Fog. The beasts shoved their bodies between Lukian and his children, and while most were dead within seconds, they succeeded in splitting him from his children.

"Father!" Gillian called as a swarm encircled him and his brothers.

Lukian's face reddened. A beast grabbed his weapon, but he twisted to release it, spun and swung down, bringing the bladed edge of his war hammer through its neck. Its head thumped to the ground with mouth still open, but as it fell, three more assumed its place. He slashed out five, six times. They fell, then the bodies multiplied.

He stepped left, jumped back, slid right, crippled one's knees, and stumbled back, barely ducking in time to miss swiping claws inadvertently slashing another, flicking droplets of blood across his face.

Time ground on like a blade on a grindstone. Eventually another lull came, and Lukian felt the fatigue of his burning muscles. His children were too far to be seen through the Fog, but he could hear them screaming.

His feet pounded as memories from years long past overcame him. *I will not fail. I will not let my children die. And when we return to the Temple, the cowards responsible will pay seven times over for the bloodshed.*

The Fog spun in violent eddies growing in intensity until the wind whistled. He slowed, feeling as if he would be lifted from the ground. Droplets of blood skipped through the air. He looked down and saw his feet rooted, but felt disconnected somehow, as if he floated far above. His gaze treaded across the blood-soaked field. The dead grasses had color once more, a macabre mixture of red on brown filtered through the gray mist of the Fog. Discernable just ahead were bodies jostling each other. There were screams, but the hissing made his ears ring. He planted one foot in front of the other, clutched the hammer in both hands, and leaned into the current as his clothing whipped his limbs.

Thoughts breached his mind. It had been long since he felt such rage. And he savored it as he swung at the nearest beast and crumpled its shoulder. It gasped and hissed as Lukian lifted the hammer and smashed its head. Others turned to face him.

"Gillian!"

The hissing swallowed his voice.

"Gillian! Where are you?"

Arms reached for him. He broke them. Legs kicked at him. He crushed them. Joints popped and oozed across the sides of his weapon, and he piled flesh upon flesh as if folding dough into a bloody crust. He clambered over bodies and screamed with each swing of his hammer until his throat swelled and his eyelids crusted with gore.

Just ahead the beasts split as if making way. "Face me!" A few ran toward him. He beat them down. Others fled as he swung his path free of stragglers. He spun and searched, and the beasts backed away.

"Gillian." His eyes burned. "My children."

He heard a low moan, almost imperceptible beneath the hissing and shuffling of the Jinn. He wondered if it had been real, but there it was again. He sprinted forward and the Jinn parted. There, only a few yards ahead, lay a pile of mangled bodies. His head shook before he realized the need to deny what he saw. The hammer fell from his hands. "No."

The Jinn were hissing and staring, but they did not reach for him. He let his gaze fall on the largest of the bodies. It was piled over the others as if even in death attempting to protect those beneath it.

"Gillian," he whispered, and his knees slid in the blood as he worked his shaking hands under his son's back. The face had been torn from the skull and hung in tatters, and Lukian let his face fall on his son's red-soaked breast.

"My beloved son." And the hissing grew as he closed his eyes and felt the warmth of Gillian's life fade in the chill of the air.

33

The Jinn's head jerked. Gorban examined the trunk-like fingers wrapped around the Jinn's skull and watched as it rose and flew out of sight. A figure towered over him, reached down, and pulled him to his feet. "Mason?" Gorban wondered if what he saw was real because the man seemed wraith-like in the mist. But Mason nodded and motioned toward Gorban's leg, which was badly wounded.

Gorban blinked. "I can manage."

Mason turned him from the sounds of battle, and though the Fog clouded Gorban's vision, he understood well enough.

"I'm not leaving," Gorban said.

Mason shoved him, and he fell. The jolt shocked the breath from his chest. He struggled to stand and scrambled for insults, but Mason was already sprinting away, disappearing into the mist.

The screams and moans of the wounded bubbled from the Fog like water from a spring, and the fear he should have felt came like a late moon peeking through cloud cover. Death was everywhere. Gorban wondered how many of his brethren lay dead or holding to life's final strands. Who would retrieve them? Who would patch their wounds?

Who will bandage my *wounds?*

He swallowed and looked where he knew the Temple should be, though the Fog concealed it. Then he braced himself and started toward it.

◆ ◆ ◆

Lukian wiped his face, but blood and bone replaced the sweat and dust. His eyes burned and his throat ached. His lips shuddered, but he could not weep. His knuckles ached against the handle of his weapon, but as he stood, his senses numbed. He saw, as if the scene were happening before him, Calebna, Terah, and Jacob resting against the wall of the Temple, rolling out the last of the bread. They reached for it with porcelain fingers, pinching fibrous lumps, and dunking them in a bowl of wine before letting the red juice stain their lips.

Lukian stood over his dead children in a field of blood and shadow. No wine to wet his tongue. No food to fill his stomach. No children, no legacy.

The monstrous half-breeds backed away until their eyes were floating flames in the cauldron of Fog. He felt a prick at his neck, and after slapping at it, brought his hand away with two pinpricks of red. He lifted the hammer to look at its gory edge. A putrid scent pinched his nostrils and stabbed his throat. He almost coughed, but instead brought the hammer level with his mouth. He leaned forward and waited, lips parted inches from the edge of the weapon. Rage bubbled up his throat from his stomach, and he shuddered as he fought against a desire he had never before felt.

No wine for the eldest son of Cain. Only blood to quench his thirst.

He pressed the metal against his face and sucked, letting the cold gel fill his teeth and stick to his face. He tipped his head back and closed his eyes as he dropped his hammer, feeling blood drip from his chin as he swallowed the rot and stifled his repulsion.

Repulsion. The soul's attitude toward the world it is ushered into, screaming and kicking and covered in . . .

Blood. It was everything and everywhere as the Fog whirled in violent eddies. He spread his arms, wondering if this was how his father felt as he killed Abel. He knew somewhere in a deep corner of his mind that this was insanity, but for the first time, he felt freed of worry. He held no concern for the future, no fear of death or pain. He simply felt the desire—the *need*—to consume life.

He should feel sorrow. But could sorrow bring breath back to his children's lungs? Could sorrow bring retribution to those responsible for their deaths?

In the case of the latter, deadly desire could. And would.

He opened his palms and let rage pour into him like a mixture of stimulant and opiate. He wondered at it. How had he known the proper response was to *accept* this moment?

And yet he knew, and dared not question it again for fear it would break the evolution. He rubbed the stinging spot on his neck and brought the hand away, smeared with thin red lines. He thought he saw a pair of silver eyes glint in the Fog, then the pain disappeared and his body shook with rage. He wrestled a rising panic to fight the shift inside him.

Run. Don't let this desire take bed in your soul.

He bit his tongue and lost himself in red waters.

◆　◆　◆

Calebna kneeled and bowed, his eyes closed more to avoid looking at the empty throne than to charge the words spilling from his tongue with passion. For he felt no passion, no emotion, no life. All was cold ritual, and he allowed it to pass through him.

"Our Father, hallowed be your name. Your kingdom live, your kingdom grow, on earth as it has in heaven. Give us today our daily bread, and forgive us our sins as we . . ." He faltered. "As we forgive those who sin against us. And lead us not into temptation, but deliver us from evil."

He thought to stand, but remained kneeling. His eyes opened and focused on the throne's square form. The candles burning on either side melted to the floor, their stump figures slouching with long trails like swollen scars. He smelled the familiar incense, felt the weight of priestly robes, lifted his hands, and closed his eyes. He breathed the words, "I have been faithful to you, as has my family. We have followed you even in the midst of great tribulation and confusion, even as we placed your elements in a tomb. So I ask you to send me a sign. Give me hope where I have none."

For a long moment, his arms floated weightless. Then they descended toward the floor and the sleeves swallowed his hands.

Did it please the Almighty to see his children fall and wallow in the consequences of others' decisions?

Calebna straightened his shoulders and pursed his lips. "I am good. I *am* a good man." He wiped his hands and stood, then licked his finger and thumb to extinguish the candles one by one, watching the curling trails of smoke float to the ceiling. He swiveled, hesitated, and bowed before turning to leave.

The door was heavy and shut hard behind him, but the cool air in the hallway lightened his lungs. As he passed open doorways, gazes trailed him and a few people called out, asking if the Almighty would save them, but the voices wrestling in the vestibule ahead drew his attention.

As he entered the vestibule, Terah, Keshra, Peth, and two other women stood around a figure lying beside one of the golden lampstands. Terah caught sight of Calebna and said, "Come quickly. It's Sarah."

"What is it?"

"She is awake."

Calebna approached and peered over his wife's shoulder. Lying on the ground, half propped up by cushions, was Cain's wife, Sarah. Her bright eyes were salient and she was saying something, but only when the others hushed could he hear her.

"What has happened?" Sarah said. "Please, someone tell me."

Calebna looked at his wife. "You haven't told her?"

"She stumbled out of the room and fell here," Terah said. "We propped her up with cushions and were just discussing what to do."

Someone said, "She looks half starved."

Another, "Her bones, her skin!"

Still another, "She smells. Those bandages should have been replaced hours ago."

Sarah's gaze bounced from woman to woman. "Where is Mason?"

Lukian's wife, Keshra, said, "I saw him leave a while ago."

Another woman hushed her. "She doesn't know what that means."

Sarah said, "Please, where is he?"

"He has joined his brothers." Calebna contemplated Sarah's malnourished figure. She had been found in the quarry a full day after Abel's death. Could it be she hadn't known Cain murdered Abel? He narrowed his eyes and said, "What do you remember?"

She swallowed and seemed to search her memory. "I don't know." She blinked. "I remember waking to Mason and a fire. He gave me water each time and once some food. But I was tired. I seem to have memories of other things, but they are so dim I can hardly grasp their detail."

The women were touching her, testing her arms and legs.

"Give her space." Calebna pushed them back and crouched. "How do you feel?"

She pulled spider-web hair behind her ear and said, "I'm thirsty, and I hurt."

"Are you hungry?"

"I feel strange."

"You've been sleeping on and off for fifteen days."

Her eyes widened, then she glared as if he were lying.

"You were asleep so long many declared you already dead, but none of us had known of your waking. It's a pity Mason can't speak. We almost gave up on you, though I suppose now we know why Mason never did."

She swallowed and looked at the hanging tapestries, the marble triangles in the floor, the gold walls and vaulted ceiling. She didn't appear to recognize her surroundings. "What has happened?"

Calebna and his wife exchanged a wary glance, and at that moment the door of the Temple burst open. They turned as Gorban hobbled in with heaving chest, and after a few hurried steps, he toppled with a moan and clapped his wrists on the stone. Gorban's wife, Peth, screamed and placed her hand over her mouth. Others whispered, their eyes wide.

Calebna looked at Terah. "Who unsealed the door?"

"I did," Keshra said.

Calebna's neck grew hot. "Why would you do such a thing? You fool!"

"No door can keep the Jinn away," Terah said.

"It will if the Almighty tells us it will."

Peth ran to Gorban and knelt beside him, whispering words of comfort, though he hushed her, already overwhelmed with pain.

Sarah's face paled. "Gorban? My son. What is happening?"

Calebna grimaced and walked to Gorban. Peth helped him lie on his back, but his leg was mangled and beneath it grew a puddle of blood. "Have your weapons failed you?" Calebna said.

"We need your help," Gorban said.

The women began to murmur. Calebna knew they waited for him to speak, but thoughts came to him of the cruel pride of Lukian's speech and of Gorban's arrogant replies at the forge. Calebna's chest rose and his shoulders angled back. "You knew the cost you might pay for choosing violence over peace."

"I'm not asking you to fight."

"Then what?" The sight of Gorban's blood in such a place dried Calebna's mouth and thickened his tongue. *He defiles the Temple with his very presence.*

"The wounded. They need help." His chest crackled as he coughed, and Peth rubbed his back.

"You ask us to place ourselves in danger for your sakes, but why should we bear the repercussions for your sins?"

"They will die on their own, but we might be able to save some if we move quickly." He gazed at Calebna as if gauging his resolve, wiped his hands on his tunic, and slipped in the blood as he tried to stand.

"Help him!" Sarah said.

Gorban's eyes widened as he noticed his mother for the first time.

Terah hurried to Gorban and braced his right side as Peth braced his left in preparation to help him stand, but Calebna held out his hand. "Stop."

"But he's wounded," Terah said.

Peth tried lifting him, but Terah did not follow, and so Peth had to set him down slowly.

Calebna thought of the danger of aiding the children of Cain, of the ability of sin to spread its defilement. He thought of the many prayers and sacrifices he had offered for the safety of his family, and the thought of letting them die in an attempt to reverse one man's deserved punishment filled him with disgust. "Let him lie in the bed he's made."

"What?" Sarah said. "Why won't you help my son?"

Terah's hands remained under Gorban's arm as she eyed her husband.

Calebna turned from them. He knew what giving in to anger would do. He needed to keep their trust, but they did not understand the depth of this decision. The depth of their danger.

Gorban shook his head. "You sent us out like sacrifices."

"We chose life, you chose death. We all are in the hands of the Almighty. Pray for forgiveness and he may yet deliver you."

Gorban laughed. "You blind fool. Have you not noticed anyone missing?"

The women's whispers grew.

Calebna twisted back, his calves tensing. "Don't test my patience."

"Philo and Tuor offered their help. We could not refuse it."

Terah stepped back. "My brothers?"

Gorban clenched the cloth around his leg and winced as Peth repositioned him. "They, at least, were man enough to fight."

"Is it true?" Terah asked.

"He is lying," Calebna said.

Peth said, "My husband is no liar." Keshra agreed.

"Would you help them and not me?" Gorban coughed and his face reddened.

"Silence!" Calebna said, and the women hushed.

Gorban laid back and shut his eyes as Peth dabbed away the dirty blood. He took a deep breath and said, "Look for your brothers. You will not find them."

Calebna swiveled on his heel and shouldered past Jacob, who was just entering the vestibule, likely drawn by the sounds of their heated discussion. Calebna sped down the hallway, searched every room, and asked everyone he saw if they had seen Philo or Tuor.

None had. The boys' rooms were empty, and the last time anyone had seen them had been the day before.

As much as Calebna could not admit it, he felt the terrible possibility grow in his mind. He wanted to scream and curse. He wanted to rage at the Almighty for allowing such stupidity.

To be betrayed by his own brothers . . .

He steadied himself against the wall of Philo's room and searched it once more for signs. It was disheveled, as if hastily sorted through. As High Priest, Calebna had been tasked with the responsibility of bridging the space between man and God. With understanding the mysteries of the Almighty so that he could, in some way, aid the people to walk between the lines. But their lives were in chaos.

He lifted his chin and breathed. If they had left, if they were really out there wounded and dying, then he would do nothing. He closed his eyes.

Let them be condemned.

He nodded slowly and let the truth settle in the cracks of his soul.

Let Judgment reign.

34

Lukian's fingernails ached. Bloody flesh stuck out from them like so many feathers, and he did not know where he was or how he had come to be there. He simply remembered the moments before plunging into the red waters of rage and violence, and letting them penetrate his soul.

He raised his hammer to get a better look at it. How many had he killed?

A body crawled through a pool of blood. Lukian turned and squinted through the Fog, but could not make it out. He approached, realizing the weakness in his limbs as the curtain of Fog rolled back from animal-like carcasses littering the soaked field. The corpses formed a wall around the crawling body who he recognized was Philo.

Lukian's first compulsion was to kill the boy, and had the inclination been stronger, he might have, but cold logic chilled the burning desire. He watched Philo struggle. The boy's right arm had been replaced by a bloody stump, but Lukian knew the gore Philo lay in was more than just his own.

What better tool to use against Calebna than his own brother?

He shook his head and frowned. What had he done by allowing the rage to pour into him?

Tears drew flesh-colored streaks across Philo's blackened cheeks. "I failed," he mumbled. "I failed, I . . ." He ran the fingers of his only hand through a human corpse's hair. "I failed you. God forgive me."

Lukian hopped the wall of dead bodies and felt a stirring in his abdomen. The boy jumped upon seeing him and cried out, but Lukian knelt and clamped his hand over his mouth. "They'll hear you and kill us. Is that what you want?"

The boy's eyes were animal-wide.

"Did you hear me?"

Philo nodded.

"Will you be quiet if I release you?"

Philo nodded again, but Lukian clamped his mouth harder and said, "If you scream, I will kill you."

The boy's eyes jerked and filled with tears.

Lukian took his hand away.

The boy began mumbling at once. "My little brother, Tuor. What have I done, cousin? He wanted to stay, but I pushed him. He was afraid. He was . . ."

"You did well. You must know that," Lukian said.

"I said terrible things to make him come."

"You were strong. Your brother was weak like your father. But you are different." Lukian licked his lips and stayed his shaking hands from the boy's blood. Why did he want to taste it?

Philo blinked pale eyelids. Dark liquid oozed down his side from the stump of his arm. His eyes glazed. "No . . . I . . ."

Sweat ran down Lukian's neck. "Your life is leaving you, but you've been brave. Will you be brave for me now?"

Philo's forehead creased, and his eyes closed. He clamped his jaw and nodded.

"You were a good brother." Lukian resisted no longer. He reached up, grabbed Philo's throat, and squeezed until the boy's eyes bulged. "Be still," he whispered. "Be still." He slid his knee onto Philo's chest and watched unblinking, feeling mild curiosity and a strange connection to Cain. The boy's eyelids closed over blood-shot white, and he convulsed and went still.

The knowledge that he had murdered Philo brought Lukian a strange sort of pleasure. He knew such pleasure was perverse, but he savored it like honey-dipped bread.

Then something shifted inside, and he fell into the bloody pool. He scrambled up, chest heaving, fingertips prickling. He grabbed his hair and pulled.

The desire. The thirst. Leave me!

It was as if a serpent were coiled inside him biting, devouring. At one moment he was repulsed. At the next he only wanted to embrace it. His soul shook, caught between extremes.

But he was weak, and the desire *grew*.

His gaze was frozen on Philo's body, the way it lay there twisted. He wanted to turn, but couldn't. He saw, as if from far away, a finger extended toward the pool of blood. The finger broke the surface, then came to Lukian's mouth, which opened wide to receive it. His lips closed over the finger, which squirmed around his mouth, but he felt nothing. He thought he saw silver eyes in the Fog, and a small figure, like a little boy whose skin was gray with death.

Lamech, he thought. *Why did I urge Lamech to run into the Fog?*

His brother's death screams had echoed on and on, calling for him to help, to do anything. But Lukian ran. He just ran.

The sensations flooded back. He gasped and realized what the wetness on his face was.

"Blood," he said, as it dripped from his lips.

◆ ◆ ◆

Sarah was crying, and she slid her arms around herself and squeezed. The memories were flooding back quicker than she could handle, and she rocked.

Do they know?

She rolled onto her side. She knew they watched, but no longer cared. She couldn't keep everything coiled inside. She knew from Gorban's wounds that something terrible had happened.

No. Lilleth's lifeless eyes floated through her mind. *Many terrible things have happened. Where are you, Cain? You promised you'd come back. You promised . . .*

God had forsaken her, and she was trapped in his Temple. Why else would she be here but to receive justice? She longed for companionship, but to open herself to another felt like a fate worse than death. Though she hated and feared Cain, he seemed to her the better of two damnations.

I don't want to die.

"What have you done?"

She jumped at Jacob's voice.

"What happened? Have you failed?" Jacob said.

Gorban's reply was sharp. "Learn respect, child."

Terah walked to her son. Her lips trembled with suppressed emotion, and she slid her arms around him and wept. Jacob held her, looking surprised and alarmed.

"My brothers are out there." Terah's voice was muffled by his shoulder.

Jacob rubbed her back.

"I know my brothers are out there," she repeated.

"Father still has not come back. "

Terah just cried.

Gorban gazed at them strangely, and Sarah wondered what was churning in his mind. Then his gaze met hers, and she looked away and clutched her robe. The fibers were rough, and the hard floor hurt her bones, weakened by days of inaction. *Has it really been fifteen days?*

Sarah closed her eyes, but the images only burned brighter. She glanced up. Gorban still watched. She turned away and hoped he mistook what he saw for anything but what it was.

For the first time since waking, she dared to touch her stomach. *I am sorry, my child.*

Gorban spoke to Jacob as his wife, Peth, cleaned his wound and bandaged it with linen. "Your father is no different from us."

"What does the son of a murderer know?" Jacob said.

"Your father has murdered too."

"You speak nonsense."

Eve entered with a small container of wine, several cups, and some of the last bits of stale bread and a handful of nuts. After hearing of Calebna's reaction, she had rushed off in grim silence to prepare refreshments for Sarah and Gorban. Now she knelt beside Sarah, who accepted a portion of the bread and a cup of wine with a nod before Eve took the rest to Gorban.

"Calebna refused to tend to the wounded," Gorban continued, ignoring what Eve placed beside him. "Has he not then pronounced judgment?"

Jacob rubbed his fingers and frowned.

Terah grabbed Jacob's face. "Think, son."

He pushed her hands away.

"Calebna plans to purchase his safety by sacrificing us." Gorban continued.

Eve laid her hand on Gorban's and said, "Peace, son of my son. You must rest." She glanced at Jacob. "We have stirred up enough strife. Let us pray instead and be silent."

35

After Eve led them in the prayer for safety and guidance, Jacob sat thinking of the sounds he heard while gazing at the Fog with his father. Words came disjointed and yet connected in ways that he knew held meaning.

"The world is dying . . . a holy thing, never to be spoken by unclean lips, never to be heard by evil ears . . . remind us who we are . . . our true nature . . . do you still want to be like me? . . . he is not Cain . . . those differences serve a purpose . . . we all have a role to fill . . . in the spring of life, I will let passion spring forth . . . am I willing to join . . . ?"

Jacob swallowed and let his soul embrace rebellion. It felt righteous. It felt holy. He wondered, *Is this what Cain felt as he murdered my grandfather?*

The blood on the floor of the Temple smelled rank. *Lives should not be wasted with such impunity. This, at least, I know is evil.*

So am I to turn to evil to fight evil?

His mother's body shook as she leaned into him again. She believed her brothers were out there, and Father would not let Jacob leave, no matter the truth. Jacob had seen changes come over Father, and the fears he suppressed only a few hours ago returned. If what they said was true, Father had embraced a God that Jacob never could—one devoid of mercy.

It would take no violence. It would demand no violation of his vow.

"We all have a role to fill . . ."

Jacob set his jaw, steadied his mother and pushed her away. Her breath caught as she looked up. Gorban stared, and despite the bitter words they traded only moments before, Jacob felt a connection with him he'd never had. He nodded, and Gorban's eyebrows crouched, but Jacob offered no explanation. He simply straightened, walked toward the door, and fulfilled his role.

◆ ◆ ◆

The sounds were so dense Mason could almost smell them. Sensations from battles long past broke forth as he rubbed his blood-crusted fingers together. The air in his lungs felt more like scraping teeth than Fog, but his legs stretched on, smashing the ground like cedar trees. He ran over fallen Jinn, popping their ribs beneath his callused feet and leaving massive impressions in the blood-soaked earth.

Piercing cries mixed into the sounds ahead. He had seen so few human bodies littering the battlefield, and that gave him hope, though only a little, and so he prayed. In the midst of the madness, when no other man truly believed, he prayed to the Almighty because he knew the Almighty had never died.

But how could a mute speak of the wondrous mysteries of God? How could a voiceless man sing of the Glorious Intervention ordained before the Spirit's breath buffeted the formless waters? Before the Word spoke and earth and fire and body and soul rolled off his tongue and into its habitation? Before Adam tasted sin, death, pain, and loss? Before Cain, his own father, murdered Abel?

Indeed, his task was not to speak, but to lay a foundation for the One to come. So he ran, and he fought, and he listened to the voice from his dreams, as he had from the very beginning when he found his mother half drowned in the storm.

Most of all, he prayed.

◆ ◆ ◆

Jacob had never seen so many corpses.

What am I doing out here? He wiped his face.

The Fog hung over the battlefield as if Time itself were suspended. Here, nothing moved. No life. Only faint sound in the distance, and he made his way toward it. He passed mangled bodies and checked them to make sure they weren't Philo or Tuor. One was Mellore, Kiile's second oldest. The other was marred beyond recognition. Neither moved.

Jacob walked on, jumping over piled carcasses and splashing through bloody grass. The bodies became fewer and soon failed altogether. He closed his eyes to shut out the world and feel safe again.

Speak to me. Give me a sign. If it be your will that I go farther, I will, but I need to know. Are you dead like everyone says?

His ringing ears strained. Had he heard something or was it only his imagination? He held his breath and waited, scanning the white for sound or sight.

Then there were footsteps, approaching hard and fast. His heart raced and he twisted to flee, but instead slipped in the blood.

The footsteps slowed. It was Lukian, and swinging at his side was a bloody hammer. He held what looked like a dead body, and upon seeing Jacob, he stopped and studied him.

Jacob scrambled up and took a step closer to the body in Lukian's arms, searching the face. Recognition burned the nape of his neck, and he closed his eyes, wondering if he would vomit.

"It is he," Lukian said.

"And what of Tuor?"

"Torn to shreds and cold to the touch. I found them together, but could carry only one."

Jacob began to weep. "Please, lead me to Tuor."

"It is too dangerous."

"It could not be far."

"I will not take the risk. You shouldn't be out here unarmed."

Jacob noted a strange twitching under Lukian's right eye, but said, "May I carry Philo home?"

Lukian approached and set Philo in Jacob's arms, and Jacob dipped his head in respect. He thought about thanking him but instead turned, said a short prayer, and began carrying his father's dead brother back.

Lukian did not follow.

Jacob glanced back, barely able to see Lukian's motionless shape through the Fog.

"What will you do?" Jacob asked.

"I must stay."

"What is out there?"

"Go!"

Tears burned Jacob's eyes, but despite his desire to stay and fight beside the man who had retrieved his uncle's body, he brought Philo to the Temple.

His tomb.

36

The hammer hung in both of Lukian's hands as he gripped it with a resurrected fury. He hungered for violence as deeply as a desert dweller thirsted for water.

Gillian. My son.

He bit his cheek.

The desire . . .

He couldn't trust himself to help the wounded. At the very least, he had made an impression on Jacob, and hopefully the boy would aid him in making an impression on the others. When the battle was over, he would need them. He only hoped this deadly desire wouldn't continue mounting.

Almighty, don't let it grow.

First he would end Calebna and any others responsible for the death of his children. Had they come to help, fewer men would have died, and maybe Gillian would still be beside him.

The time for peace has ended. The time for violence has begun. Once Calebna is out of the way, they all will follow me. It is survival, evolution, progression.

But what about Jacob? The boy was different. He had risked his life for Philo, and yet he had shown his weakness through tears.

A scream opened the Fog before him like a screeching gate. He sprinted forward, the path lit by dull gray light. Ahead, a mass roiled like dark waves on a pale shore, but soon more details leapt into the light. It was a throng of Jinn, possibly one hundred or more, arranged in a circle around what he could only guess was the final bastion of Lukian's brothers and nephews.

Lukian poised his hammer low and leaned forward, bursting

into a sprint. He lifted his hammer high and reveled in the crack of hammer against skull. He spread the beasts and glimpsed Machael fighting alongside his sons from the inside. Machael's eyes widened as he slashed a Jinn's arms off at the elbows and his boys opened up a path for him. Lukian rejoined and saw Kiile, though the man's youngest and oldest were gone.

Together the brothers and sons fought, and the demons fell like insects. Lukian noticed beasts turning in confusion. Then, bursting through the ranks, came Mason, crushing skulls with stone-hard knuckles. He split three heads in five strikes, then joined the group.

"You're late," Lukian said.

Mason peered into Lukian's eyes, and Lukian looked at the blood dripping from Mason's fingers. The red juice drew him, but with a glance up at Mason, he saw the man's eyes glint.

Lukian lifted his hammer, feeling its weight like never before. But with Mason at his side, and Machael and Kiile and their children, he would bathe in blood until he drowned.

◆ ◆ ◆

"You should have left Philo outside the Temple," Calebna said as he resealed the Temple with iron bars. To Jacob, he looked bent and aged, more a vulture than a man, and the lines about his mouth ran deeper than his frown.

"How could I?" Jacob said.

"Holiness is only difficult to those who deny its power." Calebna's eyes strayed to Gorban, whose leg was bandaged. Then he looked at Philo, whose skin was paler than the stone he lay upon.

There was long silence. Philo's wounds no longer bled, and one simple, inescapable fact bound their tongues. He was dead. Jacob couldn't stop wondering when it happened. He wanted to know the moment, the spot he had stood upon when the boy's soul left his body. As much as he didn't want to admit it, Calebna's contempt burned to the center of his chest. "I think he might have died in Lukian's arms."

"I'm sure he did."

"At least Lukian had the kindness to bring Philo back." Jacob didn't know why he was defending Lukian, but something about his father's demeanor made him bristle.

Calebna's eyes twitched, and Jacob wondered if his father would strike him. "Philo disowned us."

"Philo died protecting us," Terah said.

Calebna glanced from Jacob to Terah, who returned his glare. Calebna sucked his teeth and nodded. "I see." He laughed and looked at the ceiling. "This is what you give me? A family of cowards?"

Eve was adjusting Sarah's cushions, but stood. "Cowardice? Is that what you think this is?"

Terah's face was red, and her hands were balled into fists by her side. "With every word you sound more like Lukian."

"I am the High Priest, the intermediary between you and the flames of Judgment."

"And what of you? Who will judge you? Are there no consequences for your decisions?" Eve said.

Calebna's eyes darkened. "I have maintained my integrity in the face of death, but who might I turn to when I cannot trust my son? My wife? I do not envy the violence stored up for you in the depths of eternity."

Terah scoffed and fell silent.

Jacob's face chilled. He said in a low voice, "For years I have feared your shame, but now you have won mine."

Gorban raised his voice, pointing at Calebna. "Cain killed one, but you've done better. You've offered us all at your altar."

Calebna slammed his fist into the wall. "I'm the servant of God!" He no longer hid his contempt. "As the Almighty spoke, 'Behold, the wicked man conceives evil and is pregnant with mischief and gives birth to lies. He makes a pit, digging it out, and falls into the hole that he has made. His mischief returns upon his own head, and on his own skull his violence descends.'"

"I pray you never feel the sting of your words," Eve said.

Jacob turned and urged his mother out of the vestibule, though she remained in place.

"Now," Calebna continued with finger pointing at Gorban, "their violence falls on others as well. We have no hope apart from the Almighty. If everyone had only listened to me, none of this would have happened. If Philo hadn't been—"

Terah said, "I take back my words."

"Come," Jacob said. "Let's go."

Terah struggled against Jacob and threw her words like javelins. "You're not a good man. You're not a man at all."

◆ ◆ ◆

"What's going on? Why are they just standing there?" Kiile said.

Lukian held his hammer outstretched.

"Why aren't they attacking?"

"Quiet," Lukian said.

The Jinn were still. Deep in the Fog footsteps crunched gravel, and the Jinn parted. A shape moved toward them, dark and slender amidst the beasts.

"Great Almighty," Kiile muttered. "Is that . . . ?"

Lukian dropped his hammer.

A man strode toward them, and the Fog peeled from his gray skin as if he were formed from it.

It is an apparition, a ghost, Lukian thought.

But it was real. Too real.

The man nodded and spoke to Lukian in that familiar, resonant bass, "Hello, Son."

PART SEVEN

BEYOND THE SANDS OF TIME

You were the seal of perfection,
Full of wisdom and perfect in beauty.
You were in Eden, the garden of God;
Every precious stone was your covering:
The sardius, topaz, and diamond,
Beryl, onyx, and jasper,
Sapphire, turquoise, and emerald with gold.
The workmanship of your timbrels and pipes
Was prepared for you on the day you were created.
You were the anointed cherub who covers;
I established you;
You were on the holy mountain of God;
You walked back and forth in the midst of fiery stones.
You were perfect in your ways from the day you
were created,
Till iniquity was found in you.

—EZEKIEL 28:12–15 NKJV

37

Waves rush past and slide the man across the Sands, some of which grind between his teeth while he hovers in the twilight of Time. He is stuck on the edge of awareness, floating. Just floating. The peace tugs him toward rest, and yet the pink glare of Light through his eyelids pains him. His head thumps against a boulder, and he opens his eyes with a moan.

He squints in the Light while sitting in the salty Water with his back to the boulder, and observes the white Sands stretching away on either side, the glittering blue-green Water, and the jungle trees guarding him from behind. Warm wind rides the waves crashing on the Sands. He breathes and rests on the heels of his hands, letting a smile form on his lips despite having no reason to feel happy. He does not know who he is, where he is, or why he is sitting on an endless shoreline. He merely knows that he is here, and that there is only "now."

Perhaps that is why he smiles. There is such peace in disregarding what *was* or *will be*. But he is startled by the vague thought of something he cannot quite remember. He tries to retrieve it and runs against a barrier. Something about existing in only the present makes his mind spin, and he feels displaced, as if he does not belong here.

But why should it matter? He smiles again. "Now." It contains everything. All that matters is "now," and everything contained within "now," which is, of course, infinite. These truths strike his mind as illogical, yet his soul revels in their robustness. All is fresh and all is stale. There is joy and peace in grappling with the oneness, and simultaneous individuality, of everything.

He stands and walks the beach to feel the sand between his

toes, the warmth of the Light and the saltiness of the air. There are jungle smells; trees, undergrowth, and mossy decay. Other scents remain too subtle to describe, but together they bloom and grow to something gestalten.

He shambles up the incline toward the line of trees and stops just short to examine the boughs laced together like the weave of a shirt. They creak, pulled by the wind in an endless dance as it leads with hands on leaves.

How many arms the wind must have to dance with so many.

He approaches to join, and when his fingers touch one of the tree trunks, it shivers. He smiles and presses his hand against it only to see it slide aside and open a path into the jungle. He pauses at the entrance, and the green-scented breeze brings whispered melodies to his ears. He stops to hear them better, but they quiet as if carried reluctantly from the forest. As he stands contemplating whether there might be Music playing within, a strange sensation stirs him to turn.

He swivels and gasps upon seeing a speck of a figure bobbing on the waves. He sprints down the Sands and arrives at the Water's edge as he realizes the speck is a young woman. The shoreline catches her with open palms, and his shadow casts long as his feet splash her shoulders. Her mouth is slightly open, and behind the heart-shaped lips are teeth like milky diamonds. She opens sea-bright eyes and smiles.

He crouches, meets her gaze, and says, "Hello."

"Hello," she replies.

He extends an arm and she slips her fingers between his, which are much darker than hers. She stands, but their hands remain entwined. They turn toward the jungle and, as they near the trees, the melodies return like the scent of roses. She looks at him.

"Care to dance?" he says.

She nods, and though he doesn't understand the strength of his desire to explore, she seems to share it, and together they walk under the leafy canopy.

The path grows longer, and all around is the Music. They laugh and run, only barely keeping their fingers clasped as the trees part with increasing speed to make way. They break through the brush into an open space filled with stone ruins, and the Music hushes.

Now comes a pregnant silence—the living space between notes.

Arches, domes, and towers lie half-fallen across the ground. He examines the constructions with wonder, and brushes fingers across porous rock lined with zigzagging patterns of fleshy plant life. The ocean air is further humidified by the ever-breathing grove that, other than the creeping vines and lichen, keeps its distance from the buildings, as if the stones poison the ground.

Her thumb rubs the back of his hand, and he turns. There is love in her gaze, and he finds no difficulty returning it. She means much to him, though he doesn't understand why. He leans in and kisses her lips, so soft and warm, and she kisses back. They admire each other and continue through the ruins.

She points to a black recess in one of the walls, and they walk to it. It is a grim opening, tarnished by weather and vine. A few of the stones lie on the ground like fallen teeth, and a staircase tumbles down its throat. He tugs her forward and they enter and find themselves in a tunnel with windows every fifteen paces or so spilling Light like Fog into the cobalt shadows. They walk with fearful reverence and arrive at a doorway in the shape of a shield with its center pressing toward them in a needlepoint. Forming a circle around the shield is an assortment of letters. They are strange, but somehow he understands them. He tips his head and brushes his finger across the chiseled words to feel their peaks and valleys. The Shrine of the Song. Who knocks?

The Music returns, marked by a tentative hush, as if the players themselves hang on every movement. The melodies twirl in gentle arpeggios, conjuring images of little rivers tumbling toward unknown bends. The man and woman look at each other and back at the shield, which stands guarding them from what lay beyond. "Who am I?" he says.

She shakes her head. "I don't know. Who am *I*?"

"I don't know. At least, I don't *think* I know."

She frowns, examines the shield, and brings her fingers up to fiddle with the point. She accidentally pricks her finger on the tip, and draws her hand back and nurses it as he fights a nearly irrepressible urge to do the same. He makes a motion as if to turn away, but his hand darts forward and presses against the tip, drawing a drop of blood and mixing with hers. He pulls his hand back and the needle retreats into the shield until it disappears. An unseen mechanism grinds, and the shield rolls away, revealing a new, expansive chamber.

The Music deepens and expands, yet retains a measured patience, and he wonders what it means. He slips his arm around her waist and nearly asks, but it seems she probes his eyes for the same.

The new room is circular and its walls are formed from polished stone. Ornate script runs along the bottom, and pillars rise like arms to support the ceiling with many hands. A single mural spans the room, and he spins to take it in, though it is steeped in shadows.

"What is this place?" he asks.

"I don't know." She squeezes his fingers as if to hold him more securely. "It makes me uncomfortable."

A cold sensation settles in his stomach as he looks at the carven wall. He approaches for a better look, but she doesn't follow out of the light, so he lets her hand slip out of his and, as his eyes adjust to the shadows, is surprised at the detail. There are countless persons in the mural, and yet he can see the expression on each face and the stitching in their clothing.

"You need to see this," he says.

"There's something here," she says.

"This is incredible."

"Come back. Hurry."

He turns and sees her back against a pillar. "What's wrong?"

She points and her green eyes frost. "What is that?"

Now, as a deeper note of the Music strikes, a silver shape advances, and darkness slips from its shoulders like a cloak. It pierces them with a hollow, metal gaze. Its arms bend at the elbows. Its legs are slightly longer than what would be normal on a human in relation to the torso, and each has two knee joints bending in opposite directions. The entire creature is bright silver with only rivets and lines where sheets begin and end to add detail.

They hold their breath, expecting the thing to continue, but it does not. The man edges toward it, but the woman pulls him back and wraps an arm around his bicep.

"Don't . . ."

Amplifying curiosity distorts his face into a frown. He asks the thing, "What are you?"

Its gaze narrows, and it speaks from some hidden mechanism, "Who am I?"

Her fingernails dig into his arm.

"Are you not more interested in knowing who you are?"

"Why do we fear you?" the man says.

"Because I have the power to puncture your skin and spill your blood on this holy ground."

Both man and woman retreat. "Stay back," the man says.

"You have little right to make demands. You cannot stop the Music."

"We want neither to hurt you nor to be hurt by you."

Machine. The word comes to him, strange and familiar at once. *That is what it is called. But how do I know that?* The woman tugs his arm as if to urge him to silence, but he refuses, for questions compel him to speak. "Why are you here? What is your purpose?"

The machine says, "I am the keeper of the Shrine."

He thinks of the fallen ruins, the unkempt entrance of broken molars, and the name on the door.

The Shrine of the Song . . .

Thoughts link through his mind. "Who owns this temple?"

"The Master."

She keeps pulling, but his desire to speak with it grows greater still. The Music splits. One line ascending, the other burrowing. He says to the machine, "Who made you?"

It does not respond.

She whispers, "Don't."

He says, "When were you made?"

"I exist."

"How? What does that mean?"

The machine says, "Time is a law of nature binding the physical realm to relatively steady movement down a unidirectional pathway, but 'now' is all that 'is' here. We sustain outside the boundaries of Time. And so there is not a *time* when I *was* made. I did not *come* to be. I *am*, as you *are*."

He nods. Of course. He knows that. Or does he? He feels exceedingly strange in this place.

"We're sorry for disturbing you," she says. "We will go now."

He scowls and says in hushed tones, "I'm not leaving. Go without me if you're so afraid."

She winces as if his words cause pain and flicks her gaze between him and the machine.

"What is this Shrine's purpose?" he asks.

The machine says, "It is a haven for all who seek something more."

"And do we seek that?"

"You are a part of the Music, are you not?"

He frowns. He is. Or at least he thinks he is. But his heartbeat strikes polyrhythms. "The doorway asked who we are but opened to our blood. Why is that?"

"You remain on the brink of both ends; a son of twilight."

"You speak in riddles."

"I speak plainly."

"Then speak more plainly."

The machine pauses. "You give your blood to the Shrine, and though the offering is symbolic, it represents your life, and the Shrine accepts you for it. This is not your home, yet it may be your resting place."

"Where then is my home?"

The machine says nothing. It merely stares, its metal eyes jerking from time to time.

Her hands wrap around his arm, and she asks, "Is the Music you speak of what is playing through the forest, and in this Shrine?"

"The Music is the Song of the Master."

They shuffle to the mural, now more fearful of the machine than the dark. The machine remains as if bolted in place, but its gaze follows them.

She brushes fingers across the mural and stifles a gasp. In the image, countless beings march in rows, carrying banners and weapons toward a City. The stone smells aged, like a tomb long sealed, but he knows that is neither an image nor a thought that belongs in this land beyond Time.

She turns to the machine and points at the leading figure in the mural, the one holding what looks to be a trumpet. "Is this it? Is this the Music?"

"It is."

"What happened to them? All these figures in the picture?"

"They make war."

"But here is a mural of them."

"They make war."

"You already said that."

"I *say* that they *make* war."

Its rebuke makes her chew her lip. "What do they war against?"

"The other Music."

She points at the marching figures. "Who are they?"

"They are the Watchers, the Sons of God."

The man thinks of the abandoned ruins outside and says, "Why is everything so empty and lifeless here?"

"It is not so empty as you think. If you wish to see more, I can show you."

She fidgets and tugs on his arm. "We have lingered long enough."

"But—"

"It is time to leave." She jerks him toward the entrance, but he does not want to leave, and his mind scrambles for some way to stall her.

"Do we have names?" he calls out.

The machine says, "You do."

She stops and offers a wary glance.

"Do you know them?" the man says.

The machine says, "If I tell you, will you stay?"

He looks at her, and she presses her lips together.

"We will stay for a time," he says.

"Your words will bind you," the machine says.

"I bind myself to my words."

"Very well. Your name is Seth, and hers, Ayla."

He tries to imagine owning that name, but his mind rejects it as unfamiliar. He looks at the woman the machine calls Ayla. That name seems strange as well, but when he mouths their names, something about their shapes feels familiar.

He looks at her, remembering her desire to leave. He points at the mural. "Where is this City? The one under attack?"

"It is the center of this world."

"And where are we now?"

"The Shrine of the Song lies on the outskirts, near the Sands that keep the Waters of Time within their borders."

"Is the City occupied?"

"A different Music plays there, and it finds discord with ours. If you wish to see more of the Song of the Shrine, I can show you."

Indeed, the desire to see the rest of the Shrine and listen to more of the Music swells in his chest. "Please, lead on."

Ayla glares, but says nothing.

The machine walks past a few pillars, and Seth pulls her to follow. It presses its arm into another shield-like door, which rolls away just like the first, revealing a long passage down into darkness. The floor is smooth, yet not steep enough to warrant danger. She stops urging him back, but her hand clutches his arm, and when it becomes too dim to see, the machine's eyes cast light such as two lamps.

Questions breach the surface of his thoughts. "You spoke of Sands that hold Time. What does that mean?"

"The Sands are where Time begins and flows outward in ever-multiplying rivulets. Without the Sands, Time would not know where to begin and end, and would flow on endlessly until all movement and depth vanished."

"How are we here?"

"Your bodies are dead."

Ayla's grip tightens on his arm. "We are dead?" Her face registers the same fear he feels as terrible realization grates his skull and numbs his tongue. He asks no more questions while they journey down the tunnel, and the only noises are of grinding metal, and the fleshy slap of foot against stone.

38

Rows of light glimmer down the corridor as more flicker to life like so many glowing insects. They hum and buzz dully as they hover, causing Seth to keep a wary distance.

"They are not alive," the machine says as Seth sidesteps one with a suspicious glance.

"Where are we?"

"The Hall of Worship, where the Watchers keep vigilance."

Seth imagines beings filling the hall and trailing after one another in reverent lines, but it is massive and bare, and imagined secrets bloom like nightshades. The machine leads them down the corridor, past pillars and opulent floors. The hall curves to the left, but ever so slightly as to be almost imperceptible. They arrive at a set of broad doors on the left-hand side, and the machine opens them. They enter another hallway, only this one is smaller, with many doors and no pillars.

The machine stops and says, "This is the Eastern Nexus, from which the Chambers of Science branch. Wish you to see them?"

"What are they?"

"They devote themselves to the Mystery of Life. It is the Master's hope that the Watchers may find greater life through the Chambers of Science."

"Lead on."

"You must choose your own path now. Each note struck here resonates the instruments till they sustain with synchronized troughs and peaks."

Seth looks at Ayla, who shrugs. "So we are to choose a door and open it?"

"Choose carefully."

He brushes his fingers over subtle artwork, like shadows burned into the wood of each door. After viewing four, they examine the doors on the opposite side. Back and forth they shuffle until they see an image of a flower. Ayla points, her eyes widening. "The Aylana, the White Flower! It's the very same I was named after, though it is black here." She frowns. "And I cannot remember who named me. This memory loss is so very strange." She looks at the machine as if desiring to ask it all her questions, but the Music rolls on, gaining volume and momentum.

Seth grabs the handle of the door with the black flower on it, his hands growing clammy, but before he opens it, he whispers, "Do you want to go in? We do not know what lies beyond."

"I am not as afraid of this one as I am of"—she pauses and glances at the beast on the next door—"the other ones."

He looks at that image, a lion with the tail of a serpent and a forked tongue springing like dancing fire from its jaws. He glances at the door in front of them and notices thorns at the base of the Aylana. "Why would this image be here if not to function as a sign? It nearly bears your name."

"Perhaps the Shrine, or maybe the Music, knows us." She nods as if conceding a begrudged truth. "But we know so little of it."

"It is causing us no pain, no discomfort. Indeed it is fascinating."

She nods, but looks hesitant.

"We will view just one room. Then, if you wish, we will turn back." He smiles, and she attempts one in return. He throws the door wide and lights glimmer as if awakened by their movement. Their glow is filtered through glass and liquid, and the kaleidoscopic reflections dance as the pair makes their way forward, the machine following with head bowed and footfalls like cymbals. Throughout the room are cylindrical vats of liquid tinged green as if by algae. Lights gaze up from the bottom of each, and floating in them is what looks like twisted branches and roots.

Seth sidesteps another hovering light and moves toward the glass. Suspended within is a rose with petals closed and drooping. Its stalk flows serpentine to the base, where a treelike root, thicker than the flower, stretches like a fist striking at the bottom of the vat.

She grimaces. "What is it?"

"I don't know." They speak quietly, pitching their voices so the machine, which lumbers close, might not hear. Seth glances at it cautiously. "Take care."

She nods and squeezes his fingers. The air holds its breath, and its pulse is like an underwater timpani. It waits for them to speak, to determine the direction of the Music, but they force it into stasis, too frightened to pluck the wrong note.

They move to the next vat and observe another plant that seems but a simple vine with leaves sprouting in symmetric patterns. Upon closer inspection, tiny bone-like projections, reminiscent of teeth, sprout from the edges of the leaves.

The air grows thick and warm.

Ayla whispers, "These plants aren't like anything I've ever seen."

"They look altered in peculiar ways."

"They do evil things here. I feel it as if it touches me this very moment." She hugs herself and rubs her arms.

"The Watchers," he says as if remembering an ancient secret.

"I do not think we belong here. It is wrong for us to be here, to open these doors at all." She presses her fingertips against the chilled glass, and the plant seems to move in response.

Something about the crossbred organisms draws him, and he cannot turn away. In subsequent vats are a bush with flowers sprouting from its roots, a flower with a pink object resembling a tongue, and another vine with bone-spines and malignant growths like bloody contusions.

Ayla turns. "I don't want to see any more."

But Seth is compelled to see more. The Music turns, descending from innocence toward skin-tingling darkness, raising the hairs on his neck and his desire to see more, to give in, to become one with the Music as a dancer's body becomes the manifestation of musical emotion.

They edge toward the door and Seth's throat dries despite being filled with saliva. He says, "The machine says we are here for a reason. I wonder what led us from the beach to the Shrine and pushed us down the stairwell."

"I think it was nothing but our own curiosity," she says.

"We cannot turn back now."

"Yes, we can."

"And go where?"

"Somewhere, anywhere."

"We are meant to see this."

"But I hate it. I hate how it makes me feel."

I should take her far from this place. He forces a smile and feels a quivering in his abdomen. "It's the Music. It is leading us. It knows who we are and what we want, and it is offering what we need."

"But what if we're here by accident, and the darkness I feel is a warning in my heart?"

"I don't believe in accidents."

Her eyes search his, and he can see her resolve crumble. She does not speak. She simply grabs his hand and follows him down the corridor.

Desire blooms into itchy satisfaction as they make their way through the endless rows of vats stretching on until they become too small for the eye to register. They return to the Eastern Nexus, find the door of the lion with the tail of a serpent, and enter together, hungry for what might be seen.

The lights flicker on, but the vats that greet them are hideous. Floating in the pinkish liquid are hardly recognizable cadavers, malformed hunks of meat suspended in torturous positions.

Why are they here?

Seth swallows and touches the glass with a shaking finger. The creature's eyes roll and lock on his. Its lungs pulse in quick, sharp movements. Its mouth is twisted open, locked in place by deformed joints, and the image becomes a blur in his pained eyes.

Ayla's fingernails dig into his hand, and he shakes his head and wipes his face. Her gaze burns his cheek, and he tries ignoring the same thoughts he knows trouble her.

What torture is this creature enduring? An eternity spent drinking in the pain of such an embryonic existence—what hell could be more terrible?

But the *Music*! It is beautiful and terrible and *growing*.

"The Master says it is one of the most beautiful sights." The machine walks to the vat and inserts its arm into the apparatus. The beast's eyes bulge as it rushes from the glass and stares at the hand in the apparatus. The water fills with gray smoke like Fog.

"What are you doing?" Seth says.

The murk disappears, as if a current is sucking it away, and the fluid is clean.

Blue water. The vat is empty.

"What is happening?"

"A morsel of Time is stolen from the Waters and suspended in the vat, and inside is woven the fabric of life. It is the Master's supreme art, performed in true Time-suspension."

Suspension, Seth thinks. *I feel suspended above black water. Such terrible darkness, such brutal addiction. I am burning with fear, and yet cannot plug my desire. I am thirsty, so thirsty . . . And Ayla?*

"Where do the creatures go?" she asks in a trembling voice.

"To the Master."

"To do what?"

"To serve."

Seth cannot look away. He cannot stop, and it seems neither can she. It is as if he only watches decisions made by another.

"Let me show you the Master's greatest creation."

Seth remembers the picture on the door, the serpent's tail, barbed and poisonous. He can feel it lurking in the Music, a whip-cord striking every measure, subtle yet relentless.

"The Master calls it Nephilim," the machine says.

It seems at first like a man, but the eyes are silver, the skin is gray, and curling out of its skull are two dirty gray projections, like the horns of a ram.

"What is it?" Ayla asks.

"It is one of you taken and transformed. A soulless half-breed.

Before Adam dies, the physical world will see it walk among its cousins. It is the next evolution of what your people call the Jinn, only as applied to humanity instead of animals."

"But if it is soulless, how then does it live?" Seth says.

"An empty body may be filled. Indeed, the intention of the Master is that the Sons of God might walk about as kings of men. Here, as well as there, I prepare the way for them."

The machine manipulates the console, but the reaction of the Nephilim is wholly different from the other creature's. Its lips slide into a skeletal smile, and it grabs its arms and digs. Wisps of red float to the top. The gray Fog comes, now disappears.

"Can you show us the rest of the Shrine?"

"You wish to move on from the Chambers of Science?"

In shaky unison, they say, "We do."

"Very well, follow me. There are many rooms left before us, and they are greater than these, though none quite so distinct."

They move on, but the hum of the Chambers continues—adding complexity upon complexity and growing in both beauty and ferocity.

39

The Shrine expands. Seth finds it strange that a building can be alive, let alone move and change, but steps continue to materialize as the machine methodically pushes the stone walls ever deeper.

Where are this puppet's strings? By what will does it move? Is the Music its life? The Song is strange—strange and powerful.

And yet, in the absence of Time, he recognizes there is something greater still, as if glimpsing a star through the cracks in a moon. What is seen is only a shell hiding the true glory, though for the present it is all they know.

The deeper they walk, the farther through the octaves the Music cascades. The staircase ends and an archway appears, gilded in silver and shining like pearls. Beyond the arch the way widens to a dome, and the machine's eyes dull reactively. In the great basin revels a pool lapping against the sides of its domain, like a crooked smile undulating in ecstasy.

"This is the bathhouse of the Watchers," the machine says.

"They bathe?" Ayla asks.

"Not such as humans do."

Somehow, Seth senses the purpose of the room is not to wash filth, but to rinse cleanliness with unbridled pleasure. The machine wades across the pool. There is no ground on which they can escape, but neither does Seth desire to. He steps toward it with veiled excitement, and as his toes touch the water, existence itself becomes indulgence. Prudence flees and he falls headfirst, gluttonizing the water through his nose, mouth, and skin. He vibrates with the hum of the pool and senses his being ravaged by the rhythms.

The meaning, which sounds at first like a muffled groan, crashes into him.

He kicks in the pool and breaches the surface, grasping for substance with hungry lungs. He feels like a drum, hollowed inside and filled with violent air thrusting against his shell.

Ayla crawls from the pool next to him, and they lie dripping in the archway next to the machine. Her eyes are ringed with darkness, sunken into tired sockets, and he wonders if his look the same. They stand and shake the remnants of the pool away, though, oddly, it seems to remain.

With terrible clarity, he realizes the Song is not what it pretends. It monotonously propounds excitement. It screams to fill the pit with sound. It kills to claim life.

Contradiction. That is its lifeblood.

What if our purpose in coming is not to experience the Song, but to stop it? What if we are appointed to sing a different Song?

She whispers for him to hold her and rub the perversity from her skin, but he feels incapable, and she reaches an arm around his waist instead. The machine turns down a new hallway as the Shrine begins expanding once more, revealing new rooms, hallways, and staircases. They follow it with a different spirit, attempting to shrug the weight planted on their shoulders by the pool.

The Music—or is it so many hammers striking anvils?—dims in the Light of a new awareness.

◆　◆　◆

"It is the heart of the Shrine." The machine sweeps its arm toward the monstrosity filling their ears with measured noise. "It is the pump of the lifeblood, the percussion in the Music. It is the Metronome."

"But Time does not exist here," Seth says.

"The Metronome is a multiplicity, an anomaly lodged between the layers. It is one of the Master's many masterpieces, and through it we can glimpse the workings of the Song in other Places. Come."

It ascends a staircase leading over the Metronome. They follow and see from their vantage what can only be described as a bubble set into the Metronome like a great eye, the surface of which is akin to a membrane of oil with iridescent markings shifting constantly.

Seth asks, "What is that bubble?"

"That is the Metronome's telescope. It reveals the glory of the Song, and though some notes may be only vague images, others are vivid phantasms."

Seth bends over the rail and peers inside. The telescope seems to expand, and he wonders if he is leaning backward or forward, for it engulfs his vision. In the ever-shifting shadows, he senses arms reaching toward him, fingers straining and sliding around him and pulling until he feels himself removed and fastened to the Metronome's belts. The movement does not frighten him. It feels natural, as if his soul were meant for such an action.

Visions appear, and some remind him of dreams he might have had while under the influence of Time, which he feels closer to, like part of him has crossed through the Metronome's eye. But he is incapable of setting both feet in any one Place, and he remains suspended as he views a piece of Time here, a scrap of life there.

He watches people with gray skin heap piles into a foundation. The foundation spreads until there is no escaping its totality, and on it, cruel empires build towers and warriors beat their chests. They march with footsteps in line with the Music, and flames rise and lick the lens.

Now comes Water—a singular element from outside the Music. It fills the foundation until it overflows like a great basin and washes the world clean. As it recedes, there comes more gray-skins who build another foundation, and from it rises a Tower whose peak pricks the stars.

The visions move on relentlessly, but all is the same. There are empires, buildings, technologies, symbols, fires, disasters, wars, and plagues, but Death is all that reveals itself. There is a simplicity, a repetition in the Music, like a measure replayed. *The Music is a circle*, Seth thinks. *It is the circumference of the telescope, a great engine sustained through the whole of Time.*

They build to tear down to build to tear down. Contradiction. An opposing statement.

Rebellion.

This is all the telescope shows. The Music rolls on and the Metronome releases him, though it sets its rhythm in his chest, and he is moved to synchronize with it.

"Now you know the beauty ordained—the inevitable thrust of the universe."

The machine's voice jars him awake. He blinks and sees his surroundings, including the Shrine, for what it is.

The Music is a mindless machine, an instrument itself.

But played by what? Or by whom?

He thinks of the people. The gray-skins. They choose the paths they walk, but seem to forfeit their will in the end. Do they then become lifeless machines? Hollow Instruments?

"Come now," the machine says. "There is another chamber I desire to show you, and it is the greatest of all."

◆ ◆ ◆

The machine leads them to a vast room that is made up of seemingly endless angles set against each other and that is filled with a singular object—a massive headless body. Instruments of every kind weave in and out of the four limbs and torso, and they play as if the fingers of many masters attend them. Seth and Ayla's mouths gape at the sight, and the machine motions them closer. More than in the bathhouse, Seth feels the sensual pull of the Music. It is more forceful, more violent, and more beautiful, and they quake in the Song's enormity.

"This is the Master's body," the machine says.

"This? This is the Master? Where is his head?"

"The Master *is* the head. The violence of the Enemy's Music separates the head from the body, but the Master's body plays on." The machine opens its chest as if peeling back flesh, and the metal separates to reveal gears, belts, and glowing parts reminiscent of organs. "And I, the machine, remain self-existent through the brilliance of the Master. I am the first of his children, my purpose to tend the great Music of the Master and prepare the way for the Sons of God to come in the skin of men."

It leaves itself exposed and stares at them. It is terrible, but they stare because the glory of the machine, and the pulse of the Music, hypnotizes them.

"The Music exists to defy the Enemy," the machine continues. "Every note is an expression of this base intention, and every chord, every melody line woven through the Music, is sung by one of the Enemy's creation."

"His creation?"

"The Sons of God and of man. Do you not wish to sing the Song? Do you not wish to become an Instrument as magnificent as I?"

Seth cannot deny that he desires it. It is truly great, truly beautiful, though it is terrible to behold, and his desires strain against each other.

But there is something missing, he thinks. *Some ruinous ghost in the hollow between notes.*

"Why should we sing this Song? Why should we become the Master's Instruments?" Ayla says.

"Because the Master longs to adopt you, to free you from the Enemy. The Song shall break the Enemy's chains, if you allow it, and if you become an Instrument of the Music, you may add to it whatever your heart desires."

"We may sing anything we want?"

"It matters not whether your Song be Power, Pleasure, or Pride. All are one with the Music of the Master."

Seth teeters on the edge of the Music's embrace. As he looks, the machine gazes as if seeing his nakedness revealed. The Music hums, and his eyelids lull as he feels himself drawn invariably toward it. He remembers the control of the Chambers, the pleasure of the Pool, and the magnificence of the Metronome, and he wants it.

He wants it all.

But in all the sensual beauty moving in seemingly perfect fluidity, a note squawks his mind awake, and he sees the Music and the machine with disgust. The allure redoubles until the room shakes so violently he can hardly see, and he feels himself once more slip under the Song's command.

Ayla's fingers slip into his, and he looks at her and sees her mouth moving. Though all sound is drowned in the violence of the Music, he hears the words in his mind.

I love you.

The Music screams, and the silver temptress is revealed for what it is—an Abomination. The smile yellows, the eyes bleed and stink, and all pleasure falls away like rotten fruit.

Seth meets Ayla's eyes, and they sprint forward, grab the machine by the arms, lift it into the air, and carry it toward the body of the Master. A metal arm swings down into Seth's abdomen, and he grunts. His knees buckle as they drop the machine and it falls into the swirling machinations of the Instrument. The Music grinds the machine to a twisted, sparking heap, and there is an ear-bursting screech like scraping strings, and a rumble of stones like falling towers.

A hush descends. The machine is in a ruinous heap, but its eyes . . .

Its eyes remain aimed at Seth.

Seth cradles his abdomen. Ayla's voice is shrill in his ear. "You're bleeding?" But the sound is nearly lost in the groaning approach of the Music as it begins anew.

"Merciful Almighty, there's so much blood. Get up. You have to get up."

He looks up and his eyes sting with the dust of falling stone. His fingers feel thick, cold, and sticky. Something strains against his arm, and he stands to relieve the pressure. It twists him around and he stumbles, sensing crumbling violence filtered through the darkness overtaking his vision.

There is Music like cruel noise, as if all is only painful percussion. No singing, only shredding screams and gargling gutturals, and the tug of . . .

Ayla. Her arm against his, so beautiful and thin and strong. And her fingers. They are cold.

Pain. He bends and gags and nearly vomits, but she jerks him up, and he stumbles forward.

"Hurry!"

"I am," he says, or does he merely think it?

Light stabs through the darkness. His heartbeat washes the Music from his ears, and jungle air is thick in his throat. She is kissing his face with those beautiful lips, so soft, so perfectly formed. She is telling him of how close they are, and that if he just stays awake, it will all be fine.

He hopes she doesn't stop, for the pain is unbearable, but her voice and lips are gone, and they are rushing forward again. His toes grab sand and he falls into Water, and the last thing he thinks, as Time engulfs him, is how Ayla's fingers feel as they slip out of his.

Then there is only the Music, rumbling and shaking the Waters with thunderous peals.

PART EIGHT

THE RETURN OF CAIN

But when you see the abomination of desolation standing where he ought not to be (let the reader understand), then let those who are in Judea flee to the mountains. Let the one who is on the housetop not go down, nor enter his house, to take anything out, and let the one who is in the field not turn back to take his cloak. . . . For false christs and false prophets will arise and perform signs and wonders, to lead astray, if possible, the elect.

—MARK 13:14–16, 22 ESV

40

Cain studied the way Lukian's eyes bored into him. Was it disgust, or hatred? Mason's arms hovered at his sides, tensed, and Cain's other sons, Kiile and Machael, stood alive and prepared for violence. The Abomination had wanted them, too, but Cain would give it no more.

Do they sense what prowls inside me, and how it lusts for the very warmth of their veins?

Mason edged toward Lukian. Kiile nudged Machael and said, "Is it him?"

Lukian shook his head. "Cain is dead." He lifted his bloodied hammer. "And even if he weren't, there's no place for him anymore."

Cain laughed, and by doing so, let the Abomination slip past. "I see," the Abomination said through Cain. "You were doing well without me? I thought you were in danger, but now I see."

Cain thrust the Abomination back and wiped away the moisture that beaded on his face. Mason's fingers twitched. Kiile shuffled left, then right. Machael stared with those half-open eyes. Lukian wrung his hands on the handle of his weapon while the children waited for their elders to react.

"It's an illusion. A demon from hell," Lukian said.

"You're right. I have changed, and return more than a man," Cain said. "Days ago, in the darkness of the wilderness, I died. But then I rose again, crawled before the Almighty's throne, and bled the life from his veins. I've brought a bit of hell back with me." His eyes widened as he fought against the Abomination's demands for control. *This is my time*, he thought, *my own.* "You know the truth, but some have yet to admit it. The Almighty is dead. And I am returning to claim what is mine."

"And that is?" Lukian said.

"Your worship."

Their legs were rooted like plants awaiting harvest, their rosy cheeks plump with blood. He quelled the pale thirst and wondered if they sensed his struggle.

"Are you insane?" Kiile said.

"Bow," Cain said.

Lukian spread his feet and gripped his weapon with both hands, and Mason drew up his knuckles. Kiile and Machael pointed their weapons forward, and their boys did likewise.

The Abomination's laugh was loud in Cain's mind. It said for his ears alone, *"Resistance can only be met with violence,"* and Cain's nostrils flared. "Would all of you rather die than follow my commands?"

"You abandoned us, but we survived your absence," Lukian said.

Cain said, "Where are your children?"

Lukian didn't respond. His face reddened.

"When you found their bodies mutilated on the ground, why didn't you breathe life back into their lungs? Why didn't you heal their wounds?" Cain said.

"Shut your mouth."

"So angry."

Lukian lifted his hammer high and burst into a sprint. Cain readied himself as Lukian swung, and just before the hammer struck, he grabbed it by the head, stopping it midswing. Lukian pitched forward as his hands slipped, and he tumbled to the ground.

Kiile yelled, and Machael and a few of the younger boys dashed forward. Lukian scrambled to his feet, brushed them off, and faced Cain, who held the hammer by the head as if it were a toy.

Silence. Mason, Kiile, Machael, and the others stared. No one moved.

"You have two choices." Cain tossed the hammer toward Lukian. "Bow to me"—he snapped his fingers, and eyes lit the Fog like stars in the sky—"or die."

Lukian grabbed his hammer and raised it. There were finger-prints pressed into the metal where Cain grabbed it.

"Think of your wives. Think of the children too weak to stray from the Temple," Cain said.

"You're a coward," Lukian said.

"No, Son. I am God."

◆ ◆ ◆

To Calebna, the Temple seemed alive with whispered prayers. The boys, including Jacob, stood in a corner of the vestibule with arms crossed, and the women sat like seeds scattered from the sower's hand. They were blinded by the simple fact that God had not saved them as Calebna had claimed. To them, Philo was not just a corpse, he was the embodiment of God's abandonment. It didn't matter that the boy had run headlong into danger. Philo's motionless body was the final emphasis to their bitter question: *"Why have faith in a dead God?"*

And Calebna stood in front of them as the last remnant of that faith.

I lost control, Calebna thought, *and Philo and Tuor died while I abased myself before the Almighty's shadowed throne.*

After all the sacrifices I spilled before your feet, after all the love I lavished on your name . . . Is the presence I sensed nothing more than the imaginings of my mind?

Almighty God, if you truly exist, then kill Lukian. Take his life before he steals my family. Remember me before I disappear.

Gorban crawled to Sarah, who lay curled into herself. Calebna was surprised he felt no hatred toward the wife of the man who had caused all of this.

But we are both scarlet letters drawn in the blood of our kin. No one could have stopped him from killing my father. I know this now for certain. Cain and Lukian, alike in so many ways.

And what of me? What of my father?

Abel had walked between the lines Cain had trampled, and for all this time, Calebna had tried carrying on his father's legacy, as he saw Lukian carrying Cain's. But he could do it no longer. Calebna was no holy man.

I'm the worst of them all. I'm a dirty man who thought himself clean.

Kill Lukian. Kill him quickly.

Terah returned through the archway, passed Calebna as if he were a ghost, and handed Ben to Keshra, of all women, the deepest insult. As Terah knelt beside Philo and pressed her face into her brother's bloody breast and wept, Ben gazed at her with disturbing solemnity.

Her opinion of me is ruined by grief. And bitterness. Or are those two separate? My brothers are dead and I feel . . . nothing.

He glanced at Gorban, who examined the red and brown soaked through the bandage on his leg. Peth came out again and replaced the soiled fabric, and Gorban cried out as the wounded skin tore with the fabric, but soon clean wool secured his leg, and the two lay in each other's arms.

Calebna stood a while longer, and as the flavor of failure made bitter his soul, three hollow knocks turned his gaze toward the Temple doors, and the last knock resonated long and hard, like a gong sounding the passing of an age. He blinked as if waking from a long dream, walked to the towering doors, slid the iron bars from the handles, and pushed the doors open enough to reveal a host of bloodied men.

Lukian, Gorban, Mason, Kiile, Michael, and their boys shouldered past him. Then a voice he knew all too well made the hair on the back of his neck prickle.

"Hello, Nephew."

From behind them entered a familiar figure leading a host of Jinn. The women screamed at the sight of the beasts, and some fled the room, but the familiar man lifted his hand, and all the world seemed to hush.

Calebna blinked. It looked just like Cain, but there were details amiss. The skin looked as if it had been cured and dyed a dusty gray, and black vertebral marks shot down his arms and lined the top of each finger like snake bones. His lips were a deep shade of red so as to appear black, but his eyes were iridescent silver. They shone in the dim torchlight like marbles polished round and popped into his eye sockets.

Calebna waved his arms, and his voice was angry. "You let demons defile the Temple of the Almighty?"

"This is no Temple anymore." Cain laughed. "It is just a cage for fools. And you've caught yourselves for me."

Calebna shivered. Gorban's hand slid to the weapon at his side, but Cain's glare swiveled toward him. "Release your weapon," Cain said.

Gorban didn't move There was dangerous silence.

"The beasts behind me will rip your throat out if you do not obey me."

Sarah grabbed Gorban's arm. There were tears in her eyes, but they seemed not to come from fear. "Do as he says."

Eve also came up beside Gorban and laid her hand on his shoulder. He let go of his weapon.

Calebna gazed at them, a tattered and broken people, driven to the edge by starvation and demonic pressures. They were at their weakest, and the demon, or man, that looked like Cain had chosen this moment to appear. Such a thing could not be a coincidence.

Cain spread his arms. "What you see is truth. I am Cain, and I have returned for my family."

Calebna's legs shook with the effort to stand, and he found his mind fighting to disbelieve. His eyes narrowed as he took in the differences between what he saw and what he remembered. *If you truly are who you appear to be . . .*

"I have come to save you from yourselves. To save you from the world my father corrupted." Cain paced. "Tell me, where is he? Where is Adam, first among men?"

"He is sick," Eve said. "Since you left." And her gaze bored into Cain.

Cain said, "Go then, and bring Father here, for I have returned to establish the New Religion and usher us into our glorious future."

Eve motioned for Machael to retrieve Adam, and so he left, though not before hesitating with his hand perilously close to the weapon at his side.

"We have reached the threshold to our future as a race. Immortality is within your reach. All that is left is to accept the invitation. You need only pledge yourselves to me, and I promise I will give you everlasting life."

Lukian turned his back to them and rolled his shoulders, and Calebna wondered what had happened on the battlefield. He scanned the men who had returned and realized none of Lukian's children were present. He knew how volatile Lukian could be. If the man's children had been murdered, there would be nothing that would stop him from exacting revenge on everyone he thought responsible.

But why would he not look at Cain?

Calebna observed the Jinn standing in the doorway. Did Cain control them? Was he in league with them? He looked back and said, "There is only one Tree of Life, and it is guarded by a cheru bim and a flaming sword. You say you will give us immortality, but you lie. It could never be so easy."

"It isn't easy," Cain said.

"Then what is it?"

"An alternative to death."

Silence.

Cain said, "I have been to the depths of hell and ascended to the throne of the Almighty. I have met the Devil and killed God. Look at you—gathered in your Temple, so afraid, so weak. You worship the dead, but I am the Living Death. I killed God and I became God. And now your God speaks." He offered them an open hand. "Follow me or die."

41

Seth opened his eyes and strained to grasp at the smallest bit of light, but found nothing. He brought his hands to his face and felt his eyes. They were open, but he saw nothing. His mind registered the stiffness in his back, and his nose was assaulted by vile smells. He twisted and threw out an arm, but his hand smashed against stone and he cried out.

Shapes and forms joined in his mind. He pulled his hand back, massaged his wrist, and winced, but in the blackness he was unsure his facial expression had changed. He carefully touched flat walls to his left and right, and with difficulty and no small amount of shimmying, edged his arm above his head and found a ceiling.

He was alone in a small, enclosed space filled with darkness. His mind raced, recalling strange images of an ocean, a forest, an underground labyrinth, endless vats filled with tortured creatures, and a machine. Melodies bloomed over remembered instrumentation, and though the sounds were no more than phantoms, he knew their shapes held meaning. It was a great Music, and he and Ayla had been drawn by it into the underground labyrinth, and followed the machine until . . .

He patted his stomach. He didn't feel any wounds.

I could be dead, he thought. *Is this what death feels like?*

But he had already died before washing up onto the Sands. The machine had attacked him, and he had bled and lost consciousness in the Water. If he weren't capable of dying again, then what did the wound mean?

He shifted onto his back and tried to clear his mind. His breath reflected hot and stale, and the smell of death permeated every inch of space. He pushed against the walls and screamed until his voice tore like a dry garment, but no answer came.

He slammed his feet against the sides, then scooted his legs up until his knees were against the wall in front of him. He held his breath and pushed until his head swelled with blood. The wall popped free and light stabbed his eyes. He gasped and recoiled, curling his knees up and covering his face with his forearm.

He slid his arm away and his eyes struggled and ached. There was an ocean of blue, and in it floated white islands. He wondered if he was high above, looking down at a vast sea. His eyes regained their focus.

"The sky," he whispered.

He grabbed the stone cover that he realized was above him and, as he leaned up, pushed it until it fell to the earth with a thud. He stood shakily and hopped onto the brown grass that cracked like dry bones. He straightened and looked at the stone tub that had encased him. It sat like an empty stomach belching stench as if filled with dead rats.

"A tomb?" He rubbed his temple with two fingers and waved the reek from his face. He spun on his heels and, for the first time, noticed the Temple on the hill behind him.

The whole world seemed dead. The trees were burnt husks, hollow chaff of a world that was no longer. Though the Temple was here, this was no longer the City of the Almighty. This was something else entirely.

His eyes traced a line over two identical boxes sitting next to his. He stared at them for a few blank moments. They were tombs, sealed shut as his had been.

Ayla!

Seth ran to the closer of the two and pressed his ear to the top. There was no sound, but that meant nothing. He tried to pull off the sealed cover, but couldn't. He dug his fingernails under the edge until he bent his nails back. He grabbed a stone and smashed it against the seal. As he made his way around, pounding the seal as he went, pieces of the stone broke off and stung his skin. He tossed his tool, pulled the lid up, and flung it away. The tomb was empty.

Who would seal an empty tomb? Had another dead man woken like me? But it was sealed . . .

A high-pitched, muffled cry prickled the hair on the back of his neck. He turned and ran to the third tomb, his heart hammering his lungs like they were bells. He smashed the seal and threw the cover to the ground, and there lay Ayla curled into herself. She screamed and squinted against the brightness. But a moment later, she stood, threw her arms around him, and sobbed into his shoulder.

"You're all right," he said. "I'm here." He rubbed her back and arms and kissed her hair. "I'm here." Upon feeling the rise and fall of her chest against his, all doubt fled, and he believed. He cried and laughed at once because she was alive. Because they were both alive.

"Was it real?" Ayla said.

"I was there. The Water. The jungle. The Song."

"I thought you were dead," she said.

He hushed her. "I'm here. So are you."

"I see it when I close my eyes."

"It's gone. And we're alive. Everything is going to be all right."

She pressed her face into his neck, and he looked out on the dead grasses and trees, the shriveled flowers and brown pall. He swallowed and his throat pressed against Ayla's head. Memories returned from before he awoke in that place beyond the edge of Time. The longer he thought, the more he remembered. And the more he remembered, the more he trembled.

I lied to her. Nothing is all right. I've escaped my dreams only to land in my nightmares. "God, wake us up," he whispered.

"What?"

"Nothing." He kissed her hair and held her tighter. "Nothing."

42

C ain crouched, plucked a blade of grass, brought it to his nose, and sniffed. His heightened senses constructed a list of the few animals that had brushed against it: a mouse, a fox, and a wild dog. But the smells were days old, and little was left of their delicate forms. He rose and scanned the rolling hills. There were patches of green here and there, the first visible signs of life during the last two days of travel.

"The curse spread quickly."

The Abomination. Cain was struck by the oddity that no one but he knew of the Abomination's existence. No one but he knew that he was possessed by the very son of the Devil.

He lifted a hand to his chest and clutched his breast where a pain had developed the last two days. The pale thirst was strong, and grew stronger every day, but to feed was to nourish the Abomination. That, of all things, was what he most feared, and so he waited.

Someone slipped loose rocks from the cliff, and the sound of them skipping into the valley of the City of the Almighty echoed on and on. Cain turned. Lukian had pulled himself over the lip and brushed sand and dust from his tunic. Kiile and Mason followed and lifted Gorban, whose leg remained unusable.

The people had grown soft in the comfort of nearly two years of safety, but the awareness of life in the wild would wake them soon.

"Lukian's mind is burning against you."

The Abomination's words kept breaking through his thoughts. He was angered by it, but felt the sting of its perception nonetheless.

"Learn your place," he whispered. "It is early still. He is my son. My eldest . . ."

"Now you taste power, but can you swallow it?"

His tongue tingled with the sensations. It was like tasting blood, like drinking life. He looked at his gray skin, saw the paleness, and wondered how many more days he could wait. Would he need to slip away unnoticed?

Mason dipped to help Sarah up. She clutched his arm as he lifted and set her atop the cliff. She stood tall and erect as she let go of her son's muscled arm, and her dress rippled against her slender frame as she stumbled on a rolling stone. Mason caught her by the forearm, but still she looked so elegant, notwithstanding how gaunt she was from days of starvation. He noticed the nearly imperceptible bump of her lower abdomen growing to accommodate what developed inside.

Pregnant, Cain thought. *My unborn child grows, just as she said. I knew it was more than a dream.*

"*So why will she not look at you, let alone touch you?*"

He clenched his hands as the Abomination returned to wag its tongue in his ear.

"*She should fear you. It is better yet that she hate you. You cannot allow any to become too comfortable in your presence. That was the mistake the Almighty made. They slipped from his grip and began to question him. And they will question you too. Suffering is the only true teacher. Be free with your rod.*"

He realized he was nodding, and Lukian was watching. Their gazes met, and Cain could hardly hear anything beyond the Abomination's exclamations. He quieted it and, with great struggle, rejected its grab for power. It had become so difficult to maintain control, and doing so now squeezed sweat through his pores. He wiped his face and shifted away.

The Abomination. Bloodthirsty destruction manifested in personhood. It wanted to consume—to *grow*—but the time was not yet ripe. The Abomination thirsted for the human soul above all else, and he could pacify it for a while with animals, but there was a chance that Lukian might still prove useful. Cain hadn't yet been able to test the Waters for the certainty he needed, but he had sensed the possibility.

He chuckled, though he knew the Abomination heard and rightly divined its cause. *The trouble with possibilities is they contain both deliverance and danger. I must wait. I must endure the chaos. Just a little while longer . . .*

Lukian stared at him, and Cain turned eastward, determined to focus on their destination.

Towering trees and leaves like fans in the morning. The smell of damp life, the relief of shade, and the touch of cool water bubbling from deep underground. A place we can begin anew. A place to observe the New Religion.

"The place where I am God," he whispered, resisting the foreboding he sensed from that place beyond Time.

The desert wilderness made him long for green life. He thought back to the days spent in the underground City of the Light Bringer, and how the relentless stone and pale light had grown to a buzzing drone. But he bit his cheek upon thinking of the dark chamber and the goblet of blood. Cain was no longer the same boy straining for Adam's acceptance. The Abomination had changed him.

Or had he changed himself? Upon giving himself to the Abomination at the edge of his life in the wilderness, both his person and body had become something new, but where had the opportunity for that change originated? Cain and the Abomination had merged in an unholy coupling, like naked bodies in the dark, and yet even then the change had not been fully realized.

He breathed and flexed his forearms to feel the strength that coursed through his veins; part gift of the Almighty, part human evolution. He savored it as he savored its beginnings through the sound of a breaking skull. He had done it. He had proved his supremacy and gained a power none had imagined.

Now he was God. He was Satan.

But inside there remained turbulence. With so much power, how could he not calm the Waters? Why had everything become so much more perilous?

Because you've set yourself in the Abomination's crucible. You've used it to gain supremacy, but at what cost?

He did not know. Perhaps the Man would have known, but the Man was dead.

Kiile whispered to Gorban, who hushed him, and Cain turned and spoke so they all could hear. "If we continue at the same pace, we will arrive a day early. Though it will be a strain on the wounded, I assure you it will be worth the struggle. The haven I have prepared for you is without equal."

Sarah shifted her eyes away as Cain neared. He was captivated by her neck and shoulders, the way the musculature wove under her delicate skin, and how the artery rolled to the rhythm of the Music—or was it the other way around? He averted his gaze and cleared his throat. "I assure you that when we arrive, everything will become clear."

Cain sensed Sarah's gaze flick his direction, but only for a moment, and looked in time to see her twirl away. Mason observed him, then turned and followed his mother.

Cain stared at the space she had occupied. The others watched him, and he suppressed the Abomination's motion for control. "We rest for the night."

43

The Temple entrance loomed as Seth reached for Ayla's fingers and remembered the smell of the air as they stood before the mouth of the ruinous Shrine of the Song. "The last time we saw this Temple, it was shrouded in darkness and storm."

Ayla nodded. "I barely reached you in time. If I hadn't seen you hobbling into the storm and followed after, what would have happened?"

"I wouldn't be here. And neither would you."

She brushed the golden doors. "This world feels so unreal in comparison. I keep wondering if maybe I am sleeping on the Sands and dreaming of us being in this place. That maybe you really are dead, as you should have been after that terrible machine . . ."

"You know this is real."

"So what was the Shrine? What was the Music? What was the machine, the forest?"

"That too was real."

"I saw it stab you. I held my hand against your deadly wound and felt your blood between my fingers. If that was real, then how are we here? *Why* are we here?"

"I don't know. But we must behave as if both worlds exist in more than just our minds." He quieted and thought once more of his nightmares.

Ayla said, "Do you think we will find ourselves there again?"

"I hope not."

"I keep thinking of what the machine said about another City where a different Music plays."

"I remember it speaking of Watchers as well, but we saw none.

Maybe the City is nothing more than a myth, something the machine used to entice us deeper into the Shrine."

"Maybe," she said. "But what if it does exist? What if that City, and the Music that plays there, was what we failed to find in the Shrine?"

Seth remembered the sensuous pull of the Song, how he had longed to give in, and where those desires brought him. What could war against such darkness but Light itself? He smiled, feeling a bit of the normalcy between them from before they opened themselves to the Music. "I thought I was the positive one."

"That's why you smile so much."

Seth's ears retuned to the deafening silence, and his smile faded like the color of the world they inhabited. He grabbed the handle of the Temple door and swung it wide. Together they entered and shut the door behind them.

After their eyes adjusted, Ayla said, "Someone is in the sacrificial chamber."

He strained to see past the ghosts of sunlight. "What do you see?"

"Torchlight, I think."

Slowly, a dim glow appeared at the far end of the room, as if from around a bend.

She squeezed his hand and whispered, "Someone is here."

He hushed her. "Don't speak until we know it is safe."

"Why?"

"Do you not remember what happened before we first came to the Temple in the storm? If everything we heard was true—as I believe it is—if Cain murdered Abel and the Almighty is gone, then this Temple is no longer what it was."

"The Almighty isn't gone," Ayla said.

"What do you mean?" he said.

"You say everything we remember is real."

"We saw his empty throne, his bloodied crown and robe."

"We saw a Place that should not exist," she said.

"What about the silence of the City of the Almighty? The dead grass and trees?"

"We *died*, but now we're *alive*," Ayla said. "You know as well as I do that we should have sunk into the depths of those Waters. Something took hold of us. That's why I let go of you."

It would make a terrible sort of sense if he weren't able to remember the nightmares that had thrown him into seizures before they passed into that world beyond worlds. "You may be sure, but I'm not. Just trust me."

She paused long, then said, "I will."

"We stay to the shadows as much as we can. And don't let go of my hand. I will not be separated from you again."

He thought she nodded, but heard no response. He sensed in her silence, in the way she moved, that she knew he was keeping something from her. He wanted to brush it off, but could no longer behave as if the world were no more than a reason to smile. He had seen the future and experienced the Song, and for her own sake, he could not tell her much. Because telling her would change her behavior and influence the outcome, and she would not survive it. However, silence held its own dangers—some that he couldn't avoid.

Seth pulled her closer as they edged through the hallway. There was a sharp smack of metal against stone, and she jumped. It happened again, and they flattened against the wall of the hallway where the shadows were deepest. Again a loud smack, and with it a grunt and the sound of toppling tables or lampstands.

He slipped past Ayla and motioned for her to stay, though she followed anyway. As they reached the end of the hall, they both peeked around the corner. She breathed sharply, and he clamped a hand over her mouth and pulled her back.

Ayla pushed his hand away. "Is that . . . ?"

He motioned for silence, but said, "Calebna."

◆　◆　◆

Calebna had carefully gathered the rugs, tapestries, lampstands, tables, and benches, and placed them in front of the altar that was still dirty from the celebration that marked the beginning of the end of his life. Calebna had to scoot the ashen bones of Abel's sheep in order to make room for the items, and still pieces tumbled down the sides.

"Sacrifice." The word echoed through the chamber, brilliant and brief, like a spark underwater. "The last servant of the Almighty stands where all things have come to an end. Here, he will join his God."

Calebna walked to the wall where the torch sat, wrapped his fingers around the wooden handle, and lifted it from its receptacle. He stood watching the flames drip, then walked to the pile and touched fire to oil. Flaming tides swept up the heap, and the fabrics burned and crackled and sent sparks to the ceiling like dying stars. Calebna stood back, raised his arms to the blaze, as if listening to some far-off Music. Oil dripped from his hands as he closed his eyes.

"As evil was born through one decision, so it will be destroyed through atonement."

Atonement. The exchange of life for life. An endless cycle.

Today, for Calebna at least, that cycle would end. He opened his eyes and walked closer, his sandals crunching glowing ashes. "They left me because I believed in you." He wiped his face with his forearm, feeling emotions claw out of hiding. "I lost everything for you. For a lie."

Calebna took another step forward. The heat of the flames urged his eyes closed, but he spread his arms wide. He thought of Terah, Jacob, and Ben. It had been two days since they left, and though he had been sure Jacob, at least, would have returned, he hadn't. No one had.

This was how God rewarded the faithful. This was the lot of the righteous. He had done everything he could to serve God and lead his family in the way the Man commanded, yet he would die alone.

By my own hand, and in the time of my choosing.

"Now." He let the word linger amongst the sizzling refuse, as if the flames would listen. He opened his eyes to examine the force that would unite him with his God. The heap was a molten, slumping mountain. Tongues of fire licked the air, and beyond them . . .

What is that?

He squinted and discerned an upright shape in the hallway beyond the sacrificial altar.

He stepped back from the flames and shuffled past the pile to see more clearly. Yes, he could see a man standing in plain sight in the entryway. A man he recognized, but who could not be there, because he had been dead for weeks.

"Seth?" Calebna's lips dried, and he passed his hand over his eyes. The man was still there. "You died. You were dead. You *should* be dead."

Seth stepped closer.

"Stay back," Calebna said.

Seth raised his palms. "I won't harm you."

Calebna pointed at him. "You came to take me with you."

Seth frowned as if confused. Speaking slowly, he said, "I have come to take you with me, but perhaps not to where you expect."

The heat of the flames seemed to singe the hair on the back of Calebna's neck. He shook his head and dropped to his knees. "Not there. You can't take me there." He clenched his teeth. "I gave my life for him."

Seth laughed. "I'm not here to usher you into the afterlife."

Calebna glanced up. "Either this is a dream, or I am dead." He looked at the fire and imagined his body lying there. Had he killed himself without realizing?

"Give me a moment to explain. Don't be impatient."

"Patience has given me only pain. I won't be swayed by the lies of a demon," Calebna said. Was he lying there, his skin crackling and bubbling in the heat?

"I am no demon. I am Seth, third son of Adam, once dead and twice alive. I have returned to this world to do something. Maybe to help you." He glanced at the flaming hump of refuse, then at Calebna.

"If you're not a demon, then tell me how you are alive. I helped seal you in your tomb. I touched your body after Mason found you dead in this very Temple."

Seth's smile faded.

Calebna waved his hand. "Enough lies. Leave me in peace if you won't give me answers."

Seth stirred and licked his lips. "Why not put your torch down and follow me outside?"

"Because I'm going to kill myself."

Seth stopped. His reaction made Calebna question if he could be real. But there had been so much death. If Seth truly were alive, why him and not Abel? Why now instead of days ago, when he needed a sign, when he pleaded for help to the point of tears? He turned away. "If only you were more than a ghost."

"Do you deny that a ghost could possess knowledge you do not?"

"I deny your existence."

"What danger lies in following me and listening, just for a moment?"

"The fire will only last so long."

"If sight and sound won't cure your doubts . . ." Seth approached and offered his hand. "Touch me. Feel my body."

Calebna stared at him.

"Grab my hand and tell me I'm not real."

Calebna reached and touched Seth's fingers. They felt thick and warm. He retreated a step, his mind reeling for a way to explain the mystery before him. "If you're not a dream, I must look like a fool."

"You look desperate."

"I suppose I am," Calebna said.

"I cannot help our family alone."

Could it be real? "A legion could not help them. The whole world is lost."

"You don't believe that."

"Why do you think I'm here?"

"You plainly had plans before I arrived," Seth said. "Leave me to fulfill them."

"First, tell me why you paused when you saw me."

Calebna tried to answer, but instead swallowed hard.

Seth continued, "What reason could there be besides that you thought it possible somehow to start over, to heal?"

"I lost my family. My God. How can you heal what's no longer there?"

"I don't know. But that does not mean it can't be done."

"There's nothing left for me now."

"Then why did you stop?"

Because I hoped you were my son, Calebna thought. But he couldn't say that. He couldn't say anything.

"I can't imagine the darkness you've endured, but maybe that's why I've returned," Seth said.

Calebna thought of his speech at the funeral, the way Eve had dipped to touch Seth's cheek, and the grind of stone as they sealed the tombs. But here Seth stood with fingers that felt all too real, and a voice that reasoned just like the man he had known.

"I was dead, but now I am alive, and I think you are the reason why," Seth said.

"How could I be?"

Seth offered his hand again. "Let me show you."

44

S arah walked to the edge of the cliff. Stars dotted the sky and lit the valley beyond the drop, and in the distance lay the walled City of the Almighty. The mountains circled it like the cupped hands of God, and the river running through it shimmered like a serpent caught between his fingers.

"It is as beautiful as when I first saw it." Sarah glanced at Mason, who sat cross-legged at the edge. He was staring at her silently, sternly. "You were too serious, even as a child." She nodded toward the City. "Do you miss it already?"

He clenched his jaw.

She folded her arms for warmth. "I wonder if we will ever return."

It seemed Mason considered the thought, then looked at his fingernails to pick the dirt from beneath them.

Sarah sat beside him and let her feet dangle over the edge. She looked below and her stomach coiled at the distance. She shifted back. "I know what you did for me."

He tipped his head.

"Peth said you never left my side."

Mason gazed at the night sky and breathed toward the City.

"You speak with your presence." She bit her cheek, resisting the emotions that had surged through her since awakening. "Thank you." And then she could resist no longer. She wiped her cheeks and nose, and leaned her head against his shoulder. He was a rock long warmed by the sun, something solid to keep her upright. Her guardian. Her protector. "I am frightened." She glanced toward the men and women by the fire thirty yards away. "I can't find Cain."

Mason's gaze flicked toward her, and his eyebrows crouched. "Your father was always a hard man, but he was never a monster." She let the silence extend. "Maybe Cain is still in there, somewhere, but something has changed. I can feel *it*, but I cannot feel *him*. No? I don't know either what I mean by that. I just feel that something isn't right with him." She stood, crossing her forearms over her belly. She caught Mason glancing at the motion and acted as if she had been brushing dust from her tunic.

In the sky, the North Star shone like the point of a sword stabbing a veil, and the moon hung beneath it naked, exposed.

"I always wondered why the Almighty never let you speak. It made me angry, all those years. Now, for the first time, I'm thankful for your silence."

◆ ◆ ◆

Calebna stared at the empty tomb of the Almighty and rubbed away the oil he had drenched himself in. "Tell me how you died."

Seth exchanged a knowing glance with Ayla, who shrugged. "When Adam returned and told us Cain had killed—" Seth stopped short and studied Calebna, as if realizing too late what he was about to say.

Calebna said, "My father has been dead for weeks. Hearing the truth can wound me no deeper."

"Forgive me. There are many things still positioning themselves in my mind," Seth said.

"You are forgiven. But hide nothing out of fear of offending me. I have grown tired of subtle deceits and hidden intentions."

Seth rubbed his fingers together and cleared his throat. "When Father told us Cain killed Abel, I thought he was lying. My mind knew it was true, but I thought that if he were dead, surely the Almighty could give life back to him. So I ran to the Temple."

"Foolishly," Ayla added. "He was injured after throwing himself against rocks."

"Why in God's name would you do such a thing?" Calebna asked, then sat on the edge of the Almighty's tomb.

"Ayla enjoys embellishing when the result is me looking foolish."

Ayla scowled. "He was assaulted by visions and thrown to the ground. I saw him fall, and when he awoke, I helped him to shelter, where Adam told us what happened. Lilleth was there, but ran into the storm. Tell me, is she with the others?"

"Mother disappeared that night and still has not been found." Calebna pressed his palms into his eyes, and for the first time, allowed himself to feel the depth of that loss. His throat ached as he said, "Every single one of Lukian's children, then Philo, Tuor, and Kiile's eldest and youngest. So many lives have been lost."

"Are you the only one left?" Ayla said.

"I'm the only one who stayed."

Seth laid a hand on his wife's leg. "We still haven't answered his questions. I, too, would like to hear what has happened, but it should wait until we finish."

Calebna once again stifled his emotions, for duty had ingrained in him the ability to do so quickly and without strain. "What did you see when you arrived at the Temple?"

"The torches were extinguished and no light reached past its doors, but I had to see the Holy of Holies before believing the Man was gone," Seth said.

"I found Seth lying facedown before the throne of the Almighty. And in the throne—" Ayla bit her lip.

"Did you see the Almighty?" Calebna rested his elbows on his knees. He sensed a hardness in his own heart, and thought bitterly of what had forced him to become so.

"We saw his torn and bloody cloak, and on top of it his crown, but not him. I could no longer deny Adam's claims. I lost myself."

"But then there was a flash, and the world went dark," Ayla said.

"Went dark?"

"All sound and sight were simply gone. The only way I can explain it is that my soul had been a tense coil, and instantly, I was released," Seth said.

Calebna eyed them.

Ayla nodded. "The world slipped away like a heavy cloak, and after floating through nothingness, I awoke on a beach with Seth, who I didn't recognize."

"You both died and somehow just ended up in the same exact place?" Calebna said.

"It was a place that should not exist. A place beyond this world."

Calebna squinted, but waved them on nonetheless. "What happened next?"

"We were drawn into a jungle by this beautiful Music. We ended up in a grove filled with ruined buildings. We entered the ruins to a place called the Shrine of the Song, where we were greeted by this . . . thing."

Calebna waited for more, but neither spoke. "Can you describe this *thing*?"

Seth chuckled and rubbed his scalp. It was a nervous habit that reminded Calebna of Cain, and he thought, *This is now Cain's only brother. I wonder what Eve would do if she knew he was alive?*

"It was like a human," Seth explained, "and yet made of metal. A word for it came to me then: *machine*. That was what I called it in my mind, though everything sounds so very strange to me now that I speak it."

"I've known much strangeness in the past few weeks," Calebna said.

Ayla stood and began to pace. "But you have never seen anything like the Shrine. It was enrapturing, and the Music walked with us. It grew and changed into something we hadn't expected, and we came to understand it was capable of affecting this world."

"What do you mean?"

Ayla glanced at Seth, who said, "The machine showed us a window through which we could view the Song's inner workings. The Music we heard in that place beyond Time is driving some sort of contention here. I think that it is somehow at the root of everything that has happened."

"You are saying the Music killed my father?"

"I'm not saying that. However, the machine claimed we could become Instruments of the Song. We're not sure we know all of what it means, but we do think that we can stop it."

"How can you stop what you don't understand?"

"The machine's speech was strange, but what we saw through that window was clear enough. We are all parts of a singular conflict, one whose origin lies beyond the Sands of Time."

"So how will you save us?"

"I can't. Not alone. The machine talked as though we were the vectors of the Song. It was as if the Music had been constructed to entice us, but its true purpose was much more sinister."

"Death," Ayla whispered.

Seth looked up. "A living death."

Calebna's scorn turned to interest. "You think the Music has done more than just influence this world. You think it has come to life."

"There is some Thing here that never should have been, and it is the centerpiece of a struggle spanning all of Time; a struggle beyond us, but for some reason conducted through us. It grows in power only as we give it power. In this way, then, I think we could stop it. Not one man alone, but together through the choices we make, through the evil we refuse to tend in our minds like Forbidden Gardens." Seth paused. "Danger and deliverance lurk in every decision, and if we stray but a little, all humanity might be lost."

Calebna leaned back, looked at his hands, and realized they were fisted. He rubbed the sweat from his palms, thought of Cain's gray skin, and said, "If what you say is true, Almighty help us all."

45

Lukian slipped away just below the edge of the forest to relieve himself while the others bustled around the fire and gathered water to boil roots dug out of the hillside. He stayed away because, judging by the stillness around him, no one seemed to have followed, and he desired solitude.

"Blood. Why blood?" He shook his head, trying to rid it of the incessant buzzing. All he wanted was to see it again—to smash a living skull and watch the life ooze out, to smell the smell and taste the taste. "Maybe it was the children."

Yes. Maybe watching his children die had broken something. Or maybe, in that instant, he had simply given himself up to something that had been there all along. Whatever it was, as he found his children murdered and knelt in their lifeblood, he was consumed by raw desire, and now that desire chewed at his insides.

A chill rushed past, and with it, a whispering voice, thin and harsh, like distant Music carried on the wind. He felt a pinch at his neck, rubbed it, and brought his hand away marked with thin lines of red. There were footsteps, and through the darkness approached a small boy whose skin was silver, as if the flesh had died and only just begun decaying. The hair on Lukian's back tingled as scar-like memories ached. "Lamech?" he said. It looked just like the twin brother he had lost to the Jinn. But how could it be?

The boy stopped and seemed to assess him. It nodded and whispered, *"I have seen the war, both outside and in, and have come from beyond to give guidance."*

"Brother?" He reached for the boy's hand, which he saw clenched and dappled with blood. Then the boy grabbed Lukian's fingers, and he realized that the apparition before him was more than just a ghost. It was real enough to touch and feel. It was soft and warm, all its blood on the inside, not on the outside as his memory had betrayed his eyes into seeing just moments ago. "Is it you?"

No answer. Just that presence. Just those fingers in his hand. Just those eyes staring into his.

Words spilled from his mouth like water over broken levees. "I shouldn't have pushed you into that cursed Fog. I should have urged you away. I should have grabbed your cloak and pulled hard enough to twist you around. I should have run before—"

"I am free." Three simple words whose impact stemmed the flood. *"And soon,"* it said, *"if you follow my guidance, you will be as well."*

"But how?" Lukian bent as if craning to see a detail too small. "What do I need to do?"

"Listen and obey. Will you promise to do that?"

"I am dreaming," he said. "This is a dream."

"Will you promise?" As if plucking it from its back, it reached behind and pulled out a pale fruit the size of a peach. It raised it so Lukian could see it unshadowed, and its skin seemed to shimmer— or was it a trick of the eyes? *"Taste and see."*

Lukian was reaching for the fruit, but didn't remember directing his hand to do so. Then the fruit was in his hand, but he didn't remember grabbing it. The world was moving in strange shifts, as though Time itself were skipping beats. The fruit was in his hand by his waist, then at his nose, now between his teeth, and the red juice dripped down his chin and chest and fingers.

Then the fruit was gone, and so was the silver boy. He looked around, wondering if he had been dreaming strange visions of death and insanity. He felt so very strange. He clenched his fist and the juice bubbled between his fingers. He looked down and saw dark fluid like blood staining his clothes. Horrified, he tore off his outer garment, comforted that only a few drops remained on his undergarment. He balled the bloodied garment and wiped his hands, face, and neck with it before stuffing it under a bush.

He turned to dash back, then thought better of it and dug a hole in the dirt with his hands. The ground a few inches down was hard and cold, and his fingernails were not strong enough to release it and one bent back. It bled and darkened, and he sucked on it as he threw the garment into the shallow hole and covered it with dirt, but it wasn't enough, so he gathered leaves and twigs and threw them over it, but that looked too intentional, so he kicked it a few times and nodded and turned away.

But how could he explain the few droplets on his garment? They would wonder if he had injured himself.

My fingernail, he thought and smeared it along his undergarment in a few other places.

Fool, he thought again, *they will wonder about your nakedness first, and for that you have no answer. What madness is overtaking you?*

Men laughed and sounds approached. He stumbled and fell before the bush beneath which he had buried his garment. Between the leaves of the shrub were dark berries he had not noticed. He plucked some and smeared them in his hand. The juice smelled and looked identical to the stains on his clothes.

He wiped the sweat from his forehead and tried to settle his breathing. *You are seeing things,* he thought. *You are imagining terrible things, conjuring ghosts of shame because you are filled with shame for letting your children die, just like you let Lamech die.*

He knelt, grabbed more berries, and burst them between his fingers. He thought he should feel comforted that the visitation with the boy had only been a vision, but he could no longer trust his perception, and that made him feel cheated.

He dug up his garment. Dirt had stuck to and caked in the wetness, but after he slapped most of it off, he slipped the tunic on, turned toward the approaching footsteps, and walked back to change his clothing and burn what he wore.

"Strange fruit," he would say. *"I tripped and fell on a bush with strange fruit that stunk like death."*

PART NINE

THE GARDEN

But the serpent said to the woman, "You will not surely die. For God knows that when you eat of it your eyes will be opened, and you will be like God, knowing good and evil." So when the woman saw that the tree was good for food, and that it was a delight to the eyes, and that the tree was to be desired to make one wise, she took of its fruit and ate, and she also gave some to her husband who was with her, and he ate. Then the eyes of both were opened, and they knew that they were naked.

—GENESIS 3:4–7 ESV

46

Cain's toes sank into the desert sands as he led his family ever forward. He strained just to keep himself upright, but knew their final destination lay just beyond the mountainous dunes ahead.

An oasis in the midst of a sea of sand. A Garden, cool and comfortable, wrought in the twilight of Time with strange seeds and no little bending of the rules that hold nature strung together.

The sun positioned itself at the edge of the horizon and tossed its red cloak high. Then, as it dove and the color faded to twilight, the vertebral marks on Cain's arms glowed. He struggled up the incline and, as he reached the top, found Sarah by Mason. Her green eyes gleamed like burning copper, and her shape seemed extracted from the world, something too vibrant to belong amid so much gray.

Soon, he thought, *her belly will become obvious, and the others will wonder if the child is mine.*

The thought struck him then as it never had before. He had been so consumed by every decision, and how their weight bent the streams of Time, that he had never actually wondered if the child's origins could be questioned. *To think Abel could be living on through Sarah's womb . . .*

He looked at her red hair and felt the desire to snuff the flame as never before.

But the Sarah you know would never stoop to such evil. You only recently felt the bond between her and Abel grow.

But sex could have been the impetus. You should kill her now.

Cain's gaze was caught in the hem of Sarah's garment, so much so he couldn't tell if he was fighting the voice of the Abomination or his own paranoia. *We loved each other once. I remember us lying with fingers entwined until sleep froze our thoughts.*

Or was that too a lie?

Uncertainty burned in his mind. He brought his hands to rub his eyes, but stopped midaction. *How could I forget the streams?*

His eyes lingered on her. Mason was staring from his peripheral, but Cain could not tear himself from the thought of being with her once more, of her body pressed against his in the warmth of total acceptance.

I could swim the pathways of Time and find the truth. I need only the opportunity. When we arrive and the others rest, I will drink, and then plunge into the past.

He crested another dune and there stood the Garden, glowing with a faint bioluminescence. The others followed and gasped at the sight of its high canopy bending with the wind like a hand in the distance waving them close. As they stilled and their glances hopped between Lukian, Cain, and the Garden, Cain wondered at the importance of this moment. There was deep resonance here, and he basked in it.

"They have chosen to follow you and wonder at the repercussions."

Cain frowned. *I myself wonder. But soon I will know, because I will test each minuscule choice against the outcome I desire. It won't be long. I will rid myself of you. There will come a day I will see you bleed.*

He walked to their new home, and Eve was the first to follow, though she still led Adam hand in hand. Next were Sarah and Mason, and some of the women and children. Finally, Kiile and Machael helped Gorban up once more to finish the final steps of their journey.

Except for the shuffling of feet and rustle of clothing, they made no sound. As they neared, the faintly luminous leaves grew against the darkening canvas of night, the moon and stars disappeared under a sweeping sheet of clouds, and the Garden seemed the only source of illumination.

As Cain passed beneath the canopy, the buzzing intensified. His ears rang, and he shook his head and tipped it to rid himself of his discomfort. They huddled together until they came to an end closed off by a tapestry of thorny vines and green globes bobbing on stems bent with their weight. The globes bobbed toward Cain, and their subtle slits peeled back to the stems, revealing what looked like red eyes that danced and glowed. As one bobbed toward Jacob, he cried out and shuffled back. Mason let them brush against him and seemed comfortable enough, but the others swatted at them when they came near.

As the whispers grew in Cain's mind, so did the movement of the eyes and the vines that slithered forward and extended sharp points toward the people.

"Prick your fingers on the vines," Cain said.

"Why?" Eve asked, and the others mumbled agreement.

"It is a rite of passage."

Lukian was the first to prick his finger, though he stared oddly at the blood as it beaded on his finger. Mason was the second, and the others followed until at last Jacob let the Garden drink its fill.

The eyeballs snapped shut and curled into the thorny vines that slithered away into the foliage on either side to reveal a passageway. There was a strange calm as they passed within, and all life seemed caught in a stillness so pervasive it swallowed even the sounds of the fluttering leaves, which were clearly moving, though not under any compulsion so natural as a breeze.

Jacob gaped at everything, and Kiile's children kept stopping to point, only to be urged along by Elsa. Lukian was staring again, searing holes into Cain's skull, and Sarah walked beside Mason, as comfortable a distance from the edge as possible. Eve strode on like the queen she was, suffering her right hand to lead Adam, though she walked as if the light of the Garden dared not touch her countenance.

Cain smiled. *This Garden is no fabrication as you think it is, dear mother.*

They entered an orchard around which lay a seemingly impenetrable wall of thorns and greenery. The bobbing globes were everywhere, though their slits were closed and their glow diminished. It seemed the grove was filled with fruit trees of every kind.

Apple, peach, mango, pomegranate, cherry, and on and on until they saw mixtures of the fruits, and what seemed to be wholly new breeds. Their bewilderment cooled, and starvation overcame their lingering fear, so that they plucked the bounty and ate in muted wonder.

Cain rubbed his face with a shaking hand and groaned. He had fasted longer than he should, but the time was not yet ripe. It was Sarah, the way she stood with her arms folded, and spun to stare at the entrance of the Garden fastened against them with thorny vines. He approached as the others moved on, though she failed to notice, seemingly too distracted by the Garden.

He pushed aside a leafy branch and she jumped at his presence. They stared into each other's eyes for the first time since his return. His chest constricted and he grappled for a breath.

"I ache for you," he said. Or had he merely thought it? He could hardly think because in her eyes lay no ambiguity, no guardedness, only a transparency that was at once terrifying and stirring. He thought of the years of kisses and injuries exchanged under sun and moon alike, and all jumbled together and pressed against his mind, buzzing with the Abomination's incessant chatter. He wanted to squeeze her arm the way he had when words were outlawed and only action could speak, but dare he open himself to her? Dare he invite her to gaze upon what he knew resided inside?

"You look the same as when we kissed under the starlight so many years ago."

She continued staring with that spellbinding transparency. What did she search for?

"Do you remember the night?" he said. "Do you remember the love on the sea breeze and the salt taste on our lips?"

The transparency smoked as she looked away. "Perhaps you have mistaken me for another."

"I remember. Even now I see you crouched over countless shells, your feet pushing the foam of the surf that is washing more ashore. You pick your favorite." He touched her chin and she met his gaze again. "And bring it home, caught between your fingers."

Sarah's eyes dimmed. "Much has faded behind memories I can never forget, behind a broken home and bloody hands, a falling sky and . . . pain. I see pain, I feel pain—I am pain."

The trees swayed and brushed their leaves against them, and Cain was struck by how violence could hide in the most benign of places. In a kiss. In a smile. In a glance. In a word. As the light dimmed, she squinted as if noticing something new.

"What?"

"Your eyes," she said. "They are not the same silver within silver. They are different. They are dark again."

Cain paused and searched for the familiar buzzing sensation, though he felt nothing but the sweat matting the clothes to his skin. He searched for the Abomination, and his jaw hung as he realized there were only the sounds of him and Sarah bathing in Garden green.

She narrowed her eyes. "What are you hiding?"

"Nothing."

"Something haunts you. If you desire my trust, why face it alone?"

He extended his arm. "Hurry. Take my hand."

47

Sarah clenched Cain's arm and silently cursed herself for so quickly abandoning her desire to remain detached for the comfort of his touch. She should have stayed in the orchard, but there were many things she *should* have done, and for reasons she thought better to ignore, her hands remained where they were. "Is someone following us?"

Cain's chin sliced left, and his profile—the one she had so often admired in sleep and in waking concentration—was silhouetted by moonlight peeking through the alley above. "It's the Garden."

"Can it hurt us?"

"It could kill you. But it won't."

Her back muscles contracted as the hiss of movement sounded behind them.

"We are almost there," Cain said.

As they passed a pair of trees with gnarled bark undulating slowly like pulsing veins, one of the branches whipped Sarah's arm and she shuffled back, noticing blood as it oozed from her shoulder. She stared at the trunks and pointed, horrified. "There are faces in the trees."

He hushed her and pushed her behind him, lingering to stare at the blood smeared across her arm. His face paled and became shadowed, but as she opened her mouth, he grabbed her and pulled her toward the space between the trees. The canopies quivered and lurched, and the branches unraveled and snaked away, revealing a hallway deeper into the Garden.

The way was lit by green globes and flowering vines arching overhead that projected a pale, pink light.

"Don't touch them," he said. "Their thorns are deadly."

She jerked back her hand and resisted the impulse to wrench herself out of his grip, for she feared the Garden over his cruelty. Ahead, a wall of green globes turned and opened. Cain slapped them away and jerked Sarah through the opening, and as she stumbled forward, caught in his arms, she squinted and gasped.

A dome of black thorns arched over a great tree, around which were thousands of flowers upturned toward the crest, where a great light floated. The light, which looked like a small sun, threw gray shadows from drooping willow-whip branches and the fruit that bent them low.

Cain gripped a fruit and twisted until it cracked from the branch. "You must be hungry. Come, eat."

Sarah took three steps forward, careful not to crush the flowers that seemed to watch her as she walked. Something about the fruit disturbed her, though she knew not what it was. She looked around. "What is this place? What have you done since leaving me in that storm?"

He bit the fruit and smiled as the juice dripped down his chin. "I wandered far and returned to bring you to your new home. Here we can live freed from struggle, freed from the hunger that forced me to labor long under sun and rain. You and I can raise our children in safety. We can live as gods."

"Safety," she intoned. The smell on his breath revived the memory of matted hair and crackling candle flame. "And if I refuse?"

"You do not know what is in my power to offer. I understand your reticence, but it is a gift, Sarah."

She let the drooping branches stream across her shoulders, then curled her fingers around a dangling fruit and felt its flesh quiver. She broke it off with a twist and brought it to her nose. It had no smell at all, and she was tempted to bite it, to taste what Cain had tasted, to try it just once. She turned. Cain examined her every movement and expression. "After so many years," she said, "there is still an element of that boy I loved. You've always struggled to impress."

"Things could be as they were. They don't need to stay how they are."

"And how are they?"

He neared, yet his arms remained at his sides. His eyes tipped to search hers. "In those many days, I tried to conjure your voice just to feel the fire of your spirit. But you are more compelling than any memory I could summon."

She bit her lower lip, and her skin tingled at the brush of his breath across it.

He slid his hands to the small of her back. "It feels like years. If only you knew what I . . ." He hesitated, his eyes probing.

"What?" A pause. "Tell me."

He set his jaw.

She turned in his grip, but he held her fast. "If you want me, show your secrets."

"And what of yours?" There was accusation in that voice.

"You left only weeks ago, but now you return with silver eyes, black marks on your skin, and—"

"And what?" The seduction was gone.

"There's something in you. I saw it when you first came. It was the tone of your voice, the look of your eyes. An evil so deep I thought it would swallow me. You bring me here and offer something I do not understand, but what reason do I have to trust you, who beat me? Who murdered your twin brother and left me to die?"

"You think me insane, but I did what was necessary."

"As do I."

He said, "Did you think I could let you follow me into the wilderness? Did you think I could take you with me to the depths of hell?"

"I wish that you had hated me. At least then I could understand why all this has happened the way it has."

Cain released her and ran his fingers through his hair, which had grown these past few weeks. The branches swayed and bent as the wind whispered through the canopy of leaves.

She nodded, and her eyes burned. "You always were a liar."

"What right do you have to judge me, after everything I've seen of you?"

"Stop being a child."

"I did it for us."

"You did it for yourself. You abandoned me. You abandoned our children, and our grandchildren have been murdered by the beasts you seem able to control."

A hint of a smile attempted itself on his face. "Ah, yes. Our children." He took a few steps forward, eyeing her stomach.

"What are you looking at?" She shuffled back.

"Little child, will you not tell us whose you are?"

Darkness settled in her toes. Her voice shook. "How dare you?"

"Innocence carries no reason for anger."

She threw the fruit and it crashed through the branches. "The only fidelity between us is my own. You may think your bitterness is justified, but I watched your eyes wander long before the thought ever entered my mind."

Cain said, "Where were you those nights I lay awake?"

"Sitting in the darkness and weeping for the love we had but somehow lost."

"You made love to Abel."

"I never touched him."

"You snuck off into the fields under the cover of darkness as if it would hide your sins."

Her face reddened. "He was a good man."

"I wonder if Lilleth knew."

"I never touched him, but now I wish I had, because then maybe this wouldn't have happened. Maybe he'd be alive, and you . . ."

The silver grew, and he approached her. She fell to her seat and scrambled away, but he climbed on top of her and struck her in the face. She screamed, "I never touched him," but he hit her again. She was weeping, and the tears wetted her hair. His fists came again and again, and she thought she would choke.

Cain stopped and fell back, the breath hissing between his teeth. Sarah lay weeping on the ground, her legs and arms pulled into herself. She cupped her face, which swelled with aching wounds. He stood, and his voice sounded alien as he said, "You may think you can choose a different way, but you and everyone else will find there is nothing now but me."

"You're a monster."

"I killed Abel, I killed God, and if I must, I will kill you and everyone who stands against me. We could have peace. We could. Why won't you listen?"

She clenched her eyes until they hurt. She could feel the heartbeat in her stomach. It ached and throbbed, and she rubbed it with her hand and prayed for her unborn child.

Cain's voice rumbled behind her. "Whether the child is Abel's or not, it will always be mine."

48

Lukian knelt alone at the edge of the Garden. The sounds of the others had traveled far enough away to become mumblings, and so he sat with a fruit in each hand and a pile before him, eating. The pale thirst had returned stronger than before, and with it came that gnawing itch.

He swallowed partly masticated chunks. The fruit in his hands oozed on his fingers, but nothing brought satisfaction. It was like scratching an itch that remained too deep to be quenched.

Quenched, he thought. *Thirsty.*

A chill wind blew past and raised his skin. He dropped the fruit, stood, and turned every direction as the whispering voice crept close. "Brother," Lukian whispered. "Is that you?" The buzz in his mind grew to a roar, and when he felt he could take no more, it stilled. The sounds of his family exploring the Garden danced on the fringes. But as he strained his ears, he heard footsteps approaching from deep in the thicket, and he shuffled closer to gain a glimpse, though the hedge was too thick.

Something pricked his neck, and he slapped at it. He brought his hand away with two spots of red and stared at them, recalling an identical moment deep in the Fog, and another in the forest.

At that moment, a pale arm extended from the thicket and pushed the branches aside. A second arm shot out and spread the gap, allowing the glow of the globes to illuminate a pair of delicate feet and slender calves, and the pale face of his little twin brother.

"Brother," Lukian said, "deliver me from this sickness."

The boy frowned with pity. *"Come close so that I may."*

Lukian knelt and offered his hand. The boy took it and smiled, a thin line cupping a lengthy nose. Lukian silently pleaded for answers. Instead, the boy pulled out a fruit different from the last, perfectly round and the color of skin. *"Taste and see . . ."*

Something in Lukian was repulsed, but the longer he stared at the fruit, the more he itched with pleasure. Not the pleasure of fruition, but of a desire too deep to ever truly own. He smiled at the fruit, then those eyes. "Are they silver like Cain's because you both died?"

"Cain found the God inside and embraced it. I came because I saw you searching for it. Because I recognized your potential—your receptivity."

Lukian licked his lips and stayed a shaking hand from snatching the fruit. He wanted to maintain a semblance of dignity. "For me?"

It nodded, its eyes insatiable. *"Taste and see. But understand that once you do, you may not return."* It paused. *"You must understand."*

So the forest was just a vision, he thought. *But what about the blood on my neck?* "What will happen to me?"

"To conquer death you must embrace it. Death, like life, is an illusion. One that you might overcome if you but embrace the truth."

"What is the truth?"

"That inside you is everything—the world, the stars, life, deity—and there you will find the power to transcend. You must no longer restrain your desire, for it is the key to finding your truth. You need only believe in yourself. Believe in what you can do, what you can become."

"The Almighty?"

"His laws held you captive. They suppressed the God inside. They forced you to abandon happiness in favor of his. Come. Taste and see . . ."

Lukian shivered. His hand reached a few inches forward, his fingers itching to grab the fruit, but more so to grab the hand. He stared into those silver eyes, and though the rims were beautiful, they seemed like open throats. *This is my brother. Why should I fear my brother?*

A voice called for him, and the boy's silver eyes shot over his shoulder. Lukian turned to see, and in the distance, between the orchard's branches, moving shadows danced long and low.

Lukian turned back, his soul longing for the fruit, but the boy and the fruit were gone. He struck the ground and suppressed the urge to scream.

Cheated, he thought. *I've been cheated again.*

◆　◆　◆

Eve felt as if she had been thrown a hundred and fifty years into the past—back to the Garden of Eden.

It looks so authentic, but I know that it is not real. It cannot be real.

Something jerked her arm, and she glanced over her shoulder and saw Adam's hand in hers. "Sorry," she said. "I did not mean to twist your arm." She let go and watched his arm swing flaccid at his side. Adam mumbled, though it took her a moment to realize she had not imagined it. She squeezed his shoulder. "What did you say?"

He mumbled again and his eyes jerked to something over her shoulder. She turned and saw a round purple fruit she had never seen before hanging off a branch. She broke the fruit off its stem and pushed it into his hand, but his fingers hung motionless. She brought the fruit to his mouth, but he puckered his lips and shifted away. She brought the fruit to her own mouth and tore the skin away. The juice was sweet and fresh, and the skin sour, and as she brought it to Adam's lips, he bit, chewed, and swallowed.

When at last only the hard pit remained, she tossed it on the ground and used the hem of her garment to wipe his face and beard. Some of the juice had dribbled down his neck, and she scrubbed it from his skin.

Eve slipped her fingers into his again, and everything but the pain in her throat fell away as she pressed her lips against his bristly cheek.

If only I had known that fruit so many years ago would, in return, sink its teeth into us. "I'll shave you soon," she whispered. "I know you hate how it itches when it gets like this." She buried her head in his neck, wishing his arms would slide around her. Wishing he would awaken. Wishing he would hold her . . . as he did now.

She jerked her head back to look. His arms were locked around her waist, and his voice was soft as he said, "When did you get so thin?"

The sound frightened her. She tried to jerk away, but failed. Her mind spun. Adam was holding her. Adam had spoken. She searched those eyes that had been dim since Abel's death, but that were as bright and alive as she remembered them being when she woke from the breath of God and the bone of his side. "Adam?"

His brow furrowed as he squeezed her. "Where are we? Is this . . . ?"

"Adam!" She buried her face in his neck.

"All is fine, is it not?"

"No." The word barely found form.

"Are you hurt?" His voice grew harsh. "Who hurt you?"

Eve shook her head. "You don't understand."

And she laughed and kissed him in the shade of the trees.

49

The vines whipped Cain's arms as he struggled through, snapping thorns as he went. He was no stranger to violence, but the desire to cut himself had never entered his mind.

So why do I want to slice my wrists and drink?

Because Sarah is right, I am a monster, a slave to rage. And if I don't kill myself, I might kill the only one I yet love. What angers me most is I chose this. But what else was there to receive me?

He struck one of the bobbing globes as its lids opened at him. It recoiled and squinted, and he stifled the urge to break it from its stem. He clenched his fists and screamed, pushing until he felt the air stab his throat.

Then he heard it. Sustained laughter bubbling out of the void, followed by quiet footsteps and cold fingers slipped between his. The Abomination stared up at him in the familiar illusion of that little silver boy.

"*You see?*" it hissed. "*You're nothing alone. You will always need me, if only to stem the flood of madness. You can never be free.*"

He tore his hand out of its grip.

"*Go on, suck the blood from your wounds. Give in. Why not?*"

"You changed me."

"*I gave you what you wanted. You're nothing but a prostitute selling yourself for the ultimate drug. You wanted a deathless body? It's yours. Transcendent power? It's yours. But in return, you will always be mine.*"

Cain wanted nothing more than to crush its skull as he had Abel's. But he couldn't. Not yet. "You speak as though freedom is a fantasy, yet in the same breath claim I chose you."

"*Life gives you one choice—who will you worship?*"

"I never chose you."

"No, you chose yourself, and even God didn't make that mistake." The Abomination paused. *"There are issues craving resolution. It is dangerous to let them rally. They're already beginning to question your divinity."*

"You speak of my father."

"Humans are emboldened by small victories. Let me have this time. I'll reward you."

Cain sensed the pale hunger in its voice and refused its violent grab for control. "Crawl back into your hole," he said, "before I force you."

It was an empty boast.

◆ ◆ ◆

Gorban tore at the wrapping on his leg until it loosed. He unwound the fabric, and as he peeled the last bloody fibers away, all that remained underneath was white skin and black hair.

"My leg."

"What's wrong with it?" Kiile asked.

"It's healed."

Kiile laughed. "Did you eat bad fruit and muddle your mind?"

"I did eat some of the fruit." Gorban stood and, when he felt no pain, jumped. "And I have no more pain."

"Impossible." Kiile grabbed Gorban's shoulder to survey the pale flesh of his thigh. His eyes widened as he craned his neck to look at both sides. "You weren't even able to walk yesterday."

"I can now."

Kiile walked off, but kept glancing at Gorban's leg.

Gorban laughed and stomped the ground. "Do you see this?"

Mason nodded and smiled broad enough to show his teeth.

Jacob jogged through the trees and skidded to a stop. Sweat matted his hair and eagerness sprinted across his face. "Come quick. Adam's in the center of the orchard with Eve." He turned and ran, and Gorban, Mason, Kiile, and Machael hurried after.

Voices were raised in exclamation. Shadows danced, and as they rounded a row of trees, they saw the group gathered in an oblong circle.

Peth called to him and he joined, but as she smiled and pointed toward Adam, she noticed his unbandaged leg. "What happened?"

"It's healed," Gorban said.

"How?"

"I think I know." Gorban called for his grandmother. The people parted.

Adam and Eve were entangled in each other's arms, and upon seeing him, Eve said, "You are healed as well?"

"You fed him the fruit," Gorban said.

"He woke immediately." Eve was beaming.

Gorban bowed. "Welcome back, Grandfather."

Adam said, "It is good to be back."

◆ ◆ ◆

Cain burst through to where his family stood in a diamond formation amidst the orchard, and said, "Now you see." They turned and hushed. "The fruit of the Garden does more than feed and sustain. It heals, though within limitations." He waved to indicate all they could see. "But this is child's play compared to the true secret of the Garden."

Adam was there, truly there, for the first time since the murder, and Cain could see the disdain in his father's gaze, that familiar expression of disappointment. Adam's face had paled upon seeing him, and Cain was struck in that moment of how disconnected they had become. Adam had not yet seen the changes in Cain, and surely seeing him evoked both fear and disgust.

Cain feigned applause. "Congratulations, Father. You've finally stepped out of your dreams."

"It seems I've done so only to step into your perverse fantasies," Adam said, looking directly into Cain's eyes.

Cain hadn't expected that voice to still carry its sting, and he set his jaw against it and lowered his voice until it seemed the two of them spoke privately. "The days I spent in your shadow have long since passed."

"Have they now?"

Cain plucked a small yellow fruit and began eating it. "Do you remember Eden?"

"I remember many things."

"Have I missed anything?" Cain swept his arm toward the vines, trees, and thorns, and tossed the finished fruit as Eve walked up beside Adam and hugged his arm.

"Nothing could compare to that paradise," Adam said.

"And yet you threw it away."

"Always passing blame," Eve said. "Will you never learn?"

"This Garden is a gift. You would do well to accept it," Cain said.

"Who do you think you are?" Adam said.

"I'm who you never could be. You were the sickness. I'm the solution."

"You're twice the sinner I ever was."

Cain laughed. "You're every bit the same as me. The only difference is you are powerless and I am not."

"And what do you think wielding that power will gain you?" Adam said.

"Not me. It will gain you. It will gain Mother. It will gain anyone who is willing to embrace the God inside." He pulled out the perfectly round, flesh-colored fruit of the new Tree of Life, so benign in appearance, and their eyes followed as he dangled it in front of them by the stem. He spoke for all to hear. "In the heart of the Garden lies a reversal of the curse. A true Tree of Life. All you need to do is taste and see." He nodded at Adam. "Began and ended through fruit. It seems fitting, doesn't it?"

There was dangerous silence. Cain felt the echoes of decisions and truth, and realized this point was another nexus. The world and all beyond hushed in anticipation of their every move, though somehow he knew this nexus more potent, more treacherous than any before. He closed his eyes and let each moment fall on his ears like terrible Music.

"I would rather die than become a curse like you," Adam said.

"*My* curse is everlasting life."

"I taught you to love. I taught you to serve the Almighty and steward the earth."

Cain's sight dimmed at his father's stupidity, and he felt the blood hot in his cheeks. "Who then taught me hate?"

"Abel listened to me. He was a good son."

"Who holds you in the crucible? Who has given sanity back to you from denial's greedy grasp?"

"Every chance I gave, you threw away. How can I applaud stupidity?" Adam kept going on as if the argument had nothing to do with the present situation. And perhaps it didn't.

Cain paused. "I've done more than sin."

"I would have questioned your humanity if you hadn't done *some* good. But ever since childhood you have done shameful things."

"And ever since I could remember, Abel absorbed every ounce of your adoration."

Eve's eyes seemed to flash at that.

"Everyone saw it," Cain said. "The moment Abel was born—*before I had my very first thought*—you loved him more, didn't you? Tell me how that is not the darkest of evils. Abandoning an innocent child merely because you were preoccupied with the beauty of another. How could you?"

"I offered you every chance to prove yourself."

Cain laughed, long and cold. "What sign did you search for? Was it something in my infant babble? Perhaps the way I gripped my toes?"

"Don't mock me, child."

"I will mock who I wish." And to press the point home, he struck his father's face.

Eve caught Adam, who wiped blood from his mouth. Adam's voice shook. "All your fury could not match him. I knew the moment he was born that he was perfect. But you . . . you troubled me."

"What was it you so hated in me?"

Adam pressed his lips together.

"Why not be forthcoming?"

Adam turned away.

Cain's voice grew until he was nearly screaming. "When you looked on my dark skin and eyes, on your sharpness of features reflected, what did you fear? That I would be like you? That I would choose Sin over God, like you did?"

Adam's voice was low. "I was right to fear what you would become."

Cain paused as new thoughts settled, and he realized that for the first time he was seeing his father clearly. His voice quieted. "You still feel the shame of that moment all those years ago. You still see your mistakes crystalized in my features, forever preserved in flesh and bone too similar to yours. That's why you hated me, isn't it? That's why you still hate me."

Adam's shoulders rolled with every breath, and his hands clenched and released.

Cain hadn't realized until that moment how much he had hoped Adam did love him, however little. Perhaps that was why Cain felt such enormous importance in this moment. Because everything, from the Abomination to the Garden, led back to that day over a century ago, when the twins were born and the father chose his favorite.

The family gazed in stunned silence. Mason's eyes were bright and cold as he stared at Cain. Lukian looked bitter and distant, and Gorban's neck was red with shame for his father, perhaps his grandfather, maybe both.

The Abomination chewed at the base of Cain's skull, its angry calls for power weaving into an unintelligible storm of vowels and consonants. It wanted to speak. To spread the fear it thought so pertinent to their survival, and Cain was wearied by the pale thirst and the crumbling of hopes he had gathered through countless years. He had never so bluntly pointed to his father's faults, and somehow by doing so and finding them firm, he felt the throb of wounds run deeper still.

"Give me emptiness," he whispered, and the Abomination thrust him into the void.

50

Mason had been waiting for the moment the silver would return, and as he stood listening to the echoes of Cain and Adam's bitter exchange, Cain's eyes melted to polished marbles, and Mason knew the monster was back.

"Enough foolishness," Cain said.

Mason's throat dried, and he shivered. This was not Father. Whatever had happened in the wilderness, Sarah was right. He had not returned alone.

"As promised, I will let you live in peace, but you must stay."

Eve touched Adam's arm, but he shrugged her away.

Cain, or something inside him, smiled. "So far my patience has proven deep, but it is not bottomless. The Garden watches. It thirsts for violence, and nothing but my promise holds it from drinking your blood with its thorny roots."

◆ ◆ ◆

Cain floated in the void hearing voices like far-off underwater mumblings. The Abomination was in control of his body, and he wondered if he should attempt reclaiming power.

No, I must take this time to search the Waters of Time; for it is only when the Abomination is distracted that I may be safe from intrusion. And it must never know what I find.

He remembered the black force that had thrown him out of the stream upon his first encounter. He knew what the black force had been even then, and though the Abomination hadn't spoken of it, he knew he had been on the verge of discovering something it wished to keep hidden.

The Abomination realized then that I know of the prophetic streams, but it cannot watch tirelessly.

I must hurry.

He closed his eyes and felt the layers arise. He reached and sifted through them, slowly descending until he realized something was drawing him toward the bottom of the layers. Upon arriving, he stood poised at the edge of that endless darkness, but something stayed him.

What would happen if I jumped? Could I find my way back? The darkness seemed to call with a voice of cold finality, but he perceived it was not yet time. He would return to that darkness all too soon—that truth resonated like a wet finger circling the edge of a glass—but he couldn't sense why, so he shifted back and ascended, grappling one arm over the other to pull himself toward the light. He arrived at the other brink and stood at the edge as he had before, prepared to jump into the stream. The Water churned and boiled.

As he stood, he remembered Sarah's shining eyes and the sound of her weeping; Mason's glare and Lukian's anger; the silver eyes of the Abomination and its arrogant nose; and Abel's blood pooling under darkness and grass.

I fear what lies in the streams of Time.

But where else might you turn? You have stalled too long already. Go. Go!

He stepped off the edge and the Water rushed up and closed its hands about him, twisting and throwing him in circles, burying his face in cold wetness. He struggled until he breached the surface. A storm raged and lightning struck. Where the jagged light stabbed the surface, the stream exploded, and as he struggled against the current, it splashed on all sides. He cried out as a flash slapped the Water in front of him, but there was no pain.

Of course. My body is walking in the Garden. I am here, and yet I am not here. Through the lens of the void, I have become an observer of the Waters of Time.

He recognized visions in the Water. As a bolt of light illuminated a suspended droplet, he caught a glimpse of a baby raised high. Though the droplet sped by, the vision was so vivid that, in an instant, ages filtered through his mind. He saw the baby wriggle and heard it squeal as it was lowered into familiar hands. A woman with red hair leaned in, crinkled her nose, and pressed it against the baby's cheek.

This is my unborn child, Cain thought. *I see the resemblance even now. The jawline, the shape of the lips—ah, but it has Sarah's nose. Yes, I see the child is older and his hair is like glowing coals. And . . . what is this?*

The boy, whose name he did not know, turned and glared, but the peculiarity remained. Dirty-white projections, like the horns of a goat, pressed out the top of his head.

The vision continued in sputtering clips. Lightning struck, and as the droplets sped by, he saw the boy grown to a man. The horns curved back upon themselves, and darkened and shimmered as if moistened by the blood of the innocent.

Cain turned away. "I will not watch this." He plunged ahead, not bothering to look at the other images that demanded attention. They screamed and howled, but he swam on. The storm intensified, the lightning struck with greater frequency, and he wondered if he could find the source of the storm. He knew, as a man knows his existence, that the stream *defined* the world, or maybe that the world defined *it*—either an equal truth—and that if a possibility lay not in the stream, it could not exist, and so the stream projected the limits of will itself.

But what is this storm?

He swam on but again became caught in the visions. They grew more violent, and as the droplets sped by, murder multiplied. Men with horns just like his yet-to-be-born son beat and tortured each other with cruel instruments.

"No," he said. "This is not the world I bought with slavery. This is not the world I wanted. Show me the way I glimpsed in the eye of my imagination. The way of progress, the way of transcendence."

But true prophetic vision was altogether different and more terrifying than imagination. He could no longer bend logic to reach the conclusion of his design. The fury of Time's brutal movement shocked his eyes wide, and as another bolt struck the surface, a vision of one of his other descendants struck his cheek. The man was ugly, and one of his horns was crooked.

Lamech. The name of the son I lost to the Jinn. Though this Lamech is one of my distant grandchildren.

Another man struck Lamech, and he struck back. Lamech tossed the man to the ground, then kicked and stomped his chest and head. Cain turned and bit his tongue. He wanted to burn the images from his mind, but they grew and festered like open wounds.

Cain rushed on and witnessed countless infants murdered and unspeakable things done to women—and through it all those beast men with horns, and flames and disintegrating towers growing ever higher.

"Dear God." Cain pressed his fingers in his eyes. "Dear God. Dear God!" His hands were shaking. "Where did this darkness come from? How could so much change in so little time? This is not what I chose."

But it is.

"What should I do? How can something so all-consuming be stopped?"

Was it not you who chose to introduce murder into the world? Is anything else more urgent? Swim on. Swim on!

Cain dove upstream as he fought the terrible sensation of duality. Part of him was repulsed, though the rest lusted for what he saw, and that sickened him all the more. He shivered and suppressed the frightening sensations the Abomination had awoken in him through the unholy coupling.

The chaos grew, and he came to a fork in the river. On the path bending right lay details of the future, but on the path bending left lay shards of the past in a great glassy bay. He realized that this was the point the Abomination had kept him from, and he plunged down the path bending left. In the storm's place came a distant rumbling. He turned and saw the stream devoured by black clouds.

Does my presence affect the stream?

Cain blinked as new knowledge resonated through him like a clear note piercing flesh and soul. *The knowledge I gather here informs my decisions, and I am the tipping point, the crux upon which the world has been balanced, so tenuously that one decision might shatter it.*

The new river was so clear that he could see his toes, and the visions that presented themselves were familiar. After he traveled a distance, they were all either of him leading his family through the wilderness, or of Calebna and . . .

He paused, confused. There, with Calebna, were two whom he recognized.

Seth and Ayla?

They were talking with Calebna. And he saw them walking the City of the Almighty while Calebna, drenched in oil, stacked endless items on the altar in the Temple, next to which still lay the shriveled remnants of his rejected offering to the Almighty.

The vision altered again, and he realized he was watching Time unfold in reverse. He shifted to compensate and made his way forward until an image caught his eye. He backtracked until the vision unfolded itself. He saw a closed tomb, but the top shifted, then flew off, and Seth crawled out.

"Impossible . . ." Cain watched the vision as Seth opened the Almighty's casket, which was empty, and helped Ayla out of hers. They embraced each other and Ayla wept.

Cain shook his head. "It cannot be."

But it was motionless Truth. He stopped the vision on the Almighty's empty tomb and swallowed to banish the fear from his throat.

They're alive. How are they alive? And what about the Man?

The Man is alive.

"But I killed him."

Did you? What of the empty tomb?

"The Light Bringer even claimed I killed him, and why would my family bury the Man if they didn't have proof he was dead?"

Fool! Does a truth disappear because you close your eyes? You thought yourself God, and so you thought yourself unmatchable, but if you had opened your eyes, you would have struggled. And it could not chance you doing that. What explanation do you have for an empty sealed tomb? None!

"But how could I ever rid myself of the Abomination? I don't even know what it is or how it came to be."

There was a bend farther down the river that led to the great bay. The distant rumblings of the storm lay so far behind that he could barely make them out amidst the deafening silence. His mouth hung as thoughts fell into place. "How the Abomination came to be . . ."

51

C ain rewatched the vision of himself play in sputtering clips.
He was standing on the top of a hill, overlooking the fields
where Abel stood silhouetted against the twilight of storm. He still
tasted the emotions and thoughts that peppered his brain as he
walked into the valley and argued with Abel. As they fought, he felt
the rock and smelled the bitter thickness of Abel's crushed head as
if it were truly happening that very moment.

He rushed the vision ahead and watched as he bent and lurched
under nausea. But as he stared at his mouth, waiting for vomit to
spew, his jaw stretched and instead of vomit, a pale child gushed
onto the ground, webbed with womb netting. The child tore and
bit at the goo until it could take in a few gasping breaths. It latched
onto him and whispered in his ear.

Cain's mind claimed that it could not be, but here he saw that
it *was*.

Abomination. Silver boy. Son of Satan and . . . of *Cain*. Now he
knew the reason for the unmistakable familiarity between himself
and the Light Bringer. He understood everything.

"*I* birthed that monster." He squeezed his eyes shut. "I birthed it,
and now—*through me*, curse it all!—it will pervert my unborn child
into something else. Something evil. Something deserving only
death and damnation." *Something like me,* his mind finished. *I could
justify damnation for the sake of my progeny's salvation, but to curse
my lineage for such a fate . . .* Cain knelt. "Almighty God, if you exist,
if you truly live, then help me. Free me from this Abomination."

The tears on his cheeks were not of sorrow, but of fear. He feared
himself. He feared what he had become, as Adam had rightfully

feared him. He feared the pale thirst, and what he knew he could do, even without the child of Sin inside him.

Capable of every abomination I saw in those visions.

He stood as a sudden thought struck him like nails in the wrists. Begun through death and ended through death. Blood for blood and fruit for fruit. It truly did seem fitting.

◆　◆　◆

Law 1: Humans are incapable of owning satisfaction. Law 2: Indulgence only feeds the mortal desires it claims to quench. Law 3: A spirit possessing a human body cannot escape Laws 1 and 2.

The Abomination had listened to the Light Bringer's words in the underground City, but only now realized their full weight. The first several weeks of possession had been exhilarating. To feel the physical world in so many dimensions—to taste the blood, feel the consummation, and revel in the pleasure—the Abomination had been drunk. Even now, still shy of the true depth of the fall, it could hardly hold itself back from killing again. Animals just didn't offer the satisfaction.

And Sarah . . .

"The time is not yet right," the Abomination said through Cain. "She still carries my future in her womb."

The Abomination smiled, feeling the pleasure only the son of the Devil could by using another's voice. It felt even more pleasure knowing the body it possessed belonged to the very soul who had birthed it.

My father, the Light Bringer, and Cain—that whore of whores—my mother.

A cruel chuckle escaped from Cain's throat, broken at the end by violent rage. Momentary sanity came in waves, followed by the fiercest upsurges of ire.

I need a second host. Another body. Lukian. The Abomination laughed again, a long, cold cackling that echoed through the Garden. It was certain Cain had no inkling of what it planned with Lukian and thought it a shame that it couldn't rely on one host, though pitting the two against each other would reap even greater joy.

To drink another's blood and simultaneously gain praise. What could be better?

It waved its hands and offered no more than a glance toward the receding thorns and bobbing globes. Their lids popped and glowed as the Abomination passed by in Cain's skin. "Dim your lamps."

The eyes obeyed and the vines slid into place behind it.

"This body is tired and fogs my mind." The Abomination entered the chamber of the Tree of Life, pulled itself out of Cain's body, and rode the wind through the leaves to find Lukian, son of Cain.

52

The vines opened and Sarah was already half turned when Cain slumped to the ground. She called his name, but he did not respond. "Are you all right?" She held her belly with a wary hand. Flowers buffeted her calves as she stepped near and caught a glimpse of his back as it rose and fell.

She knelt beside him. He lay facedown, his body crumpled awkwardly. She nudged him and whispered his name. She worked her fingers under him and heaved him onto his back. His right arm remained twisted underneath, but after a few moments of struggle, she slipped that out as well.

Sarah sat beside Cain and hugged her knees. In the mixture of silver and green light his face looked sickly pale, but its shape held a regality that could not be missed. His dark lips, full enough to balance their length, looked strangely beautiful.

But what those lips have touched.

She looked at the fruit hanging around them and stifled repulsion. How could he enjoy the taste of blood? She had smelled it on his breath and saw the thick redness of it.

He has dipped into darkness so deep it stained his skin.

She nearly reached out to trace the marks lining his arms and neck.

Why am I attracted to what repulses me?

"I miss you," she whispered, and nodded as if to convince herself that was the only reason. "If you truly can make everything how it was . . ."

His eyes fluttered open and searched hers, and though her first instinct was to flee, something froze her muscles. "Is it you?" Sarah said.

Cain's eyes, devoid of silver, zeroed in on the swelling wounds on her face. He laid his head back and breathed through flared nostrils.

Her fear dissolved, and in its place came urgency. "What is it?"

He sat up and again she thought to flee, but she knew the monster was gone, and for the first time she could see the reason she followed him to this grove.

I stay to help the man I love rid himself of the monster I hate. The vows we made, the life we shared, the pain we felt—it was not all for naught.

He slid his warm hands over her shoulders. "Sarah, you must listen to me, and you must remember."

Her eyes were sealed to savor his touch as she pressed a shaking hand against his cheek. "I know already."

He squeezed her shoulders until she felt pain. "Tell me you're listening. Promise to remember."

"I promise you my life."

"Do you love me?"

"How could you ask that?"

He shook her hard. "Do you love me?" His voice was edged with fear and passion, a quality altogether different from the sharpness of anger.

"*Yes!*" she said.

"Then kill me."

Her face contorted. "How could I?"

"How could you not?"

"I'd rather die."

"Stop trying to save me."

"I can't lose you. Not now. Not after you took so many away from me. What do I have left? Do not sentence me to such loneliness."

He paused. "I was never yours."

"Stop lying." She wanted to embrace and be embraced by him. Amidst the hate, scars, and fresh wounds, she loved him now more than ever before. The desperation for his affection, for his mere countenance, had grown without her knowing like vines through her ruined soul, and it toppled her. "No," she whispered, and then she shouted, "I won't kill you."

Cain slapped her, and she held her cheek, remembering moments not so long passed and feeling fresh bruises throb.

"If you knew what I know, you would break a thorn and thrust it into my chest."

"Then tell me what you know."

"The world will shatter if you fail. They are coming. The bane of our race—soulless half-breeds born from human wombs. The Jinn were a mere dabbling in the craft. But through me Death has been perfected. They found a way to touch the children, to pervert them into something else. There were barriers before that kept them away but—"

"Who? Kept who away?"

"Kill me. Before it returns!"

"There must be another way."

He slapped her again, and the crack of it echoed. "There was never another way."

She couldn't make sense of his words, nor could she stifle her tears.

Cain looked at her and all the hardness melted. His fingers poised as if to take back the wounds. His mouth hung and his eyes shone in the light of the Garden, and her soul quickened. But as quickly as he turned, the transparency muddled.

He strode to the Tree of Life and grabbed hold of the hanging branches. They were strong, yet pliable. He pulled himself up one and, with legs crossed around the branch he hung on, twisted another branch around itself and knotted the loop. "Someday I hope you will understand. I pray to God that you do." He swallowed. "Just remember . . ." He paused, closed his eyes, and pulled the knotted loop around his neck.

What? Sarah thought. *Tell me, you fool!*

He was suspended, hanging from the Tree of Life, and holding back words they both knew he should speak. He fell. His neck twisted, strained by the weight of his body. His feet swept through the flowers, but did not touch ground. His face reddened and his body convulsed.

She scrambled up, wrapped her arms around his waist, and lifted. She thought of Lilleth lying on the floor of her house, the maw in her throat gushing blood. Now Cain was killing himself too.

"Tell me," she screamed as she tried to lift him out of the knot. "I know what you were going to say."

He kicked her away and she fell. Everything was a distortion through rough waters. "I wish you never loved me." She moaned. "I wish you never had."

◆ ◆ ◆

Lukian felt the tug at his hand and hardly began turning before he was jerked into the brush. He nearly yelled, but delicate fingers covered his mouth. He looked up at silver eyes surrounded by pale skin.

"*I have had patience.*"

Lukian frowned and, as the boy's fingers slipped away from his mouth, he said, "What have I done?"

"*You've listened poorly, brother.*"

"I've done what you said."

"*Eat the fruit.*"

The boy lifted the fruit and pressed it against his face, but he turned away. "Why?"

Its fist pounded Lukian's head, and he saw stars and cried out, only to receive its cold fingers on his mouth again. "*Eat it.*"

"No." Lukian made to sit up and leave, but those little hands held him down with unnatural strength. A strange stirring in his abdomen chilled his breath and spun his mind. "Why are you doing this?"

"*Eat it!*"

It stuck its fingers between his teeth and wrenched his jaw open, then jammed the fruit against his teeth until the juice leaked down his throat. Lukian coughed and spat, but it continued shoving the fruit down his throat, and he choked and convulsed.

"Eat!" Its voice was altogether too large, and it rumbled and shook the ground.

Lukian clawed at his throat and then its arm. His eyesight blackened and flashed at once, and he convulsed and vomited the fruit up. He coughed and held his throat, feeling as though it had kicked him there.

The boy twisted and stared into the thicket. Its eyes were strangely focused, as if it could see through the hedge. It screamed. The sound rose to a pitch higher than he thought possible, and he stopped his ears and closed his eyes until its voice sharpened to a point so high it disappeared.

When Lukian opened his eyes, it was nowhere . . . and blood was everywhere.

53

C ain felt his eyes would burst. His mind claimed that at this very moment he was hanging by his throat from the Tree of Life to die, but the irony was distant behind the blackness of closed eyes and pain. Pain that overwhelmed at first, and yet rapidly dulled.

Forgive me. Please, forgive me. I wish I would never have done what I did. I wish I could take back my actions. But these realizations have come far too late.

The washing heartbeat no longer sounded in his ears, and Sarah's weeping had disappeared. There was no more pain, no more sensation except that of vague emptiness. He shifted, opened his mouth, and yelled. The sound echoed endlessly.

Is this what death feels like?

He felt his body with numb fingers and sensed himself floating, though upon straining his eyes found nothing to see.

"You think I would let you kill yourself?" The Abomination's voice echoed through the darkness and throbbed with fury.

So, he thought, and the action of thinking it was like salting a wound, *the Abomination has pushed me back into the void.*

Cain closed his eyes to test the fact, and the layers arose as he expected. He sifted through the sheets of reality slowly, methodically peeking through them to see what lay smashed between.

I don't even have the power to kill myself. How great a failure can one be?

You should not be surprised.

But why should I not think on these facts? The Abomination will live on through me to pervert mankind, and violence and sin will spread until it overwhelms the world. Sarah will be crushed between the Abomination's jaws while I float in embryonic darkness, only to be born again into a world unrecognizable. A world filled with demons in human skin. A world I no longer have the power to change.

There is still a way.

There was never a way. Never any chance of success. I knew it the moment I murdered my brother. My bones shook with that one truth, but with all of Time coursing through my veins, I blinded myself to the most basic of truths. For what is the future but a present to come? And I built my future on an Abomination. How could it become anything less? I should have listened to the Almighty.

What stays you from listening now? Do you not remember the Man's promise?

He stared into the abyss at the bottom of the layers, and part of him wondered, *Could the abyss be the escape my soul desires? Is this what the Man meant when he said there would always be a way?*

What else could he have meant? The only other choice was between death and the Abomination.

I should have chosen death.

Perhaps. But you could choose this now.

What will happen to me upon jumping into the darkness?

What else might you lose but pain itself?

He paused at the brink, wondering if he could see Sarah again. More than anything, he wanted to hold her, to slip his fingers between hers, to kiss her, and to smell her hair.

But it would only tear the wounds afresh. Maybe, in the end, it would be better if she came to believe you never loved her at all.

He nodded. *And perhaps I never did.*

◆　◆　◆

Cain's body swung, convulsing, but his body jerked and stilled. Sarah thought him unconscious, but his body lifted and the vine around his neck slackened.

She crawled away with a start. His eyes were open to silver gemstones. No white, no black, only iridescent silver. His hand tore the vine from his throat, and he descended until his feet touched the ground.

Sarah screamed, ran for the guarded entrance, and cut her hands on the thorns. She cursed and commanded them to let her through, but the way would not open. The green globes bobbed close and stared.

"Stop looking at me," she yelled and punched one. It recoiled and the others squinted. Deliberate footsteps sounded behind her, and she spun.

It was smiling at her.

"Who are you? What have you done with Cain?"

"Come now, you know me, as I know you."

"Get away from me." She rushed up the hill and slid behind the Tree. She breathed hard with her back to the trunk, examined her hands, and wiped the blood on her dress. The wounds throbbed, and she wondered how deep the thorns had gone.

"You've met me in the dark halls of your deepest thoughts."

The footsteps seemed to echo. She twisted and heard them from differing angles.

"I've watched you curse when you thought yourself alone. I've whispered in your ear and you've repeated lies."

She held her breath and twisted, but the branches hid all but a few feet in any direction.

"I am the darkness within darkness that you fear. I am the child of Sin."

A fruit thudded to the ground next to her, and she jumped and screamed.

"Are you hurt?" it mocked.

God help me, she prayed. *If you exist, if you ever existed, deliver me from this place.*

"I can feel the pulse in your throat as if it were pressed against my teeth. Come before I grow angry. You won't like me angry."

She could not escape. She could bide her time trying to dodge it in the grove, but she had seen the monster's rage, and of that she was most fearful. She placed a hand on her abdomen and shivered. *If it beat me again, it might take you from me. But I won't let it do that. No, dear child, I would endure anything before that.*

54

C ain gazed into the boiling darkness beneath the layers and felt it his final home. Like a pilgrim through the lands of Sin, he realized the darkness just over the edge was his final bed, his resting place. Though shame would have stilled him at any other moment, he knelt and prayed with a fervency reminiscent of Abel.

God, if there is nothing you can do to stop what I've set into motion, only keep Sarah safe. Do what you will with me, but if there would be anything you would have me do before I die, I would do it.

There was no response, though the silence seemed to speak in its own way. *"Come and bear the consequences,"* it said. *"Experience the everlasting darkness prepared for you in the fullness of Time."*

And so he jumped. For a moment, the sensation of falling into that darkness was similar to falling into the streams of Time. But the darkness peeled back to a Light so violent it penetrated his very soul, and he crumpled into himself in the attempt to guard his eyes from the burning fury, though every shifting shadow was eradicated in its presence.

"My son."

Cain shivered at the familiarity of the Man's voice, but there was no anger or disdain, only sorrow and relief, as potent as mixed wine, and he wondered at it.

"There is no hope left to prevent the evil you've born and borne, but there is hope. For you have severed its connection to the streams of Time, and its power is diminished."

Cain opened his mouth to speak, but found his tongue too parched from the heat of the Light. He was dust and emotion, barely held together by the residue of Time quickly curing.

"*I heard your words and have given you one last chance to change the outcome, to mitigate at least a portion of the pain.*"

And after? he thought, for he was incapable of speech.

"*And after,*" the Man replied, for in the Light were no hidden places, "*you will go to the place I have prepared for you.*"

He shook with fear, but though there was ambiguity in the Man's answer, he sensed justice in the Light which rightfully burned him away. For Cain was Sin—broken, bloody, brutal Sin. Whether the place prepared was darkness or Light, Cain thought either would be equally terrible.

"*Hurry along,*" the Man said, and to Cain's surprise there was a humor behind the words.

You laugh at me?

"*You've no need for a cloak such as pride. Nothing could hide you now.*"

What could keep me from burning away? How could anyone endure this?

"*Blood,*" came the answer. "*But not blood such as you've drunk. My blood. For I bear Abel's wounds. I hold Sarah's scars in my hands. I feel the teeth of the serpent at my heels, the same serpent which fed at your throat.*"

Cain nodded, feeling that familiar resonation of Truth, but realizing now that it came from the Light. Indeed, the Man had spoken to him all along, even as he had thought it his own wisdom.

Why? Why would you bear such suffering?

"*For you.*"

Cain's vision swam as he wept in the pain of the Light. Emotion threaded itself through him, and he realized it was the emotion of the Man—the sorrow of an eternity of separation, of love and loss. Of true divinity. And he realized now that much more than power differentiated God from man.

"*Go, quickly,*" the Man said. "*Back to the place of darkness, for that is where men's dreams are formed. It is a place the Abomination could never touch, a place I have blinded it to. There you will find a guide to show you how to weave the fabric of the future into mortal minds and to speak to them in visions. Because of your faith, you will be given a small portion of Time in which you may give men dreams, but afterward you will continue on to the place prepared for you."*

Cain nodded, though he wanted to stay, even as he felt the dross of his life dissipating in the heat and sensed there would soon be nothing left. Obediently, he walked where the Man directed, and came to the darkness.

There he met another familiar figure.

"Hello, brother," the man said, and the words fell like silk on his ears.

◆ ◆ ◆

The Abomination watched the woman walk from behind the tree. *So courageous. What beauty. Now I know how I will kill her.*

"What are you happy about?" Sarah asked.

The Abomination approached and struck her, but her only reaction was a flaring of the nostrils.

"I've not found such strength in the others. You're a formidable woman."

She chewed her lip to stop its movement, but kept her gaze on the Abomination's.

"Why have you stayed with him all these years?"

Tears moistened her eyes. "What have you done to Cain?"

"I thought you knew him."

"Why are you doing this?"

"You don't care."

"You know nothing of what I care about."

"He is gone. You were a fool to stay, a fool to hope. Such tragedy . . ."

She wept silently, and her beauty was magnified through Cain's silvered eyes. To see the world colored through another's emotions was a strange experience, one that the Abomination thought it would never tire of.

"In truth, I pity you. To love someone so absorbed by hatred is a bitter fate. If only I had come sooner. Maybe you would have been

spared the pain." It raised its finger and pressed it into her forehead, then skipped the barriers and plunged through the fibrous
pathways of her brain, plucking infinitesimal sparks and scattering
them until all darkened and she slackened in its arms.

It laid her unconscious body on a bed of flowers and heard, as
if carried by a sudden wind, quiet Music. The Abomination smiled,
rested a hand on her abdomen, and recalled images from the rivers
of Time. Hollow men in white coats, wearing masks and controlling
machines alien to this millennia, turned a lens that clicked to the
rhythm of the Music until it magnified an embryo on the surface
before them. They gazed through the lens and, using the machines,
cut and spliced twirling helixes together, adding and detracting,
changing and molding.

The Abomination did similar work on the child in Sarah's
womb. But the Abomination's abilities were more sophisticated
and more primal than those of the men in the vision. It smiled,
sensing the child struggle for life. But the changes were too rapid,
too violent, and the soul could not remain. It slipped away, and in
its place came . . .

Emptiness.

The Abomination withdrew from her womb and whispered,
"My dear Sarah. You will wake, and you will live, and the child
inside you will grow. But after it is born with little horns, I will
come for it, and for you. Then I promise you will feel pain such
as none you've felt before, but in the vastness of eternity, it will be
only a moment." It caressed her unconscious face and kissed her
motionless lips. "Merely a moment."

PART TEN

REDEMPTION

*When man began to multiply on the face of the
land and daughters were born to them, the sons of
God saw that the daughters of man were attractive.
And they took as their wives any they chose. . . .
The Nephilim were on the earth in those days, and
also afterward, when the sons of God came in to
the daughters of man and they bore children to
them. These were the mighty men who were of old,
the men of renown.*

—Genesis 6:1–2, 4 ESV

55

S eth woke sweating.

"I've been watching you." Calebna's voice was low, though sharp.

Seth forced his fingers to relax and realized he had been holding his breath. He sat up and tried to steady the shaking from the nightmare. Calebna sat like a tombstone by the remnants of the fire they had risked, and all was quiet silver under the moon and stars as Calebna rubbed the necklace by his throat.

"Who is it you talk to?"

"The dead." Seth looked at his wife's sleeping figure, then at the puffs of clouds migrating through the sky.

"Dawn is many hours away."

Seth nodded, pulled the cloak over his shoulders, and cinched it in his hand. The two sat hunched in the chill of autumn, and Seth's mind sucked on thoughts like wet cotton. He knew why Calebna couldn't sleep—why neither of them could sleep. It was the dreams. "I saw eyes," Seth said.

Calebna scraped the ashes with a crooked stick, drawing meandering black lines through the gray.

"They were on fire."

The stick dropped from Calebna's hand. "I keep thinking of Terah, Jacob, and Ben. What if they don't want me? What if they tossed what little love they had left?"

"I don't think such a thing is possible."

"Then why did they leave?"

"I think that fear, not hate, drove them away."

"Then their love was never love at all." Calebna stood and stared westward, toward the City they had left for a hope hidden behind danger. "When we arrive, promise me something."

"Anything."

"Promise you will do one simple thing after all this is over with."

Seth waited for Calebna to continue, but the man didn't. "What?"

"I'm waiting for you to promise," Calebna said.

"But I don't know what you—"

"Just do it."

Ayla shifted next to Seth, then settled back into heavy breathing. "All right, I promise."

Calebna hung his head and heaved another sigh. He sat and drew with his fingers in the slag. "Do you think God did it? Do you think he let Cain murder my father—your brother?"

"I think he could have stopped it, but didn't."

There was long silence marked only by the scratch of Calebna's fingers in the dust. "We buried him. We buried God."

"It seems a habit of man to try to swallow what he can't understand," Seth said.

"Better we had choked on it."

"I think we all did."

Ayla moaned and thrust her arm out in search of Seth, who laid his hand in hers. Her fingers curled around his and squeezed.

"How long until we reach the Garden?" Calebna asked.

"Three days."

"Seth?" Ayla said.

"I'm here."

"I dreamt I was pregnant," she said. "And the baby looked like you. I didn't give birth. I just knew what it looked like."

The fear of his nightmares burned anew. "Was it a boy or a girl?"

"A girl. She was perfect."

Relief. "Then it certainly was your daughter." Seth closed his eyes and drank in the darkness, wishing he could stay and forget all he had seen. Wishing he could abandon all he had been called to do.

"Did you dream?" Ayla asked.

His smile fell. "I dreamed." And he opened his eyes again.

56

The Abomination smiled at Sarah's unconscious figure outlined by blue flowers. It shifted as if to leave Cain but found itself fixed. Again it tried to detach from Cain's body, but failed.

It closed its eyes and searched for the womb from which it had been born, the same hole the Abomination threw Cain into so often, but the void was gone. It snapped branches and ate fruit after fruit after fruit, but nothing changed.

The meaning came slowly. *I'll kill your family. I'll flay them alive and drink their blood. I'll tear their limbs off one by one, and I'll kill Sarah last and most painfully.* It waited, listening, hoping against hope that Cain was still there, somehow hidden from its sight.

But Cain and the void were not misplaced. They were simply gone. Vanished.

The Abomination thought of the layers—those gateways to other worlds—and the rivers of Time that ran through them. Could it be Cain had found a way to osmose the barrier?

But there was nothing other than the layers and the Waters flowing through them. The Abomination had searched them time and again with meticulous intensity. It found nothing else. There could be nothing else.

Unless . . .

It cursed Cain and sprinted for the orchard in his body.

◆ ◆ ◆

The desert sands drank the moisture from Seth's feet and burned it from his tongue. If it had been the middle of the summer, they might not have made it so far, but when the frozen months came near, the sands could be safely traversed. Soon the dunes would frost at night, and the sun would burn less at midday, but always it remained a land of extremes.

Ayla stumbled and fell shoulder first into Seth, who caught both himself and her. She mumbled an apology, and he waved it off with a limp wrist and licked his flaking lips. A shadow sprinted past, and Seth winced at the sun to find the moving shape beneath it.

A bird, he thought.

Then another shadow or was it several?

"Look," Calebna croaked, and pointed from atop a mountainous dune.

They hurried up on hands and feet and saw in the distance an oasis undulating in the heat of the desert.

"It's dancing," Ayla said.

"Is it real?" Calebna asked.

Seth stumbled forward and they followed. Of course it was real. He had seen it in countless dreams. It called like strange Music, and for reasons he could not explain, he felt he could do nothing but walk toward that singular point.

The Garden. A place of beginnings and a place of endings. Like the East is to the West, or the summer is to the winter, each singularity no more or less an equal and opposite expression of another. The Garden of Eden to this new perverse substitute.

Contradiction. The word bowled down the hill of his mind, gaining speed and size as if rolled of snow. As they neared the Garden, it began to remind him of that world beyond the Sands of Time. Perhaps it was the movement of the trees and undergrowth, so tightly woven together that it seemed any movement should crack limbs. Perhaps it was the memory of an endless shoreline, and a forest filled with Music, though there was no moisture here, and apart from the rustling of wind through the leaves, he sensed no violent Music, though he knew violence grew within. *Contradiction.*

He wiped his face and itched the stubble. His body stunk, though he had long since let the upper half of his tunic beat at his thighs. He thought of what awaited them and worried at what he couldn't foresee, for there was darkness amidst the prophecies, valleys of shadow cast by Death.

As they entered the shade of the Garden, he sensed for the first time the glow cast by the plants. It sickened Ayla's pale skin and made her cheeks appear sunken. She caught him gazing at her and said, "What?"

Seth shook his head as vines slithered toward them and extended sharp points. The hair on his neck tingled as he remembered the entrance to the Shrine of the Song. He lifted a finger and pressed it against the vine's tip, feeling a sharp pinch and watching the vine drink a drop before slithering away. Ayla had already done the same, though Calebna hesitated and only followed after a nod from them both.

"This place feels evil," Calebna said.

"It is," Seth said.

"What do we do now?" Ayla took in the surroundings with rapt attention.

The Garden opened to receive them, and Calebna took a step back, for it seemed at first that they heard the tinkling of chimes.

"We change the Music," Seth said.

Ayla grabbed his hand, which had that chilled sweat feel in the cool breeze wafting from the Garden. "It's just like the Shrine."

"Yes. But I won't fail again by pushing you into darkness and danger. No, this time you will stay here," Seth said.

"But I perceive that you will have need of me before the end," Ayla said.

He laughed out of love, for there was no humor left to fuel it. "I will need you safe, not dead beside me."

"Nothing could make me let you do this alone."

"I will not—"

She dug her fingernails into his wrist. "I swore to never let you hurt like that again. I would rather die."

Seth stared into the eyes of the woman he loved and wondered what he had just asked of her. That she lay down love for self-interest? That she let him die to live alone, when all her life was enfolded into every detail of his?

He couldn't ask her to do what he himself could not do, so instead he leaned in, wrapped his arms around her, and kissed the side of her head.

And with that they entered the Garden, and Calebna followed with wringing hands and damp brow.

57

Calebna's clammy fingers stuck together. *I had claimed suicide was courageous, though if I had been honest with myself, I knew then that I should endure the pain. But how easy it can become to close your eyes and exhale, never to struggle for breath again.*

Movement gathered like a buzz at the edge of Calebna's awareness, sharpened to a bitter tip trained toward that singular goal he had come to accept only after days of struggle. *I must become a martyr for a hope I shall never own.*

For their redemption, if not for my own.

God forgive us. God keep us. God save us all.

As they walked the hallway of deadly vines, Calebna remembered the words of the voice in his dreams. The voice of the man he now knew was dead. The voice of the man whose body still walked among men. The voice of the man he would violate his vow to kill.

"The pain will last but a moment if you succeed, but if you fail . . . You must not fail."

◆　◆　◆

This is not my father, Lukian thought. He had known since Cain stepped out of the Fog that something had changed. But now he knew there was nothing left but a manic monster trapped in human skin.

Such power. Lukian examined the black vertebra set under his father's skin and those silver-within-silver eyes. Strange but provocative. He wanted it. Only he couldn't understand how to gain it. The boy had yet to return, and he ached for its presence. The creature was not his brother, or if it were, it was like Cain, hollowed out inside and replaced with something altogether different. Something evil.

I will steal your power no matter the cost. Just come back to me.

A new thought struck him. What if the boy was inside Cain? After all, why would Cain's eyes shift from silver to brown and back again? Why would he have grayed skin? And how else could he have such strange power?

Cain was wringing his hands and glancing about. Sweat beaded across his skin and stuck the tunic to his body. Mason stood with Gorban, Adam, Eve, Jacob, and the others, and Lukian wondered why they stared at him. He remembered the blood still glistening on his skin from his encounter with the boy almost an hour ago, and he tried to brush it away, though it was thick and sticky. He grimaced and flicked his hands. Still they stared.

He plucked another fruit and ate it. He tried to clean away the blood with the juice of the fruit. It did help, though only a little.

He asked Cain, or whatever was inside him, "What are you searching for?"

Cain hushed him with a hiss. He seemed to be listening, and Lukian thought he heard a slithering sound, as if the Garden were opening again. Cain's face seemed to become shadowed, his silver eyes glinting. Sweat dripped down his neck and his hands shook.

"What is coming?"

Cain did not respond. He only stood there shaking.

The trees, brush, and vines at the edge of the orchard creaked and separated, opening a pathway through which walked familiar shapes, but Lukian's eyesight darkened upon seeing them.

Cain, or whatever was inside him, cried out, "The Enemy! He's cheated!" and screamed a string of profanities.

These three figures should not be here, Lukian thought. *How could it be?*

Eve called out the names of her youngest son and daughter as she ran to them and threw her arms over their shoulders. "Is it real? Are you alive? But I saw you dead. I saw them close your tombs. And you! How are you here with them, Calebna?" Eve gripped her children as if afraid they were phantoms.

"God took us away to show us a glimpse of what was to come," Seth said.

Ayla smiled. "And God has brought us back to you."

"Praise the Almighty." Eve cupped their faces with her hands.

Calebna stepped toward Cain, and the family watched in stunned silence.

Cain pointed at them and shifted back, though his eyes were locked on Calebna. "You don't belong here."

"You thought to leave me for dead, but the Almighty directs my course," Calebna said.

Cain spat on Calebna's foot. "You're a charlatan. A blood-stained hypocrite."

"I will not deny the truth. I was going to kill myself there at the altar. I was going to lay myself down on the same stone upon which I laid so many other offerings."

Cain's face was twisted tight. "You're worthless. Your own God abandoned you."

"You can no longer shame me. I know that I am no holy man, and I've come to pay the price. What about you? Why don't you finish what you started?" Calebna opened his arms and pointed to his chest. "Strike me down. Destroy the bloodline as you intended from the beginning."

Cain's silver eyes flashed, and he stepped closer, hand poised at his hip as if ready to grab a veiled weapon. Suddenly Cain cried, "He knows!" and Calebna lunged like a bolt of lightning, right hand clutching a knife extended and plunging into Cain's chest. Cain screamed and swung his arms wildly. Lukian caught the glint of cold metal in Cain's hand as well, then silence, broken only by a crackling in both men's throats.

Then came screaming and a flurry of motion. Seth, Jacob, and Mason ran for Calebna while Gorban sprinted to his father. Mason tore the men apart, and Seth dragged Calebna away while Jacob pawed at Calebna's wounded chest and screamed his name.

Cain was gasping on the ground in a growing pool of red, and Gorban stood near, pale faced and staring at his father. Some of the women screamed, others collapsed with their arms over their heads as if the Garden would strike them down.

Lukian stood in a cloud of euphoria. He stared at the blood on Cain and wondered how it could be. He looked at Calebna, whose blood spilled out the corner of his mouth as well as down the side of his chest.

"You're going to be all right," Seth said as he bent over Calebna. "You're not going to die."

Calebna replied, "I have peace," and clutched Seth's hand. He coughed and the veins in his neck bulged with the strain. "He told me what to do. He told me it would be all right, that it wasn't really him, that he had crippled it."

Ayla was pulling Seth's arm, her eyes pleading as she said, "We need to get him out of here."

"What do you mean? *Who* told you that?" Seth said.

"Leave." Calebna squeezed Seth's hand.

"No."

"You promised."

Seth's eyes grew with recognition and he struck the ground. "Don't speak like a fool."

"Don't add your sin to the foundation."

Seth raised his voice. "Tell me who told you."

"You already know." Blood sputtered in Calebna's throat.

The pool grew around Seth's feet and trickled toward Lukian, who knelt and watched the liquid come, first like a creek, then like a river, lastly like an ocean.

"He's dead," Gorban said in seeming disbelief as he stood over his father, Cain, but the words were distant as Lukian plunged the tip of his finger into streams of red. He heard the silver boy's voice. First distant, then beside him, lastly inside him. "*You have work to do.*"

58

Sarah woke in pain to a world spinning with colors, to swirls of green and brown encircling a spot of white so brilliant it seemed to stab her. She closed her eyes and grabbed the skin of her forehead with her cold fingers.

Where was she? She remembered the smell of blood on Cain's breath and those silver within silver eyes.

No, she thought. *Not Cain. A silver-eyed monster.*

She stood and held her belly with trembling fingers. Half-eaten fruit lay like severed heads amidst the flowers, and the smell of death was as thick as it had been the night all this evil was born. Wind whispered through the thorns, and she thought she heard far-off Music. It trickled through the vines and rattled the leaves, and she closed her eyes and strained to listen. It went as quickly as it came. Like innocence in an infant. Like beauty and love and all the good things of the world. It was a different Music than she had heard before, and she wondered if there could be something just beyond what was visible. A Light hidden under branch and leaf. A diamond buried in the crust of the world. A seed lying under scorched ground.

Then she stepped on a thorn and her blood joined the scattered red. Just ahead was an archway leading through the Garden. It hadn't shut after Cain. Had he been in a hurry?

She nursed her foot and made her way slowly forward, careful not to touch the vines or the deadly flowers. With every step, she felt her strength revive until at last she saw clearly and moved boldly. She rounded a bend and passed the trees with faces. They watched, but she ignored them and struggled through brambles. They grabbed her arms and legs and clothing, and by the time she escaped, she was scraped and bleeding. As the Garden's clamped mouth opened to the orchard, she saw a confused mass of people scattered about. Jacob knelt by a man she recognized as Calebna, and whose chest was wet with . . . blood?

She clutched her mouth and whispered, "Dear God . . . Calebna. Calebna?"

Her mind was reeling in an attempt to absorb the sounds and sights, and how it all could be. Not far from Calebna lay another figure drenched in blood, and as Gorban turned and met her gaze, she recognized the wounded man.

"Cain!" She screamed and ran to him, wrapping her arms under his shoulders. "You're bleeding." She looked up and searched Gorban's expression. "What happened to him?"

"He's dead," Gorban said.

But that couldn't be. She had just saved him. How could he have died? How could . . . ?

But she knew. She knew and she beat Cain's chest and screamed at the bitterness of it all.

Gorban tore her away. "What are you doing?"

"He did it," was all she could say. "He did it . . ."

Now there truly was no hope left to resurrect the man she both hated and loved. Mason approached and lifted her. She leaned against him and struck his chest with her fists. "None of this should have happened."

Eve knelt, paler than a pillar of ivory, and Adam stood close by shaking his head and rubbing his eyes. Terah and Jacob wept, and everyone and everything else became a blur. Mason held her, and for the first time, she truly wept for Cain.

◆ ◆ ◆

Seth pressed his fingers to Calebna's neck and felt nothing. The man's chest no longer moved, and the blood no longer seeped out of his wound. Seth stood, grabbed Jacob's shoulder, and shook him. "Quick, make torches."

"What?"

"Make fire."

Jacob looked at Calebna.

"Cry later. Your father died to save us, but we will only live if you make fire. Now."

The boy nodded, and he, Machael, Kiile, and several others broke branches and bundled them together. A bonfire was lit, and torches lay in the hands of nearly half of them. Jacob shuffled close.

Seth pointed. "The Garden."

Jacob nodded and cast wary glances toward the globes that seemed to stare through green slits, and the vines that slithered here and there. Seth's sister Sarah was still weeping in Mason's arms, and the wails of all the others soared through the canopy above.

Eve knelt next to Calebna, but she did not weep, and she did not look at her grandson. Instead, she stared at Adam, who knelt beside Cain and silently cradled his firstborn son, as if to repent for turning his back on him all those years ago out of pride and shame. But it was too late. Cain had claimed to be a reversal of the curse, but instead had become the fulfillment of it. The sin of the father had cultivated the sin of the son, and on and on it would go, a seemingly endless cycle from the first to the last Adam, just as he had seen through the vision the Metronome offered.

Ayla laid one hand on Seth's forearm and held a torch in the other. "Is it over so soon?"

"Is what over?" Jacob's eyes hardened.

"It is just beginning," Seth said.

"Did you know this would happen to my father?"

"I still don't know all of what has happened," Seth said.

Jacob's voice rose. "Why didn't you stop him?"

Seth glanced at the boy. "Why did you leave your father behind? You knew he would die alone in the Temple, so why do you grow angry now?"

Jacob turned and waved as if to dismiss the question. "It does not matter. I have lost him again."

Seth started two more torches and handed them to Eve and Terah.

"What will we do with their bodies?" Ayla asked.

"Mother?" Seth laid a hand on Eve's shoulder.

She turned, and her eyes were like wastelands.

"We need to leave."

She nodded and stood, but her gaze shot over his shoulder, and Seth turned too late to see what she looked at. He felt the familiar sensation of metal piercing flesh and remembered the attack of the machine—that Abomination from the world beyond—and grunted and doubled over.

Thrust into his abdomen was a knife. He walked his eyes up the arm that held it to sharp features and silver eyes, and wondered if somehow Cain could still be alive.

Then he realized who it was and gasped for breath as Ayla screamed, "Lukian!"

The Music had found a new Instrument.

59

The Abomination savored the violence, wishing it had time to drink Seth's blood. Its aspirations had been destroyed, but it could still salvage a portion of the glorious future.

I will not fail you, Father. I will not let the Enemy win.

It cursed the complexity the Man had woven through the streams of Time. It could not kill them all, for that, too, would shatter the glorious future. It must choose its victim carefully, one and no more. So the Abomination pulled the knife out and stabbed Seth again and again. The man's insides rolled out over Lukian's hand, and the brutality would have continued but for the hand that grasped Lukian's neck and threw him to the ground.

The Abomination forced Lukian's body to turn, but already those huge hands grappled him with frightening strength. It was Mason, and as the bloodthirsty Abomination forced Lukian to stab Mason once in the shoulder and once in the thigh, the man broke first Lukian's left arm, then his right. Mason snapped Lukian's neck, and the Abomination spoke to the darkness. *"So ends Lukian, son of Cain, grandson of Adam, slave to Sin . . ."*

◆ ◆ ◆

Gorban's eyes were wide with shock as he watched Lukian stab Seth with the knife he had retrieved from Cain's motionless hand. But the sight of Mason breaking Lukian's body swept him up into action. He grabbed Adam and Sarah and jerked them along, pulling them toward the entrance of the Garden, though Eve called Adam's name and Adam tore out of his grip to run to her.

"Keep moving," he said to Sarah, who had glanced at Cain's motionless figure.

The others were already setting fire to the Garden, and when he found Keshra and Peth, who had torches in their hands, he grabbed them and they ran together with Sarah toward the entrance.

Gorban stole Peth's torch and threatened the vines with it. The plants slithered away, and as they pushed their torches forward, they found that by grouping together they could make their way safely. As they exited the Garden, they glanced back to see flames consuming the canopy and belching black plumes.

Sarah knelt in the sand, but Gorban said, "We cannot rest yet."

"What about the others?" Peth said.

"We can do no more," he said. "We must get out of the desert heat."

"Where will we go?" Keshra asked.

Gorban knew that she had years ago lost what little love she had left for her husband, Lukian, but to see her dry eyes was disturbing nonetheless. They all saw the madness overtaking Lukian after his children were murdered by the Jinn, but what if that same madness could overcome Keshra in the loss of both her children and her husband? He suppressed his fears. "We will flee east, far from the desert, far from the City of the Almighty. And if they have any sense, they will follow."

Gorban pushed Peth and Keshra, and Sarah stood but did not follow. He turned to stare at his mother, and Peth and Keshra walked several paces before noticing.

Sarah's eyes were filled with tears. Gorban felt the tightness in his throat, the longing he had for the love of his father that now neither of them would receive.

He approached and they embraced.

"We must go." He gazed at the flames licking the Garden canopy.

"I know," she said.

"And we must never return."

"But I will never forget him." She offered him her hand, and he took it in both of his and knelt.

"I will never ask you to," Gorban promised.

60

M ason held his wounds, which burned with a scorching pain. Seth was still alive, if only barely, and he lay in Ayla's lap. The woman wailed, and as the others formed a circle around them, Mason approached.

"Don't leave me, Seth," Ayla said. "Don't leave me."

Eve's gaze looked to be carved from a glacier while Machael, Kiile, and their sons, daughters, and wives gathered around. Jacob and Terah wept for the loss of Calebna, and Ayla wept for what she was losing.

Flames grew about them and the heat nearly singed their skin. Soon the entire Garden would be aflame, and if they did not flee, they would be as well.

Adam heard Eve's call, ran to them, curled his arms under his final son's body, and lifted him out of Ayla's lap. Mason, bleeding from two knife wounds, lifted Calebna's dead body over his shoulder and joined the rough line following their patriarch. When they exited the Garden and walked a distance away, Adam set Seth on the sand, and Mason set Calebna next to him.

Mason remembered the words spoken to him in his final dream. *"Those you flee with will have need of your strength. You must stay with them and never leave. Even though the love inside you might yearn to break these bonds, doing so will only bring greater harm. This will be the last day you will see your mother or your brother Gorban. But you need protect them no longer."*

He had no idea how Gorban, Keshra, Peth and Sarah could have slipped away without him noticing, for he had decided to follow them anyway. But they were gone, and he was here. And wisdom bade him to stay.

◆ ◆ ◆

Seth felt sand beneath him and remembered that place beyond Time. There was darkness, but pain remained. Then—*through* the pain—came gentle melodies and rhythms. At first they were filled with an immeasurable sorrow. In the end the most mournful notes became the most joyful, the most triumphant, and he realized this Music was altogether different from the Song they heard within the Shrine.

"You were right," he whispered to Ayla, though he was unsure whether she heard him.

As the Music grew, a figure approached and knelt beside him. His countenance was a searing white, but Seth recognized him all the same.

"*Your time has not yet come,*" the Man said.

Seth asked, "Is this real?"

"*As real as Sin. As real as the Music. As real as your life, which is in my hands.*"

"I must be dreaming," he said.

"*Look at my face.*"

Seth stared. "We thought you were dead. If you weren't, then how could all this be? How could you allow such violence?"

The Man looked closely at Seth. "*Would you rather I never gave you breath? Would you rather I never brought you life?*"

"I would rather avoid the pain, the evil, the Sin."

"*Then why didn't you?*"

"How could I?"

"*You, not I, chose Sin,*" the Man said.

"What about Abel? What about Lilleth? What about the rest?"

"*Everyone chooses their own curse, but their stories do not concern you. What you must understand is you, like Cain and all the others, have birthed death; but I, and only I, have birthed life.*"

"You let them destroy each other."

The Man pointed downward, and Seth looked at the Man's heels, which were wounded. "*I let them destroy me. In place of*

Adam. In place of Cain. In place of you. Your words are tall, but you see so little. Do you really think death is the End? I am the End, just as I am the Beginning."

"Then what will happen?"

"I will make all things new. You need only trust me."

Seth nodded and wrapped his fingers around the Man's wrist, which also was scarred. Tears came to Seth's eyes as he remembered the change he heard in the Music, from sorrow to joy. "I am sorry I doubted you. Forgive me. I . . ." He averted his gaze and closed his eyes, suddenly feeling how pocked with darkness he was. The Man was Light incarnate, but Seth felt himself murky and smudged with gray. "I am not worthy."

The Man lifted his chin with a touch so gentle it made him weep. *"You are not worthy, but because of your faith, I bore your unworthiness, and by doing so I call you worthy, and so does my Father, the Almighty."*

"Never leave me. Please—"

"I am sending you back."

"I don't want to go."

"You must go."

"Why?"

"The End has not yet come. The blood that bore the evil of the world will come through your line, and in that day, you will rise to be with me. Then I promise I will never leave you nor forsake you. Only remember me and trust that the Music I am weaving will be more glorious than you could ever imagine. Then you will see."

"What? What will I see?"

The Man smiled. *"Me."*

"Why not now?"

"Your eyes are not my eyes. Your ways are not my ways. Your wisdom is not my wisdom. Your love is not my love. Only trust in me. Only trust me."

And the echo of the Man's voice went on and on as Seth felt the wholeness of life rush into him like blinding Light. He opened his eyes to a smoke-blackened sky and his loved ones weeping around him. Their eyes were closed and their heads were bowed, and none saw him awake. He looked down. There was no wound, no blood, but Calebna's dead body was beside him and the wound in his chest was still open and wet with blood.

Why had the Man healed him and not Calebna? Why had any of this happened? Why had so many suffered? He felt a righteous anger grow in his chest like hot coals.

But then he remembered the Man's words, and it seemed as though he heard them anew, like a man fully answered, "*Your eyes are not my eyes. Your ways are not my ways. Your wisdom is not my wisdom. Your love is not my love. Only trust in me. Only trust me.*"

And after his family opened their eyes and shed their tears of disbelief, Eve looked at him. "I feel as I did when I gave birth to you. God has given me a new offspring, for Cain killed Abel. And though having you doesn't erase the pain, the joy of this moment somehow makes all of life glow brighter. Even the parts I had thought held only darkness."

Seth wrapped his arms around Ayla and said, "It seems redemption looks back for some as it looks forward for others." Ayla reached up and kissed him more passionately than ever before. He said, "I feel a new wind in the air."

And they rode it to new lands and a new era. But as every man returns to the dust of the ground and the hands of his Maker, so all eras come to an end, and most in terrible violence.

Epilogue

*She was pregnant and was crying out in birth pains and the
agony of giving birth. And another sign appeared in heaven:
behold, a great red dragon, with seven heads and ten horns,
and on his heads seven diadems. His tail swept down a third
of the stars of heaven and cast them to the earth. And the
dragon stood before the woman who was about to give birth,
so that when she bore her child he might devour it.*

—Revelation 12:2–4 ESV

In a cave in the wilderness, Sarah lay screaming. She dug her
fingernails into Keshra's hand, but the woman calmly brushed
Sarah's hair from her face and wiped the sweat from her forehead.
The sunset threw a hue of gold that slowly darkened to a red so
deep it fell toward black. Finally, guarded from the pale silver eye of
the moon, Sarah gave birth to a son.

Keshra cleaned the newborn and handed it to Sarah, who
received her child with rapture. She crinkled her nose and nuzzled
the baby's cheek, but though he seemed healthy and whole, two
sharp points sprouted out the top of his head.

"What will you call him?" Keshra said.

"Enoch," Sarah said, and mouthed the name to feel it on her
lips again.

Keshra played with Enoch's toes. "'A New Beginning.' What a
beautiful name. But what is this?" She lightly pressed Enoch's little
horns.

Sarah suddenly cried out in pain. It seemed at first an isolated
occurrence, but then the agony increased, and Keshra handed the
newborn to Peth and slipped her hand into Sarah's once more.

"Sarah," Keshra whispered, though she did not reply, too distracted by pain. "Sarah."

She said through bared teeth, "What?"

"I think another child is coming."

Sarah's muscles contracted and her back arced as she screamed. From the darkness of her womb to the darkness of the world, came a shriveled corpse. Keshra brought it to Sarah, who waved and said, "Take it away. Take it away."

Tears came to Sarah's eyes as Keshra disposed of the dead child. Keshra and Peth returned, and Gorban leaned against the mouth of the cave. Peth handed Enoch to Sarah, and though Sarah's mind claimed it would be better to abandon the child in the wilderness and let wild animals tear him to pieces, she held her baby close.

He looks just like you, Sarah thought. *Just like you . . .*

Keshra spoke after a minute of quiet. "Where will we go? What will we do?"

Sarah said, "We will build a great city and name it after my son. But for generations it will be known as the city Cain built, for that will be the truth." She splayed Enoch's fingers and squeezed his tiny fingernails, though Enoch looked up at her with silver eyes that knew more than any newborn could, until she looked away.

Peth didn't seem to have noticed, for she was examining her own protruding belly, and smiled at Gorban. "In only a few months my first child will be born as well, and we will grow to a great people and spread across the earth."

"Yes." Sarah's countenance darkened.

The widowed and childless Keshra said, "Do you think we will ever see the others again?"

Sarah stopped playing with Enoch's hand and patted Keshra's leg. "I am weary. Will you tend to Enoch while I rest?"

Keshra took Enoch from her again and, with one hand feeling the horns on the top of his head, she, Peth, and Gorban left Sarah alone in the dark. And there came to Sarah then a quiet Music. A Music that used its tenderness to hide a violence yet unmatched in the world.

READING GROUP GUIDE

PART 1

1. Eve says, "His intention is for us to live joyful, peaceful lives. He wants us to prosper. If he didn't, why would we serve him?" Do you agree or disagree? What should be our motivation for serving God? Why do you think this?

2. Cain and Sarah's relationship is deeply wounded. Why do you think Sarah has stayed with Cain all these years? And why do you think Cain still feels a desire for her?

3. In chapter 2, we see that the Almighty promised the people, "*While you dwell in me, no danger will reach past the walls I have constructed. Not sickness, not demon, not nature.*" But as Adam is searching for Abel, he finds a cancerous lump on a sheep. How can this be?

PART 2

1. Why did the voice say, "*Give it to me and I will show you the way. He is calling us*"? What is it demanding from Cain? And who do you think is calling Cain?

2. What do you think Cain was feeling in chapter 9 as he left Sarah behind?

3. If Sarah could have stopped Cain but didn't, does that make her as guilty as Cain? What about the Almighty? Is he culpable as well?

PART 3

1. What exactly happened when Cain made the wager with the silver boy? How could he justify doing such a thing?

2. Seth and Ayla find three items on the Almighty's throne. What is the significance of each item? What does each one represent?

3. What do you think was going through Adam's mind as Eve and Calebna left to see the bodies of their loved ones and the proof that the Almighty was gone? Why did Adam not respond when Eve returned?

PART 4

1. Cain thinks the Almighty banished humanity from the Garden of Eden out of fear. What else might have compelled the Almighty to do so?

2. Why does the Light Bringer urge Cain to drink blood? And why does Cain have such a strong desire for it?

3. Who is the Man and how could Cain have killed him?

PART 5

1. Why do you think the people made a tomb for the Almighty as well as for Seth and Ayla?

2. If you were present, would you side with Lukian or Calebna? Why? Do you think your natural choice would be the *right* choice?

3. Eve admits, *I hate his not being here. I hate his silence. His love for Abel.* Is she right to feel the way she does? What do you think you would feel in her position?

PART 6

1. Do you think there was more to Calebna's sealing the Temple doors than just his desire to keep danger out?

2. After Lukian finds his children, the theme of consuming blood returns. What is the connection between the prick Lukian feels on his neck and the "shift" he senses in himself?

3. Why did Cain choose this particular time to return?

PART 7

1. What is the connection between the Shrine of the Song and the Jinn? What exactly was the machine?

2. The machine shows Seth and Ayla three distinct areas in the Shrine: the Chambers of Science, the bathhouse, and the Metronome. What motivation could push "the Master" to build these three areas?

3. The Music grows in intensity as Seth and Ayla walk further into the Shrine. When all is said and done, it is "shaking the Waters with thunderous peals." If the Music can so powerfully impact all of Time, could the rest of Seth and Ayla's family have sensed it? Can you give any examples from earlier sections of the story that might point to this?

PART 8

1. Calebna is perhaps the first person on earth to have struggled with suicidal thoughts. Being the High Priest, he would have known that suicide is against the Almighty's will. But what impact do you think the lack of historical examples would have on his ability to cope

with the pressures he was experiencing? Do you think the imagery of the Spirit of God being an "all-consuming fire" would have played into his desire to use fire as the "uniting force"?

2. Seth says, "In this way, then, I think we could stop it. Not one man alone, but together through the choices we make, through the evil we refuse to tend in our minds like Forbidden Gardens." The language he uses seems to imply that, though we can refuse to tend evil, its seeds are still imbedded within us. Is it enough to refuse to tend the evil inside of us? Or, like a weed, will it sprout and grow nonetheless?

3. Lukian is struggling against the same madness that overtook Cain. Why do you think he, of all the family, has become the Abomination's favorite target?

Part 9

1. When Cain finally confronts his father, and for the first time understands why Adam never showed him the love he longed for, his reaction is to completely disengage. Why?

2. This book deals with multiple generations and the impact of fatherhood. Do you think that if Adam had behaved differently, Cain might not have killed his brother? How do you think it might have changed Cain's personality?

3. What do you think happened to Cain in the end? Do you think his repentance was sincere?

PART 10

1. What are some of the symbolic connections between Seth's experience in the Shrine and his experience in the perverse substitute for the Garden of Eden?

2. When Seth awakens next to Calebna, he struggles with why God would allow some terrible consequences and not others. Why is this question (and the Man's answer) so important? How does it square with your theology?

3. The core of this novel deals with the idea of worship. What exactly is worship? And how does this theme weave throughout the book and impact the characters and their relationships?

About the Author

B rennan S. McPherson has always wanted to tell stories, but it wasn't until his junior year in college that he built up the nerve to try. Three years later, *Cain*, his first novel, was born. Brennan is married to his best friend, works full time at a small nonprofit, and plays the drums in his spare time.

Acknowledgments

T hank you, Jesus, for setting me free and showing me what it means to live.

To my wife, best friend, constant companion, crutch when I'm weak, warmth when I'm cold, Anna—where to start? Nothing I write is enough. You are a queen, and I can't wait to see what God does with you and your incredible talent.

Thanks to: My mom and dad, for giving me life and loving each other every day. My grandmother, Nonnie, for babysitting me and showing me good books. My teacher, Sandy Weber, for pouring years into me—without you, my head would be one empty vessel. My good friend, Don Boyer, for marking the daylights out of my early work with red ink (for good reason), yet still somehow encouraging me. All the guys at BroadStreet, for investing in a kid with a weird book. The superb editor of this novel, Natalie Hanemann, for tirelessly pouring through the manuscript, seeing what I couldn't see, excising the junk and beefing up the thin spots.

Finally . . . dear reader, THANK YOU! What a blessing to share this adventure with you.